Tour Wives

A novel by Leigh Foley

ISBN-13: 978-0-9967897-2-1

For my drummer, J. I love you always.

Tour Wives, 2025

r/AmItheAsshole • posted by showersanger Feb. 3, 2023

Am I wrong for lying to my girlfriend?

Throwaway since gf has access to my main account.

Some background. Me (M38) and gf (F25) have been dating for five months. I'm a musician and she's an aspiring filmmaker, but mostly she bounces from thing to thing, asking mommy and daddy for money when she needs it. Lame, I know, but as long as she pays half the rent, she can whine to her parents all she wants.

Last week, gf came up with an idea for a documentary. She wants to film me and my band as we "process" a crucial moment, whatever that means. Seems like she wants to use my fame to launch her film career, but she insisted that wasn't true. I was kind of hard on her about it, telling her to earn her own way instead of sleeping with the singer to sneak into the spotlight. She cried but got over it. Good thing because I hate seeing her face when it's red and snotty. It's disgusting.

Here's where I might have gone too far. gf doesn't know I was kicked out of my band, and I didn't say anything when we discussed her documentary idea. The other members voted me out last November, after a misunderstanding they took way too seriously. It's been a few months though, and I'm going to show up at Sunday's practice to convince them that they need me. Because they do. They're nothing without me.

Should I keep lying to my gf about the band? They'll let me back in soon, which means this whole situation isn't a big deal, but my gf keeps nagging me about her film idea, and I'm not sure what to tell her. What can I say to get her off my back? My career isn't really any of her business, but she won't shut up.

Give me an outside perspective. Do I owe my gf the truth?

Chapter 1 – Karina

{February 4, 2023}

An out-of-tune wail launches from the bathroom and lands in Karina's ears, ripping her attention from her phone. She listens to the high-pitched sounds for a moment before rolling her eyes. "Seriously?" she asks the empty room. "Tell me again why I'm dating a singer."

Porcelain tiles boost her boyfriend's voice, the awful sound traveling from the shower straight to their bed. This morning, Dante belts out nineties pop an octave too high, yodeling and swallowing the words until they blend into a cat-like yowl.

Karina has heard his shower singing before, but she's still baffled by the racket. How can a man with a platinum record sound this terrible? They've been together for five months, and she still doesn't have an answer.

The clock on the wall says it's 8:30, which is way too early for an auditory assault, especially after Karina and Dante stayed up late, sipping booze. Of course, that led to drunken naked time, and 3:00 AM arrived before they crashed into an exhausted heap. They had fun, and Karina has no regrets, but another hour of quiet would be nice.

"Hey babe, can you keep it down? I'm trying to read," she yells.

Dante doesn't respond. He probably can't hear her over his personal karaoke session.

Sighing, Karina lowers her eyes to her phone. Sometimes, she wants to record his crooning and blast it on social media. The video would only need to be thirty seconds long—not even an entire song—but just that little clip would make his fans lose their minds. They love learning about their favorite singer's private life. And the post would boost her follower count, something she desperately needs. It would be a win-win for them both, but Dante would hate it. He's picky about the content he allows her to share. So, instead of filming his rendition of "Hit Me Baby One More Time," Karina gets back to her email, trying her best to focus on the inbox despite Dante's tuneless voice.

There are thirty-three new messages, mostly junk. Promos get deleted. Social notifications as well. One email survives the purge.

Re: Query: WHAT HAPPENS NOW? –
a deep dive into the music industry

Her heart hammers and queasiness rips through her stomach as she reads the subject line. She's staring at a reply from Hellcat Pictures. More than likely, the message will be the next rejection in a string of hundreds. But maybe not. Maybe it's the yes she's been waiting for.

Since graduating with an MFA, Karina's efforts have gone toward breaking into the film industry. Two weeks ago, she made the first step toward that goal. During an intense ketamine retreat, she visualized an amazing documentary idea—an in-depth look at the music industry, made with the help of Dante's band, A Box of Stars. Very cutting-edge. Last week, she sent off a handful of pitches, doubting she'd get a single response, hoping like mad everyone would reply.

After four days, Hellcat Pictures is the first to get back to her. They're a smaller company, but they jumped into the spotlight after one of their films pulled in 100 million streaming hours and won a handful of awards. Good press and deep-pocketed donors followed, and Hellcat became the agency aspiring screenwriters frothed over. Karina's pitch to them was a long shot, and the answer to that gamble sits in front of her, waiting to be read.

Karina fights through her hangover as she stares at the email. Her brain is in turmoil. Doubt and anticipation seesaw through her mind, titling back and forth at a sickening speed. Did they reject or accept her? Karina whispers the question while working up the courage to open the message. After a few deep breaths, she's calm enough to learn her fate.

But Dante interrupts.

"Karina, are you up?" he calls out.

"Yep. Thanks to your singing." She aims for a neutral voice, but a dash of sarcasm sneaks in. "But no worries. I'm not mad, just tired," she adds for reassurance, trying to prevent an early morning argument, even though she'd much rather finish reading her email than soothe her boyfriend. His whininess grates her nerves.

Dante emerges from the bathroom, dark hair slicked back, cheeks pink from the steam. Thankfully, a smile fills his face. "Hope you liked the personal concert. Not many people get to hear me practice. You're a lucky girl."

"Loved it," Karina says through clenched teeth. She glances at her phone as he approaches, peeking at the reply before he reaches the bed. *Hi Karina.* Good start. *Thanks for reaching out.* Still positive.

But before she gets further, Dante stands in front of her, lips pressed out in a pout. "I'll take that." He plucks her phone away and sets it on the bedside table. "How about you pay attention to me."

Annoyance zips through her, but Karina stares at her boyfriend, taking him in from head to toe. The water glistening on his chest causes heat to surge through her body. He's too sexy for his own good. For her own good too. She can hardly believe this is real life. Dante Wilder wants attention from her, the person who was just a fan not too long ago. The singer from A Box of Stars is her boyfriend. It's surreal. It's a dream come true.

Excitement overtakes her. Lust too. She throws back the comforter, patting the mattress beside her. "There's room for one more."

Dante grins. "That's more like it." He hops into the bed, and thoughts of her email vanish as desire overtakes her.

***

They nap after they're done and roll out of bed at 9:45. Karina is starving. Luckily, Dante is too. They head to The Broke Yolk, their favorite brunch spot, and slide into a corner booth less than an hour later. After ordering the usual—coffee and egg white omelets—the couple settles into the plush cushions and waits for their caffeine.

"I wish you didn't have to leave," Karina says, rubbing her temples, trying to relieve her head's dull ache.

"I have to. You know how it is. There's no use complaining." He crosses his arms over his chest, gaze icy. "I'll be home before you know it."

"Three weeks feels like an eternity when you're gone. The house is so empty and quiet." She's whining, and she knows it, but she just can't help herself. She'll miss him so much.

"I'll text when I'm not busy." He moves his hand to cup her chin. Karina shivers as his thumb traces her jaw. "Maybe you can come to a show. I know you like watching me sing."

Exhilaration rushes through her. She's so lucky. "Really? I would love to see another show."

"Yeah. I'll have our manager put you on the list if there's room." Dante leans in for a kiss, a brush of the lips that leaves her wanting more. He pulls away but pauses a few inches from her face. His arctic blue eyes stare into her chestnut ones. "And listen. When I'm gone, take it easy on the video calls. Last tour you blew up my phone. I'm a busy man, Karina, and bothering me isn't cool. Understand?" She tries lowering her head, but he holds it in place. "Just answer," he demands.

"But I only called once—"

Dante cuts her off. "How 'bout you don't call at all? Text if you need something. I'll reply if I can."

She blinks hard, trying not to cry. Making a scene would be embarrassing. "I won't call as much. I'm sorry." Her tone is even, placating. Karina hates this part of their relationship, but it's a necessity. When he's angry, her world gets dark. Preventing his bad moods is her only defense.

After a rough squeeze, Dante releases her chin. "Good. I'm glad we got that sorted." He leans back in the booth. "What are you going to do when I'm gone?"

Karina responds quickly, knowing he hates to wait. "Not much. Maybe I'll mock out a shooting schedule for the new film." Her mind flickers back to the email from Hellcat Pictures, and she reaches for her phone. "That reminds me. I got an email from an agency this morning."

"What did they say?"

"Not sure." She gives him a light shove, hoping he's in the mood for playfulness. "Someone interrupted me with their glistening chest before I could get to it." She lays her cell on the table, typing in the password. "Let's read it together. I'm pretty nervous. What if it's another no?"

"If it is, there's no need to whine about it. Rejection will toughen you up." He drapes an arm over her shoulder. "But I am curious. Let's see what it says."

Karina taps the app and stares at the unread email. What do you have to say Hellcat Pictures? She closes her eyes for a moment, manifesting positivity. When she opens them, she's ready. With a touch of her pointer finger, the message opens, and she leans in to read what it contains.

Hi Karina,

Thanks for reaching out. You have an intriguing premise here, and I'd love to hear more about it. Do you have time for a call later this week? I'm available from 1-2:30 PM PST on Wednesday and Thursday. Let me know what works for you, and I'll add you to my calendar. Looking forward to connecting!

-Valerie Hart
Senior Agent

As she goes through the message, anxiety surges through her brain, and she's expecting the worst, so she flies through the words, not quite comprehending what they say. She slows herself down for a second read-through, and despite fearing that the sentences will morph into a rejection, they don't change as she studies them. The email remains positive. Thrilling. Everything she's been waiting for.

"Is…is this real?" Karina's hands shake as she glances at Dante. Excitement makes her heart race.

He finishes reading the message and darkens the phone. "Looks real to me."

"Can we celebrate?" Tears well in her eyes. "Just a little. Before you leave."

He checks the time on his watch. "It's still brunch. How about some mimosas? I could use a drink."

As if on cue, the server returns with their coffee. Karina grabs a mug and brings it to her nose, inhaling the rich aroma. "Yum. This smells amazing."

"Sorry it took so long, folks. I needed to brew a fresh pot." The waitress plunks a stack of napkins on the table, then squints at Dante. "I feel like I know you from somewhere. Do you go to Yoga Palace on 39th and Elm?"

He shakes his head, giving her an appraising look. "Nope. I'm more of a running man. I've never been the flexible type."

"I guess I mistook you for someone else." She lets out a chuckle. "The guy I'm thinking of can bend like a pretzel."

"Can we order two mimosas?" Karina cuts in. She doesn't want the server to realize who Dante is and flip out. It happens way too often, and last time, he ended up ditching her for some groupies. For that bender, he didn't come home until the next morning, reeking of whisky and cigarettes, promising nothing happened. Her brain didn't believe him—she knew he cheated—but her heart refused to listen.

The server's attention shifts to Karina. "Of course. Would you like to upgrade to bottomless? It's only ten dollars more."

"Sounds good to me," Dante answers. "You in, K?"

"I have to take you to the airport," she reminds him, glancing at her phone for the time. "In three hours. I can't get wasted and drive."

He snaps, "I'll get a ride, Karina." He notices her flinch and softens his tone. They're in public, after all. "We're celebrating you, remember? Get as drunk as you want."

She looks between him and the waitress, both wearing expectant expressions. In truth, she should stay sober and reply to the email in her inbox. That would be the professional thing to do. But how often does she get life-changing news? Never. And if she doesn't mark the occasion with Dante now, she'd have to wait until he returned. Three weeks is way too long to delay some fun.

"Okay, you win. We'll take the bottomless mimosas, please. And a piece of key lime pie, because why not?" Karina beams as the order gets written down. When the server leaves, she turns to Dante. "Ready to day drink?"

"I'm always up for that challenge." He reaches under the table, finding her thigh. "Then we can mess up the bed one more time before I leave."

She lifts her coffee, tilting the mug toward him. "Cheers to that."

Dante taps his cup against hers. "Cheers to you finally getting a job. It's about time."

They drain their mugs. The liquid warms Karina, and her hangover dulls the slightest bit. Everything is okay. "I'm glad we found out together. It means we can work through the details of our plan." She leans against him. "Better not get too drunk. I wouldn't want you to forget anything."

He stiffens. "You're talking to a pro, Karina. There's no such thing as too drunk for me."

"You're right. I'm sorry." He relaxes at the apology, and she presses into his arms, delighting in the feel of his body against hers.

After a minute, the server emerges from the kitchen balancing their glasses on a tray. Excitement rushes through Karina. She's glad they upgraded. Her head throbs slightly, but she knows the first sip of champagne will soothe the ache, and the next swallow will elevate her to a mellow buzz. Tipsy is the perfect state for a celebration, and one drink wouldn't have been enough to get there.

Karina flashes her biggest smile as the server places the mimosas down. "Thank you. You just made our day better."

Her cheeks redden. "You guys are cute." The waitress grabs the empty coffee cups and sets them on her tray. "I'll be back soon with your food. Congratulations on whatever it is you're celebrating."

"Thanks again," Karina says as the server hustles away. Dante's eyes follow the departing figure into the kitchen, leering as her hips sway back and forth. Why does he have to be so obvious? Karina reaches for her glass and swallows the liquid inside. Champagne is for celebrating. And for numbing the pain of a cheating boyfriend. The drink captures the uncertainty inside her.

Dante doesn't notice her mood shift. Typical. He reaches for his glass, draining the contents. "Aren't you glad we got bottomless?"

"Yep. Great idea." When their server reappears, Karina waves her over. "Another round. And keep them coming."

They float on the bubbles until noon.

***

An ambulance rouses Karina, its blaring siren cutting through the house's thin walls. She shakes her head to clear the fuzz and reaches for the water that's a permanent fixture on the nightstand. The liquid is heaven. Her parched lips and throat delight at the hydration. She must have been sleeping hard.

Day drinking always gets her. She should have stopped at three refills, but she and Dante were having so much fun. Alcohol always changes his attitude. Most times for the worse, but not this morning. At brunch, Karina's boyfriend was more cheerful than usual, and he kept talking about the things they were going to do with her advance funds from Hellcat, which he was sure would be a huge amount. Listening to him plan their future was beautiful. His attitude helped her feel better about their relationship, something she's worried about since they started dating. As they talked and drank, he reminded her of the goofy, upbeat, romantic person she fell in love with, the one who disappeared during their arguments. Dante's enthusiasm was worth any aches and pains the bubbly caused. Karina would rather deal with a hangover than a fight. It was a small price to pay for peace.

Lying there, she struggles to remember what happened after they left the restaurant. Some parts are clear. She knows they checked on the car to make sure it wouldn't get towed. Then they hailed a cab. There was some fooling around in the backseat that earned them an eye-roll from the driver, but they tipped him well, so he didn't complain.

Home is where she loses the thread. Snapshots of passion and snippets of conversation cloud Karina's recollection, confusing her. Dante's mouth trailed across her skin, but was that before or after they discussed his steps for the documentary? She squeezes her eyes shut, trying to unearth the memories.

She pictures them speaking, sitting on the edge of the bed, shoulder to shoulder. Dante nodded at her words and responded with yeses to whatever she said. He was busy while they talked. His fingers tiptoed along her leg until they found her boyshorts. He strummed the silky material, making her squirm. Karina wanted him, of course, but she pushed away because he needed to listen. He couldn't mess her plan up. The consequences were deadly if he did.

And then the flashback goes blank. No matter how hard she closes her eyes and focuses, she can't recall past that point.

Karina's attention returns to the present. The room's darkness is soothing, and it's tempting to stay buried under the covers, but she must get up. Wasting the entire day is pointless. Laziness won't bring her closer to her dreams, but old habits are hard to shake. The slacker lifestyle is easy to fall into.

During the ketamine retreat, when Karina visualized her documentary topic, she also dove into a deep self-reflection. She peeled back her inner layers, assessing the characteristics that blocked her from realizing her potential. Recognizing her faults was tough and painfully uncomfortable—there were lots of tears and cursing, plus a scream or two—but it was a necessary step on the journey to success.

After the retreat, she vowed to embrace maturity. No more late nights partying. No more passing out until lunch. No more ignoring emails, texts, or calls. No more begging Mom and Dad for money. She had decided to leave childhood behind and finally accept adulthood. Twenty-five was the perfect age to enter this productive phase.

Until today, Karina's done great. Anger floods her body, and she clenches her fists, mad that she slipped up. Luckily, it can be fixed. If she gets out of bed and replies to the email from Hellcat, she'll give herself a pass and release her irritation. After that, she won't let it happen again. Although the screw-up is minor, she knows that too many stumbles can create a huge setback, and she doesn't want to regress.

Momentum is the key. A little stretch will get her moving. She raises her arms above her head, reaching as far as possible, releasing the tension in her shoulders. After a thirty count, she swings her arms to the right. A lump in the bed stops her from completing the movement.

"What the hell, Karina?" the lump grumbles.

"Dante? Oh God, this isn't good." She rolls onto the floor, grabbing her clothes in a panic. "We have to get to the airport. You missed your flight, but there should be something else heading to Atlanta. At least you weren't flying to the middle of nowhere."

He squints, giving her a puzzled look. "What are you talking about? We have plenty of time. Your alarm hasn't even gone off yet." His gaze flicks from his girlfriend to the clock and his eyes widen. "That can't be right. Tell me it's not 6:30."

"It is." She pulls a tank top over her head, dressing as fast as possible. "I don't know how we slept this late."

"I do. You got wasted and forgot to set your alarm." Dante's nostrils flare. "Because of you, I'll be late to practice." He rips the blanket off, stomping onto the floor. "I can't trust you with anything, can I? Whenever I do, you screw it up."

Karina freezes at his accusation, and waves of dread wash over her body. "I'm sorry, Dante. I didn't mean to cause any trouble." Her voice hitches on the last syllable, but she manages to blink back the tears clouding her eyes.

"Great. Now you're all emotional." A sneer twists his handsome features into a mocking mask. "I don't have time to comfort you, Karina, especially since you're the one who messed up." He picks up his clothes and heads to the bathroom, slamming the door behind him.

She shimmies into her skirt and collapses onto the bed. As she stares at the ceiling, she begs her mind to recall what happened before their nap. Did Dante ask her to wake him? The answer refuses to surface. Her memory remains a dead end.

Maybe she set an alarm but forgot to arm it. A few weeks ago, Karina missed a meeting that way, so it's a possible explanation. She snags her phone and unlocks it, checking the screen for clues. All that pops up is the notes app, which is where she jots film ideas. There's no evidence of a failed alarm.

To the left is her boyfriend's nightstand. Resting on top is his cell. Karina knows the passcode—he gave it to her in a show of trust after an argument—but she's never used it. There hasn't been a reason until today when she suddenly needs to defend herself. He sounded sure when he accused her of messing up, but she doesn't remember agreeing to wake him. What if he was the one who forgot?

She listens to his footsteps, following his movements in the bathroom. He clomps from the sink to the closet where hangers begin to rattle. While he's occupied with packing, Karina races to his side of the bed. A flash of uncertainty grips her, but she shakes it off. This isn't her being jealous or paranoid. This is her digging for the truth. She has the right to search for this single item. If she doesn't find it immediately, she won't look further.

3-6-6-9-5. The numbers unlock the phone, and she scans the text message that pops onto the screen. Holy. Crap. Right away, she realizes she's found something worse than an unset alarm. A chill runs down her spine, and shivers ripple through her.

When was he going to tell Karina?

What she sees changes everything for Dante. And for her too.

A Box of Stars –
Edgy Rock With Super Nova Appeal

The five-piece indie rock group from Gainesville, FL is shaking up the East Coast with their debut album *Gravity Bound*. With celestial melodies and catchy hooks, A Box of Stars has something for everyone. Even your music snob bestie.

by Alexis Grimmpel on July 2, 2016

I'm picky about what goes into my ears. If you don't believe me, read my review of the wildly popular Downtonal (hint: six-year-olds could write better songs). So, when I was given a promo copy of A Box of Star's (ABOS) debut, I was skeptical. With a name like that, I expected emo whining and overused riffs to dominate the album's twelve songs, but *Gravity Bound* surprised me with floaty tones and complex yet accessible rhythms.

Founded in 2014 by bassist **Jake Devlin** and drummer **Trev Branch**, ABOS quickly ignited the Gainesville scene. They started out playing local clubs and were picked up by Florida Man Records when the label noticed they packed the house no matter the venue. With guitarists **Pearl Williams** and **Rory Ramirez**, and singer **Dante Wilder** rounding out the band, the quintet is a powerhouse who takes you on a journey through the galaxy of sound.

Let's start with vocals. Wilder's voice is rich with feeling throughout the album, and his lyrics are powerful, gripping, and brooding. The chorus from "Dark Energy" lives rent-free in my head:

> Lose the way to pain.
> Never feel the hurt again.
> Weightless in the stars.
> Emptiness is ours.

Musically, *Gravity Bound's* first track, "Owing to Lunacy" opens with dreamy ambiance then winds its way through deeper emotions using a drum build-up that stopped my heart for a few beats. The next two tracks, "Disaster Recoil" and "Sun Spun" continue with blistering percussion, but the songs somehow manage to maintain their indie feel, something I didn't think was possible. "Retrograde" and "Auroral" bring the mood back to the hypnotic with meandering guitar lines, and "Dancing on Mercury" is a twinkling interlude that lightens the ambiance. The second half of the album is a repeat of the first, but this isn't a bad thing at all. During the last six songs, listeners are taken from the ephemeral to the dramatic then back again, all in the span of twenty minutes.

The highs and the lows of the album are what make it special. They grab you and don't want to let go. Not that you'll want to escape. You'll be perfectly happy losing yourself in the music.

Rating: 8.5/10

Band: A Box of Stars · **Album:** Gravity Bound · **Tracks:** Owing to Lunacy · Disaster Recoil · Sun Spun · Retrograde · Auroral · Dancing on Mercury · Losing Balance · Rings Aglow · Dark Energy · Nebula Memorial · Rocket to Oblivion

Chapter 2 – Maggie

{February 5, 2023}

Maggie is deep into a smutty ghost story when a charred scent pulls her back to reality. She inhales deeply and the stench of burnt toast floods her nose. Her daughter Danica must be in the kitchen trying to make breakfast by herself. She's fifteen, and despite the culinary lessons she's received, the girl can't cook. At all. Normally, Danica grabs fruit and yogurt before school, but from the smell of things, she tried to use the toaster oven and failed spectacularly.

Sighing, Maggie closes her book, regretting her daughter's timing. She's pages from discovering what happens between Lady Daphne and her murdered husband. Would a séance bring him back? Will they make love one last time? Sadly, instead of continuing the smoking hot ghost erotica, Maggie gets to deal with something far less sexy—smoking hot bread.

Parenting a teenager is tough, but little moments of joy make it bearable. That's what reading does for her. Every morning, while Danica gets ready for school, books become her escape. For twenty minutes, as her daughter decides which of her clothes she hates least, Maggie immerses herself in the cheesiest romances imaginable. The stuff she calls brain candy. It's not fancy pants literature, but nothing makes her happier than a swoon-worthy story. Sentences full of longing or lust put a smile on her face, which means she's in a good mood during breakfast. This positive attitude is the perfect armor for Danica's sarcasm, and most days the pair is able to get through their meal without strife.

Her reading tactic becomes less of a distraction and more of a lifesaver when her wife Pearl plays guitar with A Box of Stars. Their daughter can be a handful when both moms are home, but she becomes touchier when it's just her and Maggie. She doesn't take the teenager's emotional shifts personally. The reaction is relatable because the same thing happens to Maggie when Pearl travels with the band. Although she considers herself fiercely independent, her wife's absences affect her, and she's less herself during the band's tours.

She and Danica are in rough shape as a duo, but since Maggie is the grownup, she perks up and smiles her way through the stress of managing the household alone. This is where novels really shine—they make life possible.

Unfortunately, today, Maggie's relaxing hobby doesn't stand a chance against her responsibilities. It's day one of a three-week ABOS tour, and she's already putting out fires at home. Literally. When she arrives in the kitchen, Danica is staring at the toaster oven, frozen in a slack-jawed expression. Small flames dance inside the appliance, and they lick at the edges of the door, trying to leave their confines.

Maggie springs into action. "Watch out," she yells.

"Mom." Her daughter blinks and shakes her head. "I don't know what happened."

"Not the time, sweetie. I need you to move." Maggie pushes past her, unplugging the toaster oven, then dragging it by the cord to the sink. The oven hisses when water hits, but the crackling stops as the charred metal cools. She opens the door, and after a few seconds, the flames inside are smothered by the deluge.

Maggie's breath bursts out. "That's one way to start the morning."

"You didn't have to shove me."

She whips around to face Danica. "Seriously? I just saved your life, and you thank me with a complaint? I barely brushed past you."

"Uh, no. You threw me into the counter." The teenager rubs her right hip. "I'm gonna have a bruise."

"A bruise is a lot better than a burn, don't you think?"

"Those are kindergarten-level debate skills, Mom." She rolls her eyes. "I prefer not to suffer an injury, period."

Maggie closes the distance between them and wraps her arms around her daughter. "I'm sorry I hurt you, my precious darling. Will you ever forgive me?" Danica tries to push away, but her mother holds tighter. "Give your mommy a proper hug."

"Let go. I don't consent to this," Danica yelps.

"As you wish, princess." Maggie steps back. "Now, tell me what happened. Why did you try to catch the house on fire?"

Hands on hips, Danica glares. "I wanted toast for breakfast. And it burned. End of story."

She looks like Pearl when she gets angry. Their annoyed expressions are identical. Seeing the resemblance makes Maggie miss her wife more, but that's life with a touring musician. "Why didn't you ask for help? You know your culinary skills are…" She pauses to think of a neutral adjective. The words flashing through her mind will most certainly offend her riled-up daughter.

"Awful." Danica finishes the sentence. "I know I can't cook. That's why I yelled for you, but you never came."

Maggie hadn't heard a thing, and sound travels well from the kitchen to the study. "You called me?"

"Yeah. And you ignored your only child. I'm guessing you were mesmerized by the ghost dick in your book. Great parenting, Mom," she says in a tone dripping with disdain.

Maggie's cheeks warm. Dammit. She hoped her daughter was clueless about her genre preference. "Watch your mouth, Danica. Ghost penis is more appropriate for a teenager. It's the scientific name."

She glowers at the correction. "Whatever."

It was time to diffuse the situation. "I'm sorry I didn't hear you, sweetie. You know I'm in another world when there's a book in my hands." A smile fills Maggie's face. "How 'bout I scramble some eggs?"

Her daughter's eyes narrow at first, and Maggie is afraid she'll talk back, but she grins instead. "Perfect." She pulls up the neck of her shirt and takes a whiff. "Can I change my clothes while you're cooking? My shirt reeks."

Maggie waves her hand, shooing the teen away. "Go on. I'll have everything ready in fifteen minutes, so don't dillydally."

"Mom, you're not old enough to use that word." Danica laughs, then scampers away, looking more like a toddler than a teenager.

After she leaves, Maggie inventories the kitchen. Her eyes water from the haze floating through the room. She opens a window and wafts smoke with a dish towel, flapping her arms in a bizarre rendition of the chicken dance. The air clears. The singed scent sticks around. Maggie loves campfire smell—there's nothing like s'mores, creepy stories, and crackling flames—but that's an experience suited to the outdoors, not inside the house. Later, she'll have to browse YouTube. Deeperest Cleaners or The_Spotless_Space will have a helpful video on their channel. Hopefully it won't take too much work to neutralize the stench.

Before her times runs out, she gets cooking. The morning started out crappy, but delicious food will make everything better, and a scramble just won't cut it. Today they need omelets, her specialty. Maggie dices peppers, onions, and mushrooms then adds the veggies to a bowl of eggs. Her hips twitch as she whisks the concoction, and by the time the food goes into the pan, she's practicing salsa to the music in her head.

Her wife loves dancing. She's incredible at it too. Pearl is graceful and has perfect rhythm, the exact opposite of Maggie's clumsy awkwardness. But their anniversary is coming up, and Maggie wants to learn salsa as a surprise. Well, a watered-down version of the dance anyway. Her oafish feet and off-tempo timing make anything else impossible.

1-2-3, 5-6-7. 1-2-3, 5-6-7. The numbers run through her head, and her legs move to the beat. Sort of. During every measure, she missteps at least twice, which sounds terrible, but it's an improvement from her starting point. A month ago, she was sitting at a 0% success rate. Now she averages around 50%. By the time Pearl's birthday rolls around, she should be in the 90+ range if they're dancing to something on the slower side. She doesn't think she'll ever master the faster tempos.

Clapping rings out behind Maggie, and she twirls to find Danica staring. Her daughter changed into a blue and teal shirt, and the colors bring out the green in her eyes. The teen's words come out between laughs. "You're cringy, but less cringy than last week. Bravo, Mom."

"That's high praise coming from you."

"And don't you forget it." She gestures to the stove. "Breakfast done?"

"Coming right up." Maggie sways while plating their meal and sashays on the way to the table. After setting their dishes down, she flourishes her arms. "Your omelet, m'lady. Eat up, then let's get rocking and rolling."

"Didn't you get enough of that while you were dancing around the kitchen?"

"No, no. That wasn't rock n' roll. But this is." Maggie raises her right pinkie and pointer, then flips her hair over in a wicked awesome headbang.

"Oh my God. Stop. Seriously."

She does, but not because her daughter told her to. She quits because her skull is throbbing. After a single headbang. Jeez. When did she get too old for thrashing? "Danica, will you grab two ibuprofen from the bathroom?

I might have overdone it." Maggie eases into her chair, sipping coffee until her daughter returns.

When Danica does, she's shaking her head. "I swear, none of my friends have parents as weird as you and Momma. They're normal. They don't injure themselves while moshing." She drops the pills into her mother's palm.

"Thank you. For both the compliment and the medicine." Maggie swallows the painkillers with a swig of coffee, then grins. "I cherish my weirdness. It's one of my best qualities."

"Hopefully, it's not hereditary." Danica sighs while sliding into her seat. After a bite, she mumbles, "Thanks for the eggs. I'm sorry for burning the toaster oven."

Warmth shoots through Maggie. She likes reminders of the sweet girl hidden inside her teenager, the one buried beneath several sarcastic layers. "You're welcome. And it's okay." She reaches over and gives Danica's hand a squeeze. "Maybe I'll get a regular toaster as a replacement. They're easier to use."

"I'll take anything that makes cooking easier. And less fiery."

"Agreed."

The pair finishes breakfast in comfortable silence, then spends the drive to school chatting about summer vacation. Pearl's tour ends in San Diego, so mother and daughter are flying to California to watch ABOS's last show, followed by a family trip to Joshua Tree. They've made it a tradition to hit at least one national park every year, and even at fifteen-years-old, Danica still looks forward to the trips, especially if she helps plan them. Her contribution this year was booking a star-gazing UFO excursion. She thinks it will be hilarious. Pearl and Maggie agree.

After dropping her daughter off, Maggie cruises to the craft store for some paint. Summer is wedding season, and orders have been flooding her inbox. Last year, her crafting venture turned a profit thanks to face-in-the-hole boards, those cheesy wooden cutout props you stick your head through. The stand-ins appeal to people with a sense of humor, and she markets them as an alternative to the tattered fake mustaches and feathered boas couples get with wedding photobooths. Want something unique that will make your big day stand out? Get one of Maggie's boards. Instant laughs, guaranteed.

Last fall, with her wife's input, Maggie created four customizable face-in-the-hole templates and launched Be Marry Boards last fall. They were an immediate hit, with social media driving sales. Potential buyers love the pictures wedding guests post, and they want a similar vibe at their receptions. Since opening, Maggie has raised prices twice—the boards require tons of work. Still, Be Marry is booked until the end of the year, a fact that gives her the warm fuzzies.

Not only do the stand-ins involve lots of labor, but they also soak up supplies. Paint is an item Maggie purchases weekly, and the cashiers at Inspiration Station know her well. Today, Beatriz, a soft-spoken twenty-something with rainbow hair, talks to her about software while she shops. B's voice is vibrant when she's pitching computer programs, less so during the small talk customers make as she rings them up.

"Mrs. Williams…" the cashier stops herself. "I mean, Maggie. I swear you'll be impressed with Illustrator. You use vectors and it really makes the design process flow. It's like, super-efficient."

"You know I'm old school, B. I use a projector. Seriously, that's it." Maggie grins and throws up her hands. "I don't think my brain could handle a program that uses vectors or layers or any of the things you're talking about."

The cashier points at Maggie's phone. "It's not any more complicated than that. And I've seen your social media posts. You know what you're doing."

Maggie doesn't hate technology, but she really enjoys flipping on her overhead projector and tracing the lines it beams out. It feels sturdy. More fixed than her computer's ever-changing screen. "I'll think about it," she says. She wouldn't, but Beatrix was nice, and there was no use being dismissive.

"Sweet." B tilts her head. "And don't forget, if you have questions about using Illustrator or any other design program, just let me know. I help my grandma when she has trouble, so I don't get frustrated easily."

Yeesh. The cashier thinks Maggie is grandmother age. Maggie hopes it's because she exudes wisdom, and not because she acts older than her thirty-six years. "You're too kind." She points to a space on the shelf. "Do you have any electric blue in the back? I'm painting an ocean themed board this week, and that color's perfect for the water."

"Lemme check." B darts off, vibrant ponytail swinging between her shoulders.

While she's gone, Maggie grabs navy, ivory, and cream, three shades made for painting waves. Orange, scarlet, and canary also go in the basket. They're the perfect trio for a sunset. The final hues she snags are aqua and turquoise, colors for the mermaid tails she'll be painting. Sexy mermaid tails to be exact. For their wedding, her clients want a stand-in board with a buxom mermaiden embracing a well-endowed merman, bulge included. If the artwork turns out well, she'll be adding the seductive sea dwellers to Be Marry's template options. Her clientele reinforces the idea that people are interesting, but Maggie enjoys catering to some of their weirder impulses.

As she's loading the last items into the cart, her phone vibrates. She sees her wife's name when the screen unlocks.

PEARL: he showed up. he came after we told him not to. he's not even in the band anymore
PEARL: I don't know what to do

Maggie knows who "he" is, and it can only mean trouble. Her hands tremble as she responds.

MAGGIE: He's a scumbag. Can you talk? I'll give you a call.

Pearl gets back right away.

PEARL: give me 5. I need to ditch him. he's hovering

"Maggie, are you okay?" The question snatches her attention from the screen. Beatriz has gone back to being soft-spoken, but her voice overflows with concern.

"I'm okay B, but I need a quick checkout today. There's something I need to take care of." Beatriz matches Maggie's pace instantly, and they rush to the cash register with quick strides.

"There was one tube of electric blue. Do you still want it?" B asks while scanning my other items.

"I do. Thank you for finding it."

She adds it to the pile and finishes scanning the order. As Maggie pays, her phone vibrates again. Beatriz hears it. "Better take that. I'll see you next week."

"See you soon, B."

Maggie throws the bags over her shoulder and presses answer as she's leaving the store. Muffled background noises fill her ears, but they don't block the sound of her wife crying.

And cursing Dante Wilder.

A Box of Star's Singer Arrested

By: Bennie Thompson • November 03, 2022

Last night, Dante Wilder, singer for indie rock group A Box of Stars, was arrested in Bellows, NJ. The arresting officer put this in the affidavit:

On 11/02/2022 at approximately 0115 hours, I was dispatched to the Overlook Suites in Bellows, NJ in relation to a domestic violence situation. Upon arrival, I met with Madison Brighton in the lobby. The victim stated she met Dante Wilder earlier in the evening at his band's concert. She agreed to drinks with Wilder after the show, and they both consumed whiskey sours from the Overlook's bar.

After 4 drinks, victim agreed to enter Wilder's room. Although Wilder had considerably more alcohol than victim - he consumed 6 doubles - victim felt safe, since Wilder was polite and showed no signs of anger.

When they entered hotel room 316, Wilder began acting in an aggressive and irritated manner, and demanded victim remove her clothing. Victim refused, and Wilder grabbed her wrist in an attempt to force compliance. Victim was able to free herself and called 911 from the hotel lobby.

After arriving on scene, I examined victim, noticing red marks on her wrists. When interviewing the hotel clerk, he stated victim came into the lobby extremely upset and crying when she asked to use the phone.

Based on testimony and victim injuries, I find Dante Wilder in violation of statute 2C:13-5. Wilder was arrested and transported to the Peters County Jail without incident.

We will update this story as more information become available.

Chapter 3 – Nicole

{February 5, 2023}

Nicole stares out the car window, watching the scenery rush past. The Atlanta skyline has changed into foliage, and sprawling oaks form a canopy over the road. Every so often, a moss-covered branch scrapes against the SUV's roof, and she hears a sharp *ssssss* as it drags across the metal.

The landscape charmed her at first, but she's over it. During the six-hour drive, she's seen more deer than houses and more opossum than deer. She and her husband are in the middle of nowhere, driving through towns smaller than the one they're from. And that's saying something because less than five thousand people live in their city. Country living is nice, but even Nicole prefers more signs of life. "How much longer, hon?" she asks her husband, a slight twang marking her words.

"Not long. Ten or fifteen minutes." Jake flashes her a grin, honey-brown eyes sparkling, before returning his attention to the road. "You're going to love where we're staying. It has treehouse-castle vibes, and it's plenty big enough for the whole band."

A treehouse-castle. Interesting. Why does Jake think she's the type of person who enjoys something matching that description? But he seems excited, so Nicole keeps her thoughts to herself. "Sounds real nice."

"Trev picked it because it's isolated, but it also happens to have a heart-shaped tub in our room." He reaches over, placing a hand on her thigh. "After practice tonight, maybe we can test it out."

How cheesy. Internally, Nicole rolls her eyes. After eight years together, her husband should know her tastes, but he usually proves that idea wrong. Luckily, he's sweet. And really, really cute. Both qualities save him from any true anger. Nicole suppresses her annoyance, keeping her voice calm while responding. "I could go for a romantic bath. Especially if there are drinks involved."

"Dylan's got that covered. He stopped on his way from the airport to grab a cooler full of stuff."

"That's smart." She peeks out the window again, frowning at the seclusion. "There's nothing close by. Not even a Dollar Store. Did he bring food too? I sure hope so."

"Yep. He hired someone local to stock the place yesterday. All we have to do is show up." He squeezes his wife's leg. "He even got you sweet tea. And the ingredients for biscuits and gravy."

Dylan is a peach. Sometimes, Nicole thinks he knows her better than Jake. "Perfect," she says while cranking up the radio. 1950s country fills the car, and she sings along with Hank Williams and Patsy Cline until they reach the BnB, a two-storied cabin a quarter mile off the road.

Nicole's hubby was half-accurate about their home for the next week. The place looks like a treehouse. Stacked logs form the exterior, and the right side of the house is built around a thick oak. Boards nailed into the trunk go up to a door on the second story. Apparently, you can access the top half of the house from an exterior ladder, although the steps appear too weathered to be safe. The sweet smell of jasmine floats on the air, adding to the outdoorsy ambiance.

There are no moats or towers, so Nicole doesn't understand the castle portion of Jake's description. Unless the place's size is what he meant. The cabin is ginormous. When they get inside, the entry's soaring ceilings add to the vastness. Nicole is thrilled. At least they won't be crowded during their stay. There's more than enough room for everyone to have their own space and then some.

Dylan meets them in the foyer dressed in fuchsia sweats and a stained navy hoodie. Nicole is used to his attire, but people meeting him for the first time often double-take at his casualness, especially those outside the music industry. He's not what they expect a tour manager to look like. After they chat with him and realize he knows his shit, they get over their silly assumptions.

Nicole blames Hollywood for the misunderstanding. They always cast managers as fast-talking suit-wearing jerks. The man overseeing A Box of Stars is anything but this stereotype. Dylan is a laidback teddy bear.

He reinforces this depiction as he greets them. Dylan pulls the couple into a hug, squeezing them together until their cheeks mash. After he releases his grip, he steps back and lets out a chuckle, eyes crinkling at the corner. "Jake, Nicole, how was the drive? We got here twenty minutes ago and almost have the van unloaded."

"D-man. It's been months." Jake shoves Dylan's shoulder, grinning from ear to ear. "The ride was long and boring, but it's over, so none of that matters anymore." His eyebrows shoot up. "I thought we got here first. I didn't see the van up front."

"Yeah, it's around back. The practice room is in the basement and there's an entrance on the other side of the cabin."

Nicole interrupts before they get too deep into their conversation. "Howdy, Dylan. It's been too long, but you look great." She grins, then sweeps her arm around the room. "Do you happen to know where our room is? I'd like to change out of my travel clothes and maybe close my eyes for a few minutes."

He points up. "You lovebirds are on the second floor."

"Thanks." She turns to Jake and plants a kiss on his cheek. "I'm going to switch into something comfy and nap. I need to clear my mind."

He grins. "That sounds good. I'll stay down here and help the crew unload and setup, then I think we're breaking for dinner. That right?" Jake asks his manager.

"Yep. I'm marinating some steaks. Should be tasty."

"Thank you, boys. See you in a bit." Nicole strolls to the stairs but pauses before heading up. "Hon, can you get my bag from the car?" she calls over her shoulder.

"Sure can," Jake answers.

His retreating footsteps echo in the foyer. Nicole waits until the door closes before facing Dylan. "Be honest with me, please. How's everything going? Without Dante, I mean. Jake didn't say much on the drive, but I could tell he was worried. He asked me if I was okay about a hundred times. He musta been projecting."

He sighs. "I think that's the consensus. We're all worried. Ever since the fallout from his arrest, he's gotten more unhinged. And that's saying a lot because he was already throwing temper tantrums every chance he got." Dylan's mouth pulls into a frown. "Hopefully he stays away. He's been warned."

A shiver runs through Nicole. She hates to think of what will happen if Dante crashes practice. "Sorry to bring it up, but it's been on my mind. The subject is off-limits with Jake too. He shuts down any conversation about it, which means I have to get my info from Maggie or Pearl. And you know how busy they are. They're either running around with their youngin' or traveling. I rarely get a text back."

Dylan reaches out and squeezes her shoulder. "No worries, Nicole. I'm here for you."

From outside, she hears a trunk slam. Time to hustle up the stairs. "I'll see you at dinner. Thanks for being you."

The band manager nods, and she scrambles to the second floor before her husband comes inside and sees her talking to Dylan instead of relaxing. She doesn't want Jake to know she's asking about Dante. He might get upset.

Rushing up the stairs causes her to pant, and she's still winded when Jake enters the room with her bag. He notices. "You okay, Coley?"

She grins at the nickname. "I'm good. Just worn out."

He wraps her in his arms. "Get some rest. If you need anything, shoot me a text." Jake raises her off the floor and their lips meet. She melts into his body, pressing her mouth against his. He nibbles her lower lip, then steps back. "You're hot, babe. Save that sexiness for later." He gestures to the gaudy red tub in the corner of the room. It's on a raised platform adorned by purple fairy lights. "Me, you, booze, and a bath. I can't lie, I'm pretty excited."

Nicole gives him a gentle nudge. "Well, hurry down to practice then. The quicker you finish with the band, the quicker we can jump in the tub."

"Yes, ma'am." Laughing, Jake jogs to the door. He drops a wink as he turns the handle. "I'll be thinking of you while we're setting up. See you at dinner, hot stuff." He waves then darts out of the room.

Nicole slips out of her jeans and into leggings. When she falls backward onto the bed, the mattress gives just the right amount. Her face settles into a contented grin, and she drifts off to sleep, happy to focus on a heart-shaped rendezvous rather than an ex-bandmember causing trouble.

***

A thirty-minute snooze clears her grogginess. There are no alerts on her phone, which means it's not time to go downstairs yet. With nothing pressing to do, she stares at the woodgrain ceiling and lets her thoughts wander to Jake and the band.

Nicole likes to send ABOS off, been doing it since the early days, when tours were only a week long and confined to a single state. Back then, she'd go to the first show, then chill with everyone until they took off for the next town. Jake would kiss her before leaving, always whispering the same thing before hopping into the band's rusty minivan, "I'll miss you, but I'll love you more when I get back." What a romantic. Is it any wonder that she married the man?

Over the past seven years, as ABOS grew popular, Nicole stayed for each tour's first leg. Usually, she watched three or four concerts from backstage and relaxed with Jake when he wasn't busy. Between soundcheck and showtime, they'd eat, drink, and shop. Or they'd hike if a park was close by. Traveling to different venues and exploring the surrounding area was a unique way to experience the world. They've visited some jaw dropping places—Austria, Brazil, Spain, lots of spots in the US—all thanks to his job.

Dante was the only one who had a problem with her coming along. When ABOS was starting out, he was fine, but as soon as their debut album hit the top twenty, that changed. All the singer wanted to do was party and he saw Nicole as a mood killer. At the venues, every time she entered the dressing room, his face would scrunch up and he'd tell Jake he was pussy whipped.

Dante's words were mean, but his attitude on the bus was way worse. When everyone hung out in the front lounge, he would ignore Nicole. He'd turn his back, walk away, and speak to anyone else instead of her. His actions were super obvious in the confined space, and she hated it. Despite several conversations with Jake, the rude behavior continued for years.

Dante's bullying stopped last November when he got arrested at a New Jersey hotel. The idiot spent three nights in jail before his parents posted bail. Even though the charges were dropped, the rest of the band knew he was trash, so they called a meeting. In a 3-to-1 vote, they kicked Dante Jerkface Wilder out of A Box of Stars.

Good riddance to bad rubbish, if you ask Nicole.

Now, the Rebound tour will be the band's emergence as a four-piece, with Pearl stepping in as lead vocalist and Rory and Jake singing backup. Press releases have been kept to a minimum, which means ABOS fans are going to go crazy when they notice one less bandmember onstage. Everyone knows about Dante's arrest. Very few people realize he's been dropped from the group.

Nicole will stick around for practice week and the kickoff show in Atlanta. She'd been hesitant to come at all—wouldn't the band want to process their massive change without a non-member peering over their shoulders? —but Jake convinced her otherwise. He thought her presence would be calming, since she's always been around. He compared her to a well-worn sweater. Her being there was good for the band.

Even with his reassurances, Nicole vowed to stay out of the way and let the band do its thing. What if they had a creative breakthrough in the cabin's basement? She'd never want to interrupt something important like that.

This hesitance is why she waits an hour to reach out to her husband.

NICOLE: Everything ok hon? I'm starting to get hungry. I can grab something for myself if you guys are still getting settled.

She gnaws at her cuticles while waiting for a reply. A minute passes. Then two. A hundred-twenty seconds is forever to wait on a text, and Jake is normally a quick responder. She counts to thirty again before sending another message.

NICOLE: Heading to the kitchen. Seems like ur busy! nbd, I can fend for myself. love you <3

She gets an immediate response.

JAKE: stay upstairs
JAKE: he's here and he's wasted

Blood pounds in her veins. She doesn't need to ask who the "he" is. Somehow, Dante found out about the cabin and he's terrorizing everyone in the basement. Like he used to do when he was drunk on the bus. Although Jake wants her to stay put, there's no way she's cowering upstairs waiting for everything to calm down. When Nicole promised to give the band their space, it had nothing to do with an emergency.

And Dante's appearance is a full-blown crisis.

She races to the first floor without having a plan. Intervention would be necessary, but how? Should she call the police? That seems excessive at this point, although technically Dante is trespassing since he isn't on the rental agreement or anyone's guest. What about causing her own scene? She can barge downstairs, screaming and throwing things in a mock rampage. Her interruption would surely divert attention away from the idiot who clearly takes pleasure in remaining a nuisance.

The more Nicole thinks about it, the better the idea seems. A distraction might break the hold Dante has over the group. It's as good a plan as any and all she can come up with on the fly. A deep breath gives her the courage she needs, and after gathering a handful of coasters and magazines from a nearby coffee table, she heads toward the basement door.

Dante's voice cuts through the barrier. He's yelling—screaming actually—and heavy footsteps strike the ground. He must be pacing while he hollers. "I have shit on all of you. Pearl, Rory, Jake. Even you, Dylan." A heavy thud makes Nicole jump. Did he hit something? Has his rage turned violent? Part of her wishes she could see, but another part is glad there's a barricade between them.

Nicole hears a slur in Dante's voice. It doesn't stop him from bellowing his next few sentences. "Are you listening to me? I'm not afraid to go public with what I know. Let's see how you like it when everyone is all up in your business like they're in mine right now."

"We're listening man, but we're not budging," Jake says. "You need to calm down and get the hell out of here. I'll call you a ride myself."

"If it isn't Mr. Perfect, trying to be the hero, just like always." I hear the sneer in Dante's voice. "Lucky your bitch wife isn't here. She wouldn't be your wife for much longer if Unkie Dante sat her down for a nice little chat." He pauses to laugh. The sound sends shivers along Nicole's spine, and she's hit with an impulse to retreat. Nothing good can come from these revelations, she knows. More than likely they're hate-fueled lies meant to provoke the band. But her feet won't budge, and honestly, she's curious about what the singer will say about her husband. What secret does a desperate man think will break up a marriage?

Dante continues, a gleeful tone giving a bounce to his words. "I'm guessing you've kept her in the dark about your twink preference."

"What does *that* mean?" Jake asks, a dark undertone giving the question a sharp edge.

Dante snorts. "You know what it means, Mr. Perfect. I've seen you in Rome and Prague flouncing around after Mrs. Devlin heads home to the good ol' US of A. Obviously, you wanted to keep your fuck buddies on the down low because you didn't bring them back to the bus, but I know what you're up to. I've seen you in the clubs, trolling for your next conquest like a horny teenager." He lets loose another chilling laugh, and Nicole pulls her hoodie tight around her. The fabric does little to fight off the coldness of the singer's words.

When he speaks again, Dante's volume has dropped. Nicole hates that she strains to hear the rest of the accusation, but she can't help herself. She's in too deep to miss anything. She has to hear the rant until the end. "For seven years, I haven't cared who you've boned. If you hook up with a thousand people, what does that have to do with me? I'm not one to slut shame. I've partied plenty and have some crazy stories of my own." He pauses, and no one speaks up during the silence. Nicole holds her breath waiting for him to resume,

When Dante starts again, his words are guttural. They drip with malice. "I still don't care who you bone, but I do care that you've made me into the bad guy and kicked me out of the band. You pricks aren't the sweethearts you claim to be, and I swear on my mother's grave that I will make your lives a living hell. As soon as I leave here, I'm calling my press contacts, and I will sell you out to the highest bidder." Another laugh, this one less chilling and more sadistic. "Have fun practicing, assholes."

She expects Dante to emerge from the room, but a frightened Pearl charges up the stairs instead. Tears stream down her cheeks, and she pushes past without a word. Nicole waits for a minute, but no one else comes up. Guess it's on her to head down. She drops the items in her hand—she doesn't think a diversion is necessary at this point—and creeps to the basement, nudging the door open when she reaches the bottom step.

Minus Pearl, the band and crew are huddled in the center of the practice space, bent over a large item on the floor. Nicole scans the faces of those standing and doesn't see Dante. Where did he go?

When she approaches the group, Jake breaks away and clutches her hand. His breath comes out in gasps. He's trembling. "Why didn't you stay in our room, Coley?"

"I was worried. And wanted to help." She glances at the object on the floor. It looks like a pile of clothing, a faded flannel and some jeans. Why is everyone staring at discarded clothes? It's odd. "What's that, hon?" She gestures toward the shirts and pants.

Trev answers, a blank expression on his face. "It's him."

"Him?" Nicole's question comes out as a shriek. Trev nods, then goes back to staring at the body, barely blinking.

It is a body. That's obvious now. But Nicole doesn't understand why everyone is calm. And silent. A person is lying on the floor, and from what she can tell, no one has called 911 or even bent down to check Dante's pulse. She understands that his last words were threats, but ignoring him isn't the answer. In her mind, that makes them just as bad as the singer. There's no way she wants to be compared to him.

She drops Jake's hand, edging closer to Dante, holding it together until she figures out the extent of what's happened. Dylan, Rory, and Trev make space for her, and she scoots around them until she's next to the body. "I'm going to check if he's breathing." No one responds, so she drops to her knees, placing trembling fingers on Dante's neck. "Someone set a timer for a minute." Again, no one speaks, but she notices her husband fiddling with his phone. She presses down firmly and waits, wanting to feel a pulse, dreading what it means if there's no movement.

After some time, Jake's alarm goes off. "That was two minutes. Did you feel anything?"

Nicole lowers her head, surprised at the tears welling in her eyes. "No. Nothing. Not a single beat."

"Should I call an ambulance?" His voice is timid.

Her reply isn't. "Yes. We need an ambulance and the police. Dante is dead, and they're going to want to know what happened down here."

peter peter noodle eater @noodlesfosho • 11hr

holy. shit. dante wilder is dead. it's sus that he died during band practice. what was abos doing in that creepy cabin? satanic rituals?

Emmy Whithouse @ems_cookie_biz • 11hr

Satanic Panic is so 1980s. But yeah, it's weird that he died in front of everyone. Why hasn't ABOS released a statement? Their silence is making everything weirder. And definitely sus.

The Lucille @lucilletheone • 11hr

Their silence is speaking volumes. THEY'RE HIDING SOMETHING!

Bleepity @bleepityboi • 11hr

they havnt said anything because dante was kicked out of the band and the timing makes them look like azzholes

ABOS Life @abos_life • 10hr

Not true. Stop spreading rumors, troll. There's an explanation for what happened, but the band is in mourning. They'll tell us when they're ready. Where are my ABOS moots? Follow for follow.

Bleepity @bleepityboi • 10hr

my source is reliable. dante was kicked out and now everyone in the band is panicking. Serves them right. theyre no talent wankers

Chapter 4 – Karina

{February 11, 2023}

Flowers (yellow roses).

Cake (chocolate, two tiered, shaped like a microphone).

Booze (old-fashioneds and whisky sours).

Social media announcement (shared forty thousand times).

Dante's parents organized his memorial service, following instructions he'd penned weeks before he died. The first time Karina met them was after his death. They asked her to speak at the event.

They want her to tell a happy story about their relationship. To raise a glass and give a toast to his tragic end. To sing a verse from his favorite song. All the things a grieving girlfriend should do.

Karina agrees, but instantly regrets the promise. She won't be around for the memorial service.

Because it's her fault that Dante's dead.

And she's turning herself in tomorrow.

Breaking News < Clementine County < City of Clemons

Girlfriend of A Box of Star's Singer Confesses to Murder

By: Devora Maltrusic • February 12, 2023

Karina Belmore was placed in police custody early this morning after posting a murder confession online. Belmore shared the following on her social media accounts:

> *Like many music fans out there, I mourn the loss of Dante Wilder. We had almost half a year together. A beautiful five months filled with love and laughter. He inspired me to pursue my dreams and was always by my side when I needed support.*
>
> *I can no longer live with what I've done. I don't eat, I can't sleep, I barely leave the house. Guilt is preventing me from functioning.*
>
> *While Dante made my life better, I made his infinitely worse. Because of me he's dead. I poisoned someone who loved me for who I was. I'm the person responsible for Dante's death.*
>
> *I'm ready to face the consequences of my actions.*

The message was shared 7.8 million times before it was removed from the web. Clemons Police escorted Belmore from her home without incident, and she is considered a person of interest in Dante Wilder's death.

*This is a breaking news story and will be updated as information becomes available.

Chapter 5 – Lala

{February 6-12, 2023}

When tour is cut short, Lala takes a week off work. She and Rory spend hours discussing Dante's death and its aftermath. They also consider next steps. Did Rory still want to be in ABOS, or was it finally time to pursue a law degree? Lala's man loves playing guitar, but his true passion is environmental conservation. During the band's prosperous period, the couple had saved more than enough for tuition, so three years in school wouldn't set them back financially. Also, the timing would be good for the planet. Earth is in terrible shape and gaining an advocate like Rory would be a huge win. He'd be thrilled to work on cases dealing with water use, pollution, or climate change.

As they weigh his options, they huddle on Potato, the brown corduroy couch from their first apartment. The sofa had traveled with them since undergrad, and it currently occupies a corner in the basement next to Rory's guitar collection. They do their best thinking on Potato, and the beat-up couch has helped them navigate some tough decisions. Lala hopes it will do the same as they discuss the next phase of their lives.

From the reluctance in his voice, she can tell Rory's hesitant to commit to the attorney path. It's not because he's afraid of the challenge. That's not it at all. His issue is more noble. Lala's husband doesn't want her to shoulder extra burdens while he's enrolled in classes. "It's not fair to you, La, and that's reason enough for me." He sips his bourbon, the fancy stuff they were saving for a celebration. Instead of enhancing a happy event, they're using it to calm their nerves after experiencing Dante's traumatic death. Rory, by witnessing it. Lala, by listening to him describe the grisly details.

And the liquor is doing its job. The first swallow sends a wave of warmth racing through Lala's body. A few more sips lend a shine to the basement. She sinks into Potato, breathing deeply while enjoying the room's rosy veneer.

When she glances at Rory, it seems like the bourbon is working for him too. There's an adorable flush on his cheeks, and he grins while swirling the spicy rye. His voice is raspy when he speaks. "For now, my decision is to stick with music. At least while I'm playing, I get a decent paycheck. Don't you want to retire before we're fifty? I sure as hell do."

Lala shakes her head. "Don't let money or fairness sway your decision. Do I need to remind you about my dissertation? You were there for me nonstop, and I'm more than happy to do the same for you. That's what being a partner means."

"But that's different. I was between tours and could devote every waking minute to your needs, Dr. Ramirez." He chuckles. "You didn't even ask much of me. Only that I always had a pot of coffee going and that I agreed to a chicken tender run whenever you needed it. Which was three or four times a week if I recall."

"Chicken tenders help me think. Never underestimate the power of protein coated in honey barbeque sauce." She shoves his shoulder. "You're trying to distract me. And it's not working. We're here to talk about you, not my weird cravings."

Rory lowers his head and stays quiet. From experience, Lala knows he's gathering his words. He likes to put just the right spin on his thoughts, so he takes time to craft his sentences. Some people get frustrated with the habit, but she finds it endearing. It's taught her to slow down and listen, a rarity in the fast-paced world.

His eyes are clear when he meets her gaze, a half-smile lifting the right side of his mouth. "Mi amor, I'm always going to do what's best for us. Right now, the band is in turmoil, but if I know the industry, any negative press will pass quickly, and we can use what happened to our benefit." His smile fades. "I hate saying it like that. Like we'll be using Dante's death as a marketing ploy because that's not exactly what will happen. We'll just be taking advantage of the eyes on ABOS, and the attention will jumpstart our transition to a four-piece group."

Rory opens his arms, and Lala moves between them, snuggling against his chest. He rests his chin on her head and keeps talking. "I'll give the band another year, then reevaluate the situation. That's when I'll decide if going back to school looks better or if I should keep playing. Either way, there's no wrong answer. I'll be content with either." He kisses the top of her head. "I'm an extremely lucky dude, Lala. Not many people get to choose between two awesome careers."

"You're right. You are lucky. But not because of your job." She turns around, facing him. Her hands find his beard and give it a gentle tug. "You managed to snag yourself one hell of a partner."

Rory's eyes sparkle as he leans forward. His lips meet Lala's, and she tastes the bourbon on his breath like she's sure he tastes it on hers. Their kiss is heated, and she wants him, but Rory pulls back. "I know you're trying to be sexy, and believe me, it's working, but I wanted to tell you how right you are before I start getting handsy. Laverne Darlene Ramirez, I'm the luckiest man alive, all because I married you."

Tears well in her eyes, and she wipes them with the back of her hand. "Damn it, Roars. You made me cry."

"Just telling the truth."

"In the sweetest way possible." She tugs his beard again. "You know I'm emotional. Here we are talking about your future—"

"Our future," he says.

"Our future. And you go and get all romantic on me, and I start weeping like a mom sending her firstborn off to kindergarten."

"It's one of my favorite things about you. You're not afraid to feel." He reaches up and clasps her hands. "Keep being sensitive."

She lowers their hands to the front of his jeans. "You're pretty sensitive too."

"That I am." He presses down. "Want to find out just how sensitive?"

"Oh yeah." They stand and kiss their way to the bedroom, where they peel off their clothes before toppling onto the bed. Throughout the night, they discover that both of them are extremely sensitive. And somehow, they have the same level of stamina from their first date, fifteen years ago. How cool is that? There's nothing like maintaining a spark through a relationship's highs and lows.

***

The remainder of the week passes the same. they chat and make out, and maybe take a chicken tender break or two.

Or four.

They actually take four. There's no shame in loving the fried, sauce-slathered delights.

Lala isn't bored by the monotony. In fact, she's reassured. Although Rory had experienced a traumatic event, their lives continued moving forward, one routine-filled day after the next. They know what will happen when they wake up in the morning, and each night, when they close their eyes, they're satisfied with the hours they've spent together.

On Sunday, out of the blue, their routine gets a shakeup. Lala lounges in her robe, enjoying the last day before the workweek, when Rory rushes into the kitchen, eyes wide, laptop in hand. "Lala, have you seen this?" He thrusts out the computer.

"Whoa. You're coming in hot." She reaches up, snags the machine, and sets it on the breakfast table next to her coffee. "Must be something important. Did the Backstreet Boys announce that they're dropping an album?" Rory isn't amused by her question. He gestures at the laptop, so Lala squints at what's on the screen. "A Karina post, huh? What's she up to today?" Usually, Karina sticks to motivational phrases or food pictures, but this post is different. Given her boyfriend's recent death, Lala expects the mood of her message to be toned down, and it is. What she's not expecting is a murder confession, but that's exactly what Karina has typed out, sharing her guilt with the entire world.

"Oh wow." Lala's eyes widen to match Rory's. "This isn't good."

"I don't believe it. How can that timid woman be responsible for Dante's death?" He shakes his head, frowning. "Both times I've been around her, she barely talked. She just hid in the dressing room until it was showtime. And the few times I saw her on the side stage, she was swaying back and forth to the songs, but like barely. Even her dancing was timid."

"I agree. She was shy when I met her, but don't you think poison would be the perfect murder weapon for someone like that?" Lala asks. "Maybe she had battered woman syndrome, and she snapped? We all know Dante was a royal jerk, but what if he was even worse in private? He got arrested for assaulting that woman in New Jersey, and I wouldn't put it past him to have hurt Karina in some way."

"Damn. I bet you're right."

"Did the news get ahold of her confession?" she asks.

"Nothing yet, but they will soon. Look how many times it's been shared."

Lala glances at the number. 250,000 shares in less than an hour. Karina is going viral for all the wrong reasons. "Should I text her? I don't want my words being used by the police, but I'm worried about her." Lala inhales sharply. "Wow. I just said I was worried about a confessed murderer. What planet is this?"

"It's Earth last time I checked." He collapses into the chair next to his wife. "I get it, though, because I feel for her too. Living with Dante must have been hell. I don't agree with murder, but it's not hard to understand her reasons for doing what she did." Rory's eyes close, and his shoulders droop. "If you could have seen him in the practice room, Lala. The way he was screaming at us until he stopped breathing. He was scary." Rory glances up. "And I'm a six-foot-tall man. Karina is what 5'1, 5'2? If Dante squared up to her, frightened would only be the beginning of what she felt."

A shudder ripples through Lala. He's right. Dante was a big dude, taller than her husband, with a broad chest and runner's build. He also had freaky eyes. They were ice blue and looked both emotionless and rage-filled. If he were towering over Lala, she'd be terrified. And plotting revenge. There's no way she'd let someone bully her without wanting to lash out.

She finishes the rest of her coffee, no longer interested in prolonging the morning. "My guess is that she'll get picked up and taken to the local PD for questioning. Her post gives the police enough probable cause to bring her in, no doubt about that, but they'll want to double check that she's not just seeking attention."

He grimaces. "People do that?"

"They sure do. Plenty of people post false statements online. I come across them a few times a year." She stands up, carrying her mug to the sink. She scrubs the cup while continuing, the monotonous activity contrasting with their morbid discussion. "Mostly, the false statements are accusations against someone else, but Karina seems to be pointing the blame at herself. The detectives on the case will want more proof, like the why and the how of it. That'll build on her social media confession and make their evidence airtight." Lala doesn't think Karina was the type to retaliate, but sometimes the most timid wallflowers carried the most rage of all.

"Can you help her at all?" Rory asks, eyebrows raised.

"Right now, I can't think of anything I can do, but I'll keep mulling it over. Tomorrow at work, I'll huddle up with the girls and we'll brainstorm. I'm sure Tina and Ellen will come up with something. They're really good at stuff like this." Lala pivots to the refrigerator and opens the freezer. "Want a smoothie?"

"Always," Rory answers.

As the fruit and yogurt blend, her mind wanders to the night of Dante's arrest. She stays out of Rory's way when he's on tour, but she does watch a show or two during most runs. Usually, seeing her husband's concert meant a long drive or flight, but that wasn't the case the evening of the arrest. The show was in Bellows, New Jersey, a twenty-minute trip from their house. Easy Peasy. Even better, the band had a day off after the show, so Lala could stay in Rory's hotel room until bus call the next afternoon. It was rare when things worked out like that, and she took advantage of the timing. She got to the Overlook Suites during the early check-in window, and her and Rory hung out (wink wink) before sound check. After that, they chilled in the dressing room until showtime.

During the concert, ABOS sounded great. Well, if the singing wasn't included. Dante's vocals were shot. There were moments when she thought his voice would completely give out, but by some miracle, he made it through the last song. When the audience erupted into applause, Lala questioned her judgment. Had she misinterpreted Dante's struggle? Did he do better than she thought?

Later, while she and the hubs lounged at the hotel bar, she asked Rory those questions. He backed up her perception. "You saw it right, La. He's been shitty for a while now. The man starts drinking whisky when he wakes up in the afternoon and finishes a pint by showtime. Almost anyone would sound terrible after that much booze."

Lala held up her drink. "Cheers to that." Her husband laughed while they clinked glasses. "Phew. I'm glad I don't have to drive back tonight. This beer is strong. You know I'm not much of a drinker."

"Yeah, Double Knot knows what's up. I like when we play near our favorite breweries." He leaned his head back, taking a deep swig of his IPA.

"Hopefully, this becomes a normal stop for you guys."

"Yeah, that would be great." Rory sighted something over her shoulder and narrowed his eyes. "Don't look now, but here comes the trainwreck," he whispered.

Lala didn't look. There was no need. The trainwreck stumbled into her sightline with a woman she'd never met.

Dante raised his hand and pointed in Lala's face. "Move down. Madison needs a seat." His breath smelled like an entire minibar.

His date interjected. "Let's sit over here, handsome, and leave your friends alone. They don't look like they want to be bothered." Madison's ruby lips stretched into a grin. She tugged Dante's arm, pulling him toward two open stools at the bar's opposite end.

He shook her off. "I want to sit here. Rory and Lala won't mind, will you guys?"

"Actually, we were just leaving, so you can have our seats." Rory stood and reached into his pocket for a twenty. "I recommend the IPA they have on draft. It's delicious." He plopped the bill down and turned his wife's way. "You ready, mi amor?"

"Yep." Lala pushed her beer away, no longer interested in the remaining quarter. "Let's get into our PJs and find a movie to watch."

"Lame," Dante said.

She swiveled her head between him and his date. Although Madison appeared sober and alert, she was going to start drinking soon, which would make her vulnerable. She was a stranger, but that didn't mean Lala wanted to see her harmed by the slime standing next to her, so Lala gave her an out. Just in case. "We're in room 423 if you guys need anything."

Dante sneered. "What would we need from you?" He pulled out the stool I'd abandoned and collapsed into it. "Nighty night, losers."

With those friendly words ringing in their ears, Rory threw an arm around his wife's shoulder, and they headed to the elevators. While waiting for a car, Lala stole a glance behind her. It was 11:30 on a Friday night, and the tavern was slammed. Madison was flagging down the bartender, oblivious to everything except scoring a drink, but Dante noticed Lala peeking. The creep raised both hands and flipped her the bird. Classy.

That was the last time she ever saw him. From the police report, Lala knew Dante tried to hurt the woman he brought to the bar. Luckily, she got help before it escalated.

After his arrest, Lala avoided anything to do with the ex-singer. He sent a few pathetic texts, whining about everyone abandoning him, but she ignored them and lived like he didn't exist. And now, he doesn't.

How's that for manifesting?

Her attention returns to the blender. The smoothies are done, but they need one more ingredient. She turns to Rory, confident he'll agree. "Is it too early to start drinking? Karina's confession is making me feel really icky, and I think some rum will help."

He nods. "I'm with you. This whole situation is strange. Can you believe we know a murderess?" He pauses. "That's probably sexist. We know a murderer. A real, live murderer." His lips pull into a frown. "We were at a show with her, babe. We spent hours hanging out with a killer." Rory reaches into the liquor cabinet and pulls out a bottle of Bacardi. "If that's not reason enough for a drink, I'm not sure what the threshold is." He hands over the bottle.

"Thank you for understanding." A healthy pour goes into their smoothies, and Lala blends them for twenty seconds before sliding Rory his drink. "I was going to take it easy on the last day of my staycation, but it seems like the universe had other plans." She raises her glass. "Bottoms up, Roars. Tomorrow, I'll start making sense of this situation. For now, let's get tipsy."

What Happened to A Box of Stars?

ABOS' third album, Deviance Driven, leaves me mourning the early days of the band. When they were good.

by Alexis Grimmpel on April 29, 2020

Sigh. It's tragic when a band you love produces terrible work, but that's exactly what happened with ABOS's third album. The early days of the pandemic were made for listening to music. What else were you supposed to do while isolating at home? But even uninterrupted listening time couldn't save Deviance Driven. It's that awful.

Honestly, I just don't get it. I'm all for musicians trying new things—that's part of the creative process—but ABOS went way too far with this album. Throughout ten songs, you'll find no floaty melodies or intense drum buildups, but it was these two factors that made the band huge. They were ABOS's calling card, and fans will be disappointed that they're missing from Deviance Driven.

Vocally, Dante Wilder lost his edge. In the previous albums, wonder and pain weaved through his voice, and the songs were just as likely to make you cry as amp you up. That was a beautiful thing. Music is supposed to move you. Unfortunately, on Deviance Driven, Wilder tries out a nasal whine he has no business touching. And it's rough. Really rough. I tried to get into the ballads because that's what the entire album is, but there was no amount of lenience that could rescue the vocals.

The music. Oh, the music. Technically everything is solid. Pearl Williams and Rory Ramirez are talented guitarists, and even through Wilder's buzzsaw wailing, you can hear their precision leaking through. There are a few licks that are worthy of a repeat. I recommend the ones during **Bleeding Kaleidoscope**'s finale. Here, Williams and Ramirez slay in what's definitely the album's highlight. On bass, Jake Devlin gets lost in the first few tracks, but by **Twinkling Tomorrows** he finds his way again. For the drums, Trev Branch is subdued throughout the album, but his apt percussion beats add polish to each track.

Overall, I say skip Deviance Driven. Instead of creating the intense masterpieces they're known for, ABOS delivers a mediocre album overflowing with the stench of try-too-hard. Maybe next time they'll return to their celestial roots.

Rating: 2/10

Band: A Box of Stars · **Album:** Deviance Driven · **Tracks:** Light Years Recaptured · Moonrise · Twinkling Tomorrows · Alienation · Seven Months to Mars · Bleeding Kaleidoscope · Constellations on the Brain · Solar Flare · Float · Absence of Sound

Chapter 6 – Brandi

{February 12, 2023}

Trev has been home for a week, and he is already bumming Brandi out.

Every day, he mopes around the house, wearing ratty sweats and hitting his vape like it is an emotional support item. When she tells him the smoke bothers her, he responds in the most patronizing way. "Vaping is way better than cigarettes, Brandi, and it doesn't cause secondhand smoke. There are studies out there if you're willing to read them." Then he would pat her head. "You're being paranoid, kiddo. Drop it."

She hated when he called her that. She was not his kiddo.

And Brandi knows he is wrong about his vape, but she is too tired to argue. Pregnancy drains her patience for stupidity.

When Trev went on tour, she was excited. Her to-do list was huge, and quiet time without his downer presence would be a gift. Babies require a ton of preparation, much more than Brandi anticipated, and up to now, she had done zero to get ready for the little one's arrival. And it is not because she is lazy. Believe her, she is type A and would be done with everything if the decisions were up to her. But they are not. She is behind because her boyfriend is incapable. Of pretty much everything.

Okay, to be fair, Trev is good at two tasks: drumming and bedroom stuff. Any other responsibilities are beyond his capacity, despite several frustrating attempts to correct his incompetence. For her own sanity, Brandi learned to cope with his helplessness. She completes everyday chores without involving him. Life is easier that way.

Obviously, prepping for an infant's arrival is outside Trev's wheelhouse, so she planned to accomplish the most critical items while he traveled with ABOS. But instead of three weeks by herself, she ended up with twenty-four hours, and stupidly, she spent the time resting because she did not know her Trev-free time would be cut short. Thanks to Dante's death.

Leave it to the deceased singer to ruin a good thing. That man was trouble. Well, he was until a bigger trouble overcame him. Bet he never thought his downfall would be a murderous girlfriend. Or maybe he did. He was known for leaving a trail of women behind him, some angrier than others.

Now, Brandi is not one to wish violence on others, but she is not sad Dante is gone. He was cruel and irresponsible. He even turned people against each other. Take her and her former bestie as an example. Dante was the reason they called it quits.

However, this morning, her ex-best friend did text her out of the blue. It was the first Brandi had heard from her in almost five months, and it figures that she was looking for help. Makes sense, though, because Karina is in a tough spot.

Brandi pulls out her phone and rereads the messages.

KARINA: I'm sorry, Bramble. Love blinded me.
KARINA: Can you forgive me? I need you more than ever.

It is too late to reply—her ex-best friend is locked up in the county jail—but Brandi wants to. So. Badly. She wants to tell Karina that she will never forgive her. She wants to say that seeing Karina use her nickname sickens her. She wants to scream that the bitch is getting what she deserves.

But Brandi will not do any of those things. In her younger days, she would have lit into Karina without a second's hesitation, but becoming a mother has changed her. Since seeing the positive sign on the pregnancy test, she has become calmer, less likely to lash out. The composure has allowed her to grow. She is no longer the feisty girl known as Bramble. She has entered her mature stage, the phase overflowing with nurturing maternalism.

Besides, ignoring Karina's pleas was punishment enough. Let her rot for all Brandi cares.

Dammit. Those types of thoughts are not good for the baby. She forces her brain away from the past and focuses on her future. The one loaded with possibility. Getting anything done today will require her to navigate Trev's presence. He's occupied with breakfast, but that will only last five minutes max. How much longer can a bagel hold someone's attention?

Maybe there is somewhere she can send him. It will have to be someplace fun, though. There's no way he will replace the milk or eggs without pitching a fit. Brandi is not exaggerating when she says this, but Trev launches into a pouting, foot-stomping tantrum whenever she asks him to do anything useful. After experiencing two blowups, she learned to get groceries by herself.

A terrible thought hits her. Her boyfriend has trained her to become his bang maid. She literally cooks and cleans up after a grown man. Gross.

Hot rage flows through her body. Why is she only realizing this now? For five months, she just accepted the embarrassing situation, shopping for groceries and scrubbing the toilet without question. The baby has been a distraction, so that is probably why she let it go on unchecked. But still, she has put herself in a less-than ideal situation. And she is furious.

Brandi's boyfriend believes that rock stars do not handle life's boring details. Those tasks are for the hired help. Or apparently, his live-in girlfriend. But there is a major flaw in his thinking—Trev is not a rockstar. At least not one who can afford an assistant or personal chef. A Box of Star's first two albums put them close to that level. The third one almost tanked those efforts. The controversy surrounding Dante's death will either help or harm the band, but it is way too soon to tell. Who knows how fans will react to their new configuration? Switching from a five-piece to a four-piece is a big deal. Some groups have survived similar changes. Others have not. Either way, Trev still lives like it is 2017 and his royalty checks are clearing six figures. But they are definitely not. The couple gets by, but there is not a lot of extra.

Brandi peeks into the dining room, taking him in. The guy is handsome, she will give him that. His ebony hair is pulled into a low ponytail, the end hanging over his shoulder, brushing against his chest. Trev's posture gives him a regal presence. He sits ramrod straight, fussily bringing an everything bagel to his mouth, not the other way around like a classless slob—his opinion, not Brandi's. As he chews, his cheekbones flash, and he manages to appear sensual without even trying. The man looks sexy while he eats. Who does that? No wonder she fell for him. She has got a thing for pretty guys, a weakness she is not afraid to admit.

Despite his tasty appearance, Trev is a nuisance. Especially right now when there is so much to do. Brandi refocuses on finding a distraction for him, using her phone to browse for anything that will motivate his departure. Annoyingly, a social media scroll brings up tons of Karina-related posts. Everyone is obsessed with her confession. They keep trying to decipher her motive. She is already being called a black widow, even though she only killed one person. Do they not know a person has to murder three victims before they are considered a serial killer? Amateurs.

Their mutual friends are the most rabid. The people who knew them both in high school cannot believe timid Karina could commit such an awful crime. Between the two of them, they probably thought Brandi would be the one arrested for murder since Karina was the golden-haired cheerleader, and Brandi was the antisocial drama nerd. Shows how much they know.

Still, she cares less about all that and more about her primary objective—getting rid of Trev. Usually, people's posts are filled with events and gatherings, but with Dante's murder capitalizing her feed, she is left with zero ideas for where to send her boyfriend. She browses a couple more sites, but they are useless. The town calendar has not been updated in months, and the webpage for the closest brewery is malfunctioning.

Brandi is out of ideas. Shit. What is she going to do with him? He needs to leave.

"Kiddo?" Trev's voice cuts through her panic.

Brandi stifles a cringe at the nickname, grinning instead. "What's up?"

"Think I'm going to drive to the coast today. I need to clear my head." He pushes back from the table, stretching to his full height. He is so proud of his perfectly polished posture. Few people know there are lifts in his shoes. "Do you mind? I'll be home before dinner." He arches an eyebrow. "I saw ribs marinating in the fridge. Wouldn't want to miss out on those."

Her smile stretches. "I don't mind at all, love bug. You have the best time."

He saunters over, then bends to leave the whisper of a kiss on her cheek. "Thanks, Brandi. You're a fine girl." Referencing the song used to make her laugh. Now it irritates her. Trev wore out the playfulness of 'Looking Glass' lyrics long ago.

Her beaming lips remain frozen until the front door closes behind him. After that, her features return to their natural state, an expression that lives between a frown and bewilderment. Others tell her she appears confused, but it is far from the truth. She is constantly observing. And learning.

Without warning, the baby delivers a nudge to her bladder. "Hey there, little guy. Good morning to you too." At five months pregnant, her belly still has not popped, but the limited space does not stop the little bean from exercising. He seems to enjoy using her insides as a personal gym. "Did you like the yogurt Mommy had for breakfast?" she chirps.

Brandi never expected to become someone who talks in baby voice. She would prefer to be the mom who sounds mature and educated, the kind of mother you know is going to produce little eggheads with impressive careers. But that is not what happened. She does not go to the extreme by using googoo or gaga or wittle. When she talks to the baby, her pitch gets so high she barely recognizes who is speaking. And it is not on purpose. Baby voice is just something that flies out of her mouth.

There is no ditching the voice either because baby boy loves it. Whenever Brandi converses with him, he wiggles like crazy. He does it now as she strolls to the guest room, chattering aloud. His gentle kicks flutter with each of her steps. As much as his movements awe her, the horror-lover part of Brandi imagines the chest-burster scene in *Alien* whenever he kicks around in there. Growing a human is weird. Who knew babies and seventies sci-fi had so much in common?

The little guy keeps grooving until she steps into the spare room. Maybe he stops because he senses its unfinished state. Brandi reassures him, "It doesn't look like much, little man, but this space has the potential for coziness. All that's missing is a crib and a changing table." She does a three-sixty, noting the scuffed walls and stained carpet. "And some elbow grease." Sighing, she lays a hand on her stomach. "But don't worry. You'll have a beautiful bedroom before you're born. Sorry, it's taking so long. I don't have any help."

There is one item that is ready to use. Brandi's childhood rocking chair sits in a corner, decked out with a sage and tan cushion. She loves the cherrywood rocker. She had dragged it with her from apartment to apartment, never expecting to use it with her own child. But there it was, slightly scuffed, wholly beautiful, and ready for baby.

"How about some music?" she asks her stomach. The answer is a kick. "You got it." As Brandi walks to the chair, song titles float through her head. She had not sung since Trev had returned home—he hates her nasally croon. That means she needs to make today's selection special. "How about a classic?" After settling into the chair, she launches into "I Will Always Love You," channeling the divas who gave the song its bittersweet mood. Of course, matching Dolly's twang and Whitney's depth is impossible, but she gives it a go, and trills through the lyrics twice.

Her singing and the chair's rocking quiet the baby. The motion lulls her too. Her head falls back onto the cushion, and long after the last words leave her mouth, she remains in the chair, zoning out. When Trev left for his drive, her energy levels had peaked. Now, that liveliness had been replaced with thoughts of a nap. Brandi tries to get up from the chair, willing her body to cooperate, but each attempt is countered by weariness. Her arms are cement, her legs granite. She cannot move. What is there to do besides close her eyes? Technically, there is a whole bunch to do, but her stamina is wiped. She gives into the exhaustion and nods off.

During her rocking chair snooze, hours pass by, and the productive morning slips away. When she wakes, it is a quarter till four, and most of the afternoon is gone, but she is revived. Brandi rubs her eyes and stretches her arms, happy for the unexpected nap. The rest was desperately needed. For weeks, she has not slept more than two hours at a stretch. She pushes through the days, dealing with the fatigue as best she can.

If Trev were not such a bed hog, the nights would be better. And if she is being honest, it is not just the evenings that would improve without him crowding her space. Breaking up with him would enhance Brandi's entire life. The man is lazy and self-absorbed, and she is not sure he will be a good father.

It is why she has refrained from telling him about the pregnancy. And why she was waiting until he left to set up the nursery. Her plan was to use the first few days of tour for thinking, to really ensure that Trev's house was the best place for a family of three. His flaws are obvious, but there are benefits to staying in a relationship with him. Stability is one factor, although that could disappear if the band took a nosedive. For now, Trev has a home, even if it needs some work, and royalty payments are deposited into his bank account four times a year. Their combined finances are enough to raise the baby without too much stress, but as a single mom, she would struggle to provide the kind of life her son deserves.

His looks are another appealing factor, and she supposes throwing his drumming abilities on the positive side is only fair. So, three items total in the plus column, and at least three times that number counting as negatives.

Such an unfavorable ratio sounds like a guaranteed trip to the Heartbreak Hotel, but she is hesitant to ditch Trev. His cons are glaring, and they outnumber the pros by far. Red flags for days, if you will.

The problem is, she works as a business analyst, and calculating risk-reward is a critical part of her job. When she encounters a product that offers more than a 15% chance at potential profit, she advises the CEO to take a calculated, moderate gamble. More often than not, these ventures pay off huge, and when they do not, the company backs out immediately, barely scathed by the lost capital.

If she treats the Trev situation as a risk-reward problem, plugging in his three positives and twelve negatives exceeds the level she needs for making a sensible gamble. Logically, Brandi knows human behavior cannot be translated into an equation, but the what-ifs of the whole thing keep dragging her back. What if all their relationship needs is a bigger investment of her time and energy? What if Trev matures when she tells him about the baby? What if they become a happy family that travels the world with A Box of Stars?

There are negative outcomes, of course, but the shiny ones are the most appealing. They are what Brandi wants her life to be. She closes her eyes and pictures Trev chasing a chubby-cheeked toddler. Fallen leaves crackle underfoot, and laughter follows the boys inside the house where the three of them gather for a homecooked meal. At night, she will read the baby a book, and Trev will tuck him in with a kiss on his downy-soft cheek. Later, the adults will sip red wine while watching a movie. Before bed, they will please each other, because they have not lost their passion to the routine of parenthood.

A chuckle erupts from Brandi's throat as she opens her eyes. The daydream is cheesy, she knows, but it could become reality if she stays where she is with Trev. He is not that bad, so maybe some unwavering attention will bring the best out of him. The investment is worth a shot because the payout could be huge.

And just like that, Brandi makes her choice. She will give life with her boyfriend a last-ditch attempt. She will lean into the bang maid role for a week and respond to his every whim without protest. If he levels up and becomes the type of partner she needs, she will tell him about the pregnancy, and they can become her daydream family. If he continues with minimal effort, then Brandi will know he cannot meet her expectations, and she and baby will peace out. Either conclusion is a path forward, which is better than waiting for something to happen. She much prefers taking charge.

Satisfied with the decision, Brandi heads to the kitchen, and begins prepping for the evening. Dinner is the easy part. The ribs are marinating. She will bake them soon. And she will roast the veggies closer to 7:00 PM. Dessert is where her skills are needed. How she sees it, playing the perfect girlfriend requires attention to Trev's sweet tooth. Before he left for tour, she whipped up a chocolate mousse that was to die for. Her boyfriend devoured three servings after dinner and more for breakfast the following morning. Tonight, strawberry coconut tarts will be an excellent way to kick off her weeklong experiment. Might as well start Trev's test with something indulgent.

As she chops berries, her phone buzzes. The caller ID reads UNKNOWN, so she lets it go to voicemail. Half a minute passes and a drawn-out vibration lets her know she has received a message. Probably a spambot pitching an amazing extended warranty. Brandi ignores her cell while whisking the flour, butter, and sugar. After covering the batter for a thirty-minute rest, she plays the recording on speaker, expecting a robot greeting. Instead, a clipped voice barks from the speaker.

"Good afternoon. This message is for Brandi Monner. My name is Lydia Crissick and I'm a partner at Crissick, Deblin, and Cordone. My clients Jenna and Martin Wilder have asked me to reach out to you about an important matter. Will you please return my call at 311-488-7777 at your earliest convenience? Thank you, I look forward to speaking with you."

Notice Regarding Estate
State of California
Clementine County

ESTATE OF Dante Patrick Wilder

(who died on February 5, 2023)

To: Brandi Monner
872 Porrus Drive
Clemons, CA 95094

Ms. Monner,

This notice has been mailed or delivered to you as required by law. The person who signed this notice has identified you as a spouse, heir at law, or beneficiary under a will of the deceased person named above.

Lydia Crissik, Esq. has been appointed as the administrator of the estate.
Address: 300 Citrus Avenue, Suite 215, Clemons, CA 95092
Telephone number: 311-488-7777

Barring contestations, the estate assets of Dante Wilder will be disbursed 30 days following the date below.

THIS NOTICE DOES NOT MEAN THAT YOU WILL RECEIVE ANY MONEY OR PROPERTY.

Thank you for your attention to this matter.

Lydia Crissik
____

Estate Administrator: Signed February 14, 2023.

Chapter 7 – Lala

{February 12-13, 2023}

After a smoothie and a snuggly power nap, Lala and Rory use Sunday evening to chill. They order Thai takeout and lounge on Potato discussing theories about Dante's murder. Rory's convinced arsenic was the weapon Karina used, while Lala picks fentanyl. Their ideas match their personalities. Her husband is adventurous and dreamy, hence the Agatha Christie method he chose. Lala is more practical and knows opioid poisoning would be an effective way to cause fatal damage. The potent drug is easy to get and even easier to disguise. Plus, the overdose rate skyrocketed during the pandemic. Fentanyl is an efficient killer—and a common one. If she were plotting a murder, she'd want to use a method that would blend in with current death trends.

Not that she's plotting a murder.

And Karina certainly isn't blending in. When the singer's girlfriend confessed online, she placed herself in the spotlight, and it isn't just Lala and Rory formulating theories with her as the main suspect. Karina's post was shared close to 100 million times before it was taken down. Everyone wants to know what happened.

The couple's conversation causes the evening to pass in a blink, and before she knows it, 11:00 PM arrives, and it's the end of the weekend. Well, almost the end. After some cuddling-turned-sexy time, the seven-day staycation officially wraps up, and Lala fades into a contented slumber until her alarm blares early the next morning.

Cloudless skies greet her when she rolls out of bed and opens their green argyle curtains. She shuffles to the kitchen for some breakfast and coffee. Thoughts of Karina swirl in her head as she eats some avocado toast, and they keep swirling while she pulls on a wrap dress and booties.

Lala is still thinking about Karina when Rory joins his wife on the front porch to send her off to work. A light breeze ruffles his shaggy coal locks. He's extra cute in his new glasses, the first pair after a lifetime of perfect vision. The frame is clear, and it gives him a hipster-professor aura, a style that looks great on him. "Glasses suit you, Roars."

He lowers his head and peers at Lala over the top of his frames. "Am I the sexy nerd of your dreams?"

"You know it."

"Thanks for helping me pick them out. Hopefully, I'll get used to them soon. Having something on my face is weird." He glances at his watch before passing over his wife's lunchbox. "Time to get moving, mi amor."

"Do I have to?" she pouts.

"You do. But you love work."

"That's true. But spending the week together was nice." She holds up her polka-dotted lunchbox. "Thanks for feeding me. You're the best."

"Sorry to say it's not chicken tenders, but I'm pretty sure you'll like what I packed." He leans over, planting a kiss on her forehead. "Have you thought any more about Karina? She's been on my mind all morning."

"Same with me." Lala swings her lunch back and forth. "It might be stupid, but my instincts are telling me to help her. Of course, I'll have to see if Tina and Ellen are on board. I won't do anything to put LegalShe at risk, and they'll tell me if Karina's case is an issue."

"It's not stupid at all, La. You want to help someone." Rory shrugs. "I mean, she's different than your normal clients, but we both know she dealt with some of the same issues they face." He shoos her with his hands. "Now, hurry and get to your office so you can tell me what Tina and Ellen say."

Lala throws a salute. "Yes, sir. I'll report back as soon as they answer my questions." Her lips stretch into a grin. "Or maybe I won't."

"You better not leave me hanging. Please, babe, I'm begging you."

"Welllll—" she twirls her hair, stretching out the phrase "—since you used the magic word." She stops speaking and caresses Rory's cheek. Her lips close the distance between them, and she presses into his mouth, kissing him with a light moan. When Lala pulls back, his eyes are half closed, his expression faraway.

Her voice has a raspy edge when she continues speaking. "Plus, I appreciate your hotness last night. Me-ow. So yes, I will tell you what my coworkers say as soon as the words leave their mouths. Or probably a minute or two later, once I have a chance to jump on my phone."

"You're fine, Lala. Like, the finest woman ever." The dreamy haze hasn't left his face. It's adorable.

"And you're a gem, my dear. A gem." She giggles, then waves. "I must be off. See you around 5:30. Love you."

"I love you too. Tell everyone I say hi."

He closes the door, and Lala waltzes down the driveway to Brownie, her 1974 Chevelle station wagon. The wagon's bronze paint shimmers in the winter morning, calling out to passersby with its irresistible sparkle. The car is Lala's pride and joy, bought with savings from her first big girl job after college.

Lala and Rory take the wagon for short trips, but the vehicle's main job is hauling her to work during the week. There's something motivating about starting the day in such a gorgeous vehicle. The post-weekend blahs don't stand a chance against Brownie. The wagon's sleek curves and smooth ride guarantee a pleasant journey to the office.

At almost 50 years old, Brownie still purrs when the key is turned. Lala's commute is ten minutes, and she uses the duration to gather her thoughts. The car's background sounds help her focus. Cheerful fifties tunes play on low, and the motor's rumble thrums almost in time. She maintains a watchful eye on the road and allows her thoughts to wander to Karina again.

What will be the best way to approach her colleagues about the case? They've never dealt with such a high-profile client, and Lala's not sure getting their business involved is the right decision. But that's where her partners come in. Tina and Ellen's perspective is less biased than hers. Any decision they make won't be clouded by a connection to the confessed murderer.

Was it smart to offer their assistance? Since the trio founded LegalShe Empowered in 2018, they'd grown from handling fifteen to sixty-five cases per year. A critical part of their success has been recognizing the situations they can't handle. They never turn women away (or the few men who seek their services), but if they aren't comfortable assisting, they find an entity or professional who will. They're definitely a powerhouse. Tina is a wicked awesome investigator, Ellen is a formidable attorney, and Lala is a psychologist who specializes in victim recovery. So, it's rare to come across something they aren't qualified to tackle, but there have been a few instances when yielding was necessary.

The last client they'd transferred was Alex, a woman who was physically and financially abused by her partner. At the onset, her case contained issues LegalShe encountered often, but after some digging, Tina discovered that their client was turning her pain into a nasty case of Munchausen Syndrome by proxy. The target of her mental illness was her six-year-old daughter, an underweight child who suffered from various maladies.

Tina compiled evidence showing the little girl's abuse. When she presented Ellen and Lala with the completed file, the LegalShe owners held a vote. With a 3-0 result, they decided to transfer their client to a local psychiatrist-psychologist team who were known for their Munchausen's work. This would address Alex's mental health needs, an urgently needed undertaking. For her legal endeavors, the trio referred her to a family court lawyer who enjoyed complicated cases, especially the morally gray ones.

Karina is like Alex in a way—both women turned their pain on another. There is a major difference between their actions, though. While Alex used her hurt against an innocent child, Karina had retaliated against the person who harmed her. This factor is crucial and is why Lala is even discussing it with her colleagues.

Laying everything out is the best approach. She'll offer her partners the impressions she has of Karina and Dante, walk them through her husband's observations of them as a couple, and outline the theories they'd come up with yesterday, although she'll probably gloss over Rory's fanciful poison selection. The evidence will be presented in a neutral way, and Lala will ask for their honest viewpoint. Should their company get involved? Is there anything they can do for the woman facing such a lengthy sentence?

Tina and Ellen won't hold back. It's part of the reason they work so well together. All of them give an unfiltered opinion when it's requested, even if the perspective is brutal. The trio has shouted and cried, argued and sulked, but they never leave the conference room until everyone's point of view is expressed. The entire spectrum of emotions has blazed through Lala during five years of meetings. There are times when she's humbled, others when she's assertive, but no matter what, she's always awed. Having friends to be honest with is one of humanity's finer experiences. Their sisterhood is special.

When Lala pulls into the parking lot, she does a scan, noting Tina's lux sedan and Ellen's sporty SUV. They're both here. She inhales deeply. There's no need for courage—her friends won't attack her, no matter what topic is broached—but she manifests some mettle anyway. A bright surge of confidence makes its way through her body, starting at her feet, wending upward to her brain. The vitality pumps her up, and in about a minute, she's ready to discuss the prospect of assisting a murderer.

She locks Brownie and strolls up the red brick walkway, humming the last song playing in the car. When Lala steps inside LegalShe's retro bungalow, Tina is at the copier, adding paper and cursing under her breath. They're due for a printer upgrade, but they've been putting it off because printers are astronomically expensive. So, they deal with a machine that's years past its prime, waiting for the day they can go Office Space on it and smash the faulty printer into a million pieces.

After the door closes behind her, Tina swivels toward her colleague, rolling her eyes. "Lala, can you save me from this monstrosity? All it needs is more paper, and that task has turned into a twenty-minute exercise in frustration." She kicks the bottom of the copier, careful to strike lightly, not wanting the metal and plastic heap to break before they can afford a replacement. "I never knew I could feel such rage toward an inanimate object, but here we are. I hate this thing."

Lala laughs and shakes her head. Their printer really is awful. "You're not the only one with irrational feelings towards it. This copier can take a flying leap, with me pushing it off the ledge." She glides toward Tina, squatting next to the printer. "Let's see if I can help." She teases open the empty drawer, jiggling the tray in a series of movements that work for some unknown reason. Tina hands her the copy paper, and she places it inside the machine. After twenty seconds pass, Lala pushes the drawer back in, and stands. "That should do it."

Tina's eyes widen as pages emerge from the device. "What wizardry have I just witnessed?"

"Despite loathing our decrepit printer, I've learned to read her. To decipher her moods and her temperament." Lala pats the machine. "We've come to an understanding, her and I, one built on mutual respect."

Tina bursts out in laughter. "Stop bullshitting, Lala. Tell me your tricks." She snags her copies from the exit tray. "Unless you want to be the only one who refills the printer. I'm okay with that too."

"I'll do the refills if you listen to a reckless idea I have."

She raises her eyebrows. "This wouldn't have anything to do with your husband's band, would it?"

"Ding ding ding. I forgot you're a world-class investigator. It's impossible to hide anything from you."

"I mean, it's all over my feed, Lala. I didn't have to do much investigating to figure that out. Just some doom scrolling."

"It's all Rory and I talked about yesterday." Lala glances at the ground, drawing in a deep breath. Was discussing Karina a dumb idea? Perhaps. But when she raises her head, Tina is smiling. Lala takes the friendly expression as a good sign. "I was hoping to bounce some thoughts off my brilliant besties. You gals help me make sense of things, and I'm too close to this murder to be objective."

"Can we huddle up around 10:00? Ellen is free until the Durango trail this afternoon." Tina shakes her head, and Lala knows she's remembering the overnight stakeouts she endured for that particular case. Mr. Durango is not only a terrible man, but he's also a sneaky one. Tina hustled to gather enough evidence to nail him, and after eight months his crimes were finally going to trial.

"That man is the worst," Lala says.

"Tell me about it." Tina shakes her head and tucks a brown curl behind her ear. "I need half an hour before we meet. I want to check the property appraiser's website for the Lincoln case. And, of course, there are emails to answer." She sags into the copier, letting her arms hang loose. "There are always emails to answer. Ughhhhh."

"Okay drama queen, 10:00 is fine with me." Lala raises a hand to her ear. "Did I just hear an incoming email alert? Better hurry before your inbox fills."

Tina sags lower. "You're a brat."

"Takes one to know one." Lala moves toward Ellen's office. "I'll pop in and let our luscious lawyer know about the meeting. See you in thirty."

After a gentle knock, her colleague responds, "Come on in."

Lala opens the door and steps into the pinkest office in existence. The shade is everywhere—the paint, the decorations, the furniture—but even among the fuchsia, blush, and salmon hues, Ellen's outfit stands out. Neon pink is the only color she wears, and the more subdued tones adorning the walls, floor, and curtains complement her slim-cut dayglo pantsuit.

In the beginning of her career, Ellen shied away from brights. She wore neutrals to court like other lawyers, never straying from more traditional navy or black jackets and skirts. But as her wins accumulated and she grew more confident in her skills, Lala's friend embraced her inner pink fanatic. A few judges balked when she ventured into their courtroom wearing the radioactive shade, but her appearance eventually faded from their focus, and her fierce lawyering took its place. The petite Latina is a force in court, and her neon suits have become a symbol of her success.

Ellen's color scheme also thrills their clients. When they see her cheerful outfit and smiling face, they're instantly comforted and more willing to divulge the terrible experiences they hire LegalShe to fight. Ellen is an asset to the team. There's no doubt about it.

She's donning a grin now. "Lala! A week is an eternity without you." She jumps from her desk, rushing over to crush Lala in a hug. When she releases the embrace, Ellen plops her hands on her hips. "Girl, I read all about Dante's death the first day you were off, then yesterday I was stunned by his girlfriend's confession. I want to ask how men like that idiot singer get girlfriends, but we see it here every day." She lets out a forceful sigh. "The kind of men who hurt women are the ones who know how to use love as a weapon. Cruelty drives them, and they stack up the bodies in their wake."

Ellen winces, back peddling her words. "That might be a bad analogy since there's actually a body in this situation."

Lala reaches out, giving her arm a squeeze. "I know what you mean. Guys like Dante are the worst."

"Exactly." Ellen grabs her friend's hand and tugs her toward a coral couch. "Come on. You have to spill the tea, Lala. Tell me everything. How are you? How's Rory? I wanted to reach out, but Tina told me to give you space. She's such a grown-up, and as much as it frustrated me at the time, I can admit that she was right." A laugh escapes her throat. "And I hate admitting when she's right."

Lala hesitates. "Well, if you want the dirt, you're going to have to come to the meeting I just scheduled. It's at 10:00 so you only have to wait—" she glances at her watch "—twenty-four minutes to hear the grubby details."

"Pleassseeeee," Ellen begs. She arranges her face into a lip-quivering pout, knowing it usually works.

Lala shakes her head. "Sorry, Ellie-belly. I'm not falling for your perfect pout today. See you at 10:00."

"Fine. I'll consider this a test of my abundant patience." Lala doubles over in laughter, and this time, Ellen nudges her toward the hallway instead of the couch. "You're lucky I love you," she says.

"You speak the truth." Lala blows her a kiss and hurries away. After closing her office door, she fires up the coffee maker, knowing the caffeine will help fuel the conversation with her colleagues.

And she needs all the spunk she can get because the meeting's topic deviates from their normal victim-oriented approach. Offering assistance to a murderer is quite the one-eighty for their business, and Lala is still not sure how to feel about Karina's actions. Were they justified or not?

Steaming coffee brings her clarity, and she spends the next twenty minutes pondering the complicated question.

Clemons Police Department Record of Interrogation
February 12, 2023
Karina Belmore re: Murder of Dante Wilder

Detective Cartridge (Det. C): Ms. Belmore, thank you for your willingness to discuss what happened with Mr. Wilder. We want to get everything down in your own words.

Detective Barnes (Det. B): Yes, we appreciate your cooperation. Do you have any questions for us before we get started?

Karina Belmore (KB): Am I under arrest? I killed my boyfriend, and you're treating me nicely. That's weird. I don't deserve any kindness.

Det. C: You're not under arrest, Ms. Belmore. We need additional information before we make that determination.

KB: I'm not making a false confession if that's what you're thinking. I did it. I murdered Dante.

Det. C: May we ask you some questions about that?

KB: Yes. Please do. I'll tell you whatever you want.

Det. C: Okay. Let's start with the day of Dante's death. Can you give us a rundown of your activities?

KB: I can, but the day before was more important.

Det. C: What do you mean?

KB: Well, that's when we finalized our plans.

Det. B: And what plans were those?

KB: Our Romeo and Juliet idea. Well, it was actually my idea. Dante hated it at first, but when I told him it would get attention on ABOS, maybe enough for him to pursue the solo career he'd been thinking about, he was in. And of course, I'd be getting something out of it too. It would totally launch my film career. I had a meeting scheduled with a production company and everything.

Det. B: Romeo and Juliet? Were you looking to make something related to Shakespeare?

KB: That's not it at all. Shakespeare documentaries don't get noticed, especially not by the younger audiences. Our work was cutting edge. We were going to make a film everyone would enjoy.

Det. C: Will you tell us about it?

KB: Can we take a break first? I need to use the bathroom.

[Interrogation pauses for ten minutes]

Chapter 8 – Karina

{February 13, 2023}

The day after getting arrested, Karina calls her parents to update them on her whereabouts. Instead of listening, they try to fix the situation like they always do. Mom and Dad waste precious minutes convincing her to take their money, and they're upset when she declines their bailout offer.

"Sweetheart, please, it's for your own good," Mom says between sobs. The agony wounds Karina, but the hurt is her fault. Accepting responsibility for her crime will be brutal. She senses that already.

Karina's father agrees with her mom. "Yes, darling. There's no need to spend any time in jail. Come home, and we'll hire a lawyer. I know a few who've been successful fighting these types of crimes. We'll take care of you." To an outsider, his voice would sound calm, controlled, but his daughter knows better. His words are tinged with an almost imperceptible disappointment.

A pounding headache pulses in Karina's jaw, so she closes her eyes and rests her forehead against the phone bank. She can barely speak through the throbbing. "I can't tell you how much your support means. Most women here have no one, and I'm lucky enough to have two wonderful people rooting for me." She squeezes her eyes tight, already regretting her next words. Accepting their help is the easy way out, the way she usually takes, but today Karina is standing on her own. Her voice trembles as she continues. "Mom, Dad, I love you more than anything. You've been the best parents. Seriously. My friends were always jealous of how awesome you treated me, and they were right to be." Karina inhales sharply, then releases the air in a rush. Excruciating words tumble out with the breath. "I'm sorry, but I can't accept your help. I did it. I killed Dante, and I need to be punished."

A scream blasts from the phone and stabs into her skull, so Karina pulls the receiver away. The misery in her brain pulses louder with every heartbeat, and her mom's wailing makes it worse. She lowers her head between her legs, putting pressure on each temple with her knees, hoping the grip counteracts the internal tension.

A guard in the corner takes notice and waves a hand, gesturing for Karina to right herself. She complies. That's what you do in jail. Comply, comply, comply. When she returns the phone to her ear, relief courses through her. Her mother is done screaming. The vice grip on her head loosens the tiniest bit.

Her dad has taken over the conversation. "Karina? Karina, are you still there?"

"I'm here," her voice is a whisper.

"Don't you ever say that again, do you hear me?" he practically growls.

"What do you mean?"

"This is going to be the fight of your life, baby girl, and you can't claim you killed someone like it's no big deal. Strike those words from your vocabulary and start using not guilty instead. That's what your plea will be during your first appearance tomorrow. Not guilty."

"But Dad, I did kill someone. I'm going to plead guilty."

"Damn it, Karina, you're going to make me lose my cool." He pauses, counting to ten under his breath. When he continues, his tone is clipped. "Promise me you won't plead guilty. Your mom wouldn't handle it well. She's already teetering on the edge of a breakdown."

"I can't promise that, Daddy." Her brain strains against its bony enclosure, and dark spots dance across her vision. This time the pain is too much. "I've got to go. I'll call you soon." The receiver gets slammed on the cradle, and her head goes back between her knees. As she rests there, nausea ripples through her stomach, distracting her from the agony in her skull. A deep inhale quiets the queasiness, but only temporarily. Once Karina releases her breath, the sickness barrels through her guts, and she opens her mouth to retch.

"Nope. No way. You better close your suck and swallow whatever's trying to come up. I am not cleaning up after you, princess." Footsteps approach, and black leather boots appear between Karina's legs. "Lift your head. This isn't a hotel, and you don't get to lounge around whenever you feel like it," a scratchy voice bellows.

Karina tries to raise her head, but it weighs a thousand pounds. Instead of lifting, her torso inches closer to the ground until she's jerked up by a fist ripping into her hair. Crimson sparks crackle along her nerves. Consciousness floats in and out. She barely holds on to reality.

Through a pinhole of vision, Karina focuses on the area in front of her. The officer who was in the corner is now in her face, sapphire eyes glinting with anger. The guard's bluntly cut auburn hair angles downward, accentuating hollow cheekbones and thin lips arranged in a scowl. In addition to her gravelly vocals, creases outline her mouth and eyes, hinting strongly at a pack-a-day cigarette habit.

The red-headed hair grabber is furious at Karina. She leans in close. "When I tell you to get up, you listen. Got that, Belmore?"

"Yes."

The guard's grip tightens. "Yes, what? I'm not your friend, so you better show some respect."

"Yes, ma'am."

"Good, that's a start." She wrenches Karina from the chair. "Phone time's over. Get out of here." The redhead pushes her toward the door, and another guard opens the steel barrier from the hallway. "Come out slowly," her new controller commands in a twangy accent. Karina trudges over, and the officer gives another order. "Stand over there. I'm waiting on Jackson and Deery to finish their calls. After that, we'll mosey to the cellblock."

Karina is placed against a scuffed gray wall, and she leans against it, using the minutes for deep breathing. Slowly, the tension in her jaw eases, and her field of vision expands. She's grateful for the reprieve.

It's quiet where they stand, so that helps. Noise is a constant in jail, and after a single day, Karina has learned to embrace silence when it arrives. Inmates chatter. Guards yell. Footsteps ricochet off concrete floors. On the way to make her call, the clatter of food preparation rang out from the chow hall, but in the phone nook, clangs are deadened, and stillness reigns.

In the small hallway, there isn't room for many yoga poses, but she can stretch her neck. Karina hangs her head forward, then back, holding each position for thirty seconds. Next is a rotation, once to the left, once to the right. The muscles loosen, and further relief ebbs through her body.

Halfway through stretching, she notices the officer watching her movements. This guard appears friendlier than the woman who guarded the phones. Her ebony hair is in a bun, but the hairstyle isn't painfully tight like most of the jail's overseers. A pink tint shades her lips, and the corners of her mouth lift in an almost smile. Her tawny skin is unlined, so she seems young, maybe mid-twenties, close to Karina's age. The guard's name is E. Vickers, according to her name badge. Is she an Elizabeth or an Erika? Karina may never know. Guards use their last names to maintain authority and distance. The effect is chilling.

Vickers speaks up after Karina completes the rightward rotation. "You got a headache or something?"

"I do."

"And those movements help?"

"Yes. It's mostly gone now."

Vickers lifts her eyebrows. "I might have to try it. There's nights where my head pounds so hard I can't sleep."

"I can show you what to do if you want." Karina throws a glance at the door, not wanting the other guard to see their interaction. Thankfully, there's no scowling face pressed against the window. Karina lets her anxiety drop a notch. "The series takes two minutes. Do you think the other ladies will stay on the phone for that long?"

Vickers looks at her watch. "Yeah. They should be occupied for another five minutes at least."

Karina takes a second panicked peek at the door. Still no face. Although her cellmates had warned her being friendly to the guards, she ignores their advice and begins instructing the officer. What can it hurt? There was no one around to witness their actions.

"Okay. First take a huge breath in, filling your lungs as much as you can. Hold the breath until I tell you to release it." Vickers inhales and holds it in. Karina counts to three. "Now, gradually release the air, and as you do, lean your head forward. Don't move your shoulders, only your neck. Inhale and exhale slowly while you hold the position" The guard follows the directions, and Karina counts to thirty. "Next, move your head backward. I like this stretch. It feels really good." Vickers transitions until her forehead is pointed toward the ceiling. During the next thirty-count, Karina notices the guard's facial expression relaxing. Her eyes become less scrunched, her mouth slacker.

That changes when sharp knocking interrupts. "Vickers, open the damn door and collect these two ingrates," the red-headed guard shouts.

Vickers, now pinched instead of serene, snaps her attention to the door. She scrambles for her badge and scans it over the lock. "Sorry, Allen," her voice apologetic.

"Yeah, you are." She snorts. "If you weren't socializing with a murderer, you'da known I needed you." Allen kicks the door jamb, and

Karina jumps at the clang. Vickers does too. When the enraged officer continues, her words brim with scorn. "One week on the job, and you're already failing. Why am I not surprised? I swear they've lowered the hiring standards since that new sheriff took office. He's bringing in a bunch of idiot kids. Like you. It's not fair that I have to depend on snot-nosed brats." Grimacing, she rakes her eyes up and down her colleague's body. "You can't be older than my daughter, and she turned twenty-four this past January." Her smirk deepens. "At least she's got her shit together. Apparently, life experience is no longer valued around here. All you need is a pulse to become a correctional officer."

"I won't let it happen again," Vickers says, her body tense, the rigid position probably building up to another headache.

"Damn right you won't. I'll have a talk with the sergeant after my shift. He'll set you right." Allen shifts her sneer Karina's way. "And you. Stop fucking with my jail. We like it orderly around here. Nothing weird, nothing out of place. There definitely isn't any room for that froufrou yoga nonsense you were distracting Vickers with. Here, you listen and comply. Nothing more, nothing less."

Karina lowers her head. "Yes, ma'am. I didn't mean to cause any trouble."

"It's not about what you meant to do, it's about what actually happened," Allen says. She turns around and shouts at the convicts standing behind her. "Get out of my face."

They shuffle to Vickers, a willowy dark-haired woman in the front, a pale muscular blonde coming next. The youthful guard places them in cuffs, directing them to the wall on either side of me.

Under Allen's watchful stare, Vickers reaches into her pocket and brings out a piece of paper. "What's your name and ID?" she asks the blonde.

"Deery, 36219," she grunts.

"Good, good," Vickers responds. "And you?" She points to the slender inmate.

"Jackson, 36375." Her voice is low-pitched and buttery. She could have had a career in voice acting, but instead, she's here with Karina, the failed documentarian. This entire place brims with crushed potential.

"Alright. And you?" Vickers points at Karina, cheeks tinged red. Karina hates that she's embarrassed. Ignoring the guard would have been a better idea, like her cellmates advised. Making enemies is a terrible way to adjust to a new environment.

Karina answers her question, filling her voice with faux confidence. "Belmore, 36695." As soon as the digits leave her mouth, she knows they're wrong. Shit. Her false bravado abandons her. "Wait. That's not right. I'm sorry."

"I really am surrounded by idiots," Allen remarks while twirling her hand in an impatient gesture. "Get on with it."

After a moment of frantic blankness, the ID pops into Karina's head. Thank God. "Belmore, 37294."

"Correct." Vickers looks to Allen, who gives her a nod before retreating into the communications room. The younger officer steps behind the inmates. "Let's hustle ladies. We're cutting it close to lunch count, and I'd hate for you to end up with a bagged nasty instead of a tray."

What was a bagged nasty? Karina probably doesn't want to know.

The jail is a maze, and her experience with the building's layout is limited. Afterall, she's spent less than twenty-four hours in lock up. Her navigation skills won't get them to the cellblock, but thankfully, she's not leading the group. Deery, the angry blonde, has that honor. All Karina needs to do is follow the woman in front of her. Easy enough.

They trudge past the chow hall, the infirmary, and the library before arriving at the women's ward. Here the caravan halts. Vickers strolls over, using her badge to open the steel door that separates their living quarters from the rest of the facility. The weighty metal groans as it slides along ancient-looking tracks, jerking so hard Karina is afraid the barrier will stop halfway through its trek. Somehow it completes its course, and their escort hurries them inside. When the door closes behind them, Vickers dismisses the inmates. "You've got five minutes till lunch count. Get back to your cells until then."

In Clementine County, and pretty much everywhere else in the world, men are arrested more often than women. Compared to the 700 men locked up, there were maybe fifty females in the Clemons Correctional Institute, most under pre-trial confinement, some serving short sentences for minor crimes. Like Karina, her bunkies are awaiting their day in court, but Karina is the only one being held for a violent felony, a major one at that. When she stumbled into the cell yesterday, they were impressed that their new bunkmate was famous, although she insisted it wasn't true.

Karina isn't well known. She'd only killed someone who was.

Apparently, her role as Dante's girlfriend had a name—tour wife. Nicole had given her the cheeky title when they met in the ABOS dressing room. Karina was a pretty terrible tour wife, though. Unlike Nicole or Maggie or Lala, she wasn't a capable person who handled the household, plus a career, plus pets or a child, all while her partner wooed the world with music. No. That wasn't her. Instead of being a badass when her boyfriend was away, Karina had hatched an idiotic plan that resulted in his death and her incarceration.

She is pretty much the opposite of the ABOS tour wives. She's pathetic.

Karina's protests didn't stop her cellmates from being impressed with her music industry connections, though. They kept her up late last night, asking questions about Dante and the rest of the band. The women were hungry for excitement, and Karina couldn't blame them. Living behind bars is a monotonous existence and celebrity dirt distracts from the repetitious nature of their lives.

Of her life now too.

Three women share a hundred-square-foot cell with Karina. Two of them, Darla and Eve, are in their twenties. Darla was arrested for a DWI at 10:30 the previous morning. Apparently, she made a series of bad decisions after she was let go from her job and dumped by her girlfriend hours apart. Those bad decisions included snorting a Valium and chugging a pint of vodka, actions not advisable under ideal conditions let alone under misery's dark shadow. Her BAC was 0.17 when police pulled her over, and by the time Karina met her, Darla was still recovering from a wicked hangover, made worse by fluorescent lighting and the rock-hard pillow on her bunk.

Eve is in for fraud. For months, the police had built a case against All Bets Are On, her auction business. During online bidding wars, she would hire people to artificially increase an article's value until a legitimate buyer paid well over its worth. Eve also fibbed about the authenticity of items, and it was this practice that got her locked up. Apparently, an older gentleman had paid $100K for what they thought was Mr. Ed's saddle, but which had actually belonged to Darby Dangerfield, a racehorse who retired in 2006. Unfortunately for her, Eve forgot to erase Darby's name from inside the leather flap, and the buyer noticed the lettering as he saddled his wife up for some horseplay. The man filed a report, and Eve's business was toast after a police investigation.

Eve learned a lesson from her arrest. It wasn't related to screwing people over, or anything like that. No, it had to do with the guy who turned her in. "Listen, ladies, stay away from horse people. They'll rat on you in a heartbeat." She shrugged her shoulders. "I don't care what a person does in their bedroom, but I do care when they involve my livelihood in their whacked-out fantasies. If that dude could pretend he was a stallion, why couldn't he stretch his imagination a little further and make believe he bought the talking horse's saddle?"

Karina didn't have an answer to her question, but she did take note of Eve's advice. Don't trust horse people. Got it.

At thirty-eight, Cici is the oldest in their cell. Her crimes are less troubling than the ones committed by her younger roommates. Almost a year ago, she was arrested for driving without a license, an action she undertook to escape a volatile relationship. Cici wasn't given jail time, but she was assigned twelve months of probation. Unfortunately, yesterday, she was scooped up on a violation—she'd forgotten to inform the system about a new address and job, two positive upgrades in her life that had turned into criminal justice issues.

Cici had been a month shy of finishing her initial sentence. To celebrate the upcoming completion, she'd scheduled a driver's test so she could get her provisional license and become legit. Now, unless she got a lenient judge, she'd earn a longer probation period and be forced to pay fines she couldn't afford. She'd also have to cancel her DMV appointment, the thing she was most upset about. Cici wanted to follow the rules, but she'd gotten tangled in legalities that wouldn't release her.

Last night, after discussing their situations, the women asked questions about Karina's crime. She answered, of course—it was only fair when they shared their own details—but her responses weren't entirely honest. While her bunkies saw her as a criminal, her perspective was different. Yes, Karina committed a terrible crime, but she was more of a naïve idiot than a violent killer. For some reason, her stupidity embarrassed her more than anything. She didn't want her bunkmates knowing her boyfriend's death was caused by a reckless documentary plotline.

So, Karina focused more on Dante's role. Darla, Eve, and Cici listened to stories of his anger and impatience, his everyday alcohol binges, and the way he treated his girlfriend in front of others. They learned about his arrest in November. How he'd not only cheated on Karina again but how he'd also hurt the woman he'd been trying to hook up with. She told them about the sometimes bruises, the marks carefully covered by sweaters and jeans, and twice with extra thick concealer.

As Karina spoke, her bunkies stared at her, nodding as she recounted the hellish relationship. Telling their twisted story was a cleansing experience. When she lived with Dante, she was focused on his rages. Her energy went toward preventing his outbursts or calming them down. Everything was centered on a monster in human form.

In a small jail cell, surrounded by women she'd just met, Karina gave herself permission to confront her true feelings about the singer. Avoiding his temper was no longer a concern. Instead, she stoked the fury inside, building her hurt into a crackling bonfire.

Karina wasted almost six months on a cruel, frightening man. Why hadn't the realization come earlier, before her freedom disappeared and she ended up in jail?

Darla and Eve hugged her, murmuring apologies and insults, the former for Karina, the latter for Dante. Cici hugged her too, then offered some words of wisdom. Her onyx eyes sparkled with tears as she spoke. "You lost yourself for a while, Karina, but that's okay. When you're up against the dark side of human nature, you often have no choice but to fold." She reached over, laying a hand on Karina's shoulder. "But here, you have the space to heal. Jail might not seem like a therapeutic environment, but it can be. You're no longer in that evil man's clutches, which is a huge step forward. Focus on yourself, and why you think you deserved someone like him." A beaming smile lit her face. "After that, you can concentrate on getting the hell out of here."

Until sleep claimed Karina, Cici's sentences bounced around her head. They were simple. Powerful. Reassuring.

This morning, she ran through Cici's words before calling her parents, loving the self-sufficiency at the core of the advice. As expected, her mom and dad's guidance went in the opposite direction. They wanted to rescue her. Although their intent wasn't awful like Dante's, they, too, wanted Karina to lose herself to their whims. While she'd submitted to them in the past, she was done with all that.

Now, with five minutes until lunch, Karina heads to her cell to seek her older bunkie's counsel. The pair share a bunk, and when Karina finds Cici, she's lounging against her pillow on the bottom bed, oblivious to the world. She clutches a paperback in her hands, a Western romance judging by the cover. Books are one way to pass the time in lockup, and Karina doesn't want to interrupt such a rapt reader.

As soon as she decides to talk to her later, Cici glances up from the pages. "Karina, how'd your parents take the news?"

"Are you sure you want to hear?" She gestures to a dogeared novel. "You looked way into the story."

Cici's tinkling laugh rings out. "I can get back to Honeytail Saloon after lunch." She sits up, patting the spot next to her.

"Okay." Karina settles onto the bed. "My parents want me to plead not guilty and hire a high-powered attorney who probably charges more than $1000 an hour. They'll foot the bill, of course."

"Is that what you want to do?"

"I'd love to be home." Karina's eyes widen. "No offense to any of you ladies. You're the best part of this place."

"None taken. I'd love to be home too."

"But, like, don't you think I'm stunting myself by depending on others for everything? I've never had to land rough. My parents always made sure there were feathers wherever I fell." Karina lowers her head as shame washes over her. "And when I was with Dante, he decided what we were going to do. He was violent, but again, I didn't have to face the consequences of my actions, because, in our relationship, I took no action."

Cici's voice is hushed when she responds, and she leans close to Karina. "There's something to be said for a person who holds themselves accountable. Too many people refuse to process the shame or guilt that comes from a bad decision. Instead, they shift responsibility to someone else, and continue with their selfish behavior, never learning, never growing." She touches Karina's chin, gently lifting her head. "I get where your parents are coming from. If I had a child, I'd want them out of this hellhole immediately. But I also get where you're coming from. You're trying to do the right thing, and that's noble."

"But what should I do? I'm torn."

"Take some time to think about it, Karina." She gestures at their cell, and Karina takes in the sparse surroundings. The concrete floor. The barely working toilet. The ever-present scent of prison food. The bars.

It's bleak.

Cici continues, "That's one thing you get here. Plenty of time to mull things over." She pats Karina's hand as the announcement for lunch count blasts throughout the ward. "And you can start thinking right after we eat."

Subject: Query: WHAT HAPPENS NOW? – a deep dive into the music industry
From: Karina Belmore Feb 1

Dear Valerie,

Music fans love learning about their favorite artists, and with books, movies, and social media posts, there's tons of information for them to consume. One perspective that's missing from these offerings is real-time coverage of a life-changing event. Often, when tragedies occur inside a band's insulated world, interviews are conducted after the fact, and we're presented with a scrubbed-down version of what happened.

Imagine if fans were in the room when Guns and Roses broke up in 1996. Or if an audience watched as David Lee Roth was given the boot from Van Halen. The proposed documentary, WHAT HAPPENS NOW?, seeks to explore similar unfiltered band interactions.

Featuring A Box of Star's singer, Dante Wilder, the film begins with a revelation that will shake ABOS to the core. The movie's remainder will follow Dante and the band through acceptance and recovery, doing so with unflinching honesty.

As Dante's partner, I have access to his personal and professional spaces, making this project far more intimate than any existing music documentary. I would be happy to discuss the details of WHAT HAPPENS NOW? with you, as well as Hellcat's role in this important film.

Thank you for your time and consideration. I look forward to hearing back.

Sincerely,
Karina Belmore

Chapter 9 – Lala

{February 13, 2023}

"Where're the donuts?" Ellen asks as Lala enters the sunny space they use for meetings.

"Donuts?" Lala responds, annoyed her colleagues beat her to the room. It's 9:57, three minutes ahead of schedule, but there they sit, grinning from across the cherrywood conference table. Usually, the two women trail behind, answering emails until the last second. But not this morning, during the one day Lala wants a quiet moment before their arrival. Oh well. Guess it's showtime. "I didn't know there was a snack requirement."

Ellen rolls her eyes. "Duh. When you call a meeting about the person who murdered someone in your husband's band, snacks are definitely needed." She looks to Tina for confirmation.

Tina nods. "Yep. That's the truth."

Lala tilts her head, pouring earnestness into her voice. "So, you want me to pause this gathering to make a donut run? With traffic, that might take close to an hour, but I'm willing to make the sacrifice. Can't have my besties being hungry."

"Nooooo, I've already waited too long to hear this." Ellen pouts, letting her thirst for gossip outweigh her desire for breakfast. "Just remember for next time."

"Honestly, I hope there isn't a next time," Lala says.

"You know what I mean." Ellen notices the laptop she's holding and rolls her eyes. "Wait. Why did you bring your computer? Did you make a spreadsheet or something? That would be so you."

Warmth floods Lala's cheeks. Her friend knew her too well. "Not a spreadsheet, but a presentation."

"Lala, did you seriously use the last twenty minutes to make a PowerPoint?" Tina asks.

"I did." Her words come out in a rush. "But only because it helps me think. The presentation organized my thoughts. They were all over the place before."

"Girl, we're just teasing. If you need to make some slides, make some slides. This is a judgment-free zone." Tina's lips curl into a grin. "But I can't lie. I'm super curious about what you're going to show us."

"Give me a minute to plug in, and I'll get started."

Lala's laptop goes on the table's middle, where waiting cables poke through a circular hole. She connects to the screen and opens a file containing a gray and red presentation. As the display warms up, she gives her partners an intro. "Over the years, I've ranted a few times about Dante Wilder, and I'm sure you know my opinion of him, but I'll state it again for clarity's sake. The man was an abusive jerk, the kind we battle every day, and I wasn't sad when he died. I felt relieved. Especially after his domestic violence arrest last November. Combine that with how he mistreated his one-night stands, and society is better off without him."

The first slide appears on the screen, and Ellen reads the title aloud. "Countering Abuse with Murder: The Karina Belmore story." She whips her head Lala's way. "Jesus, girl. What are you, a true crime junkie?"

Ellen would know the answer to that question if she knew how many murder podcasts her friend consumes. Rory calls his wife an addict, but Lala only uses the episodes for research. Since her career is based on helping people recover from hurt, learning about humanity's violent side prepares her for the individuals who walk into her business seeking help. The clients who hire LegalShe carry trauma, anguish, desperation—all burdens that can destroy them. And while Tina and Ellen assist with legalities, Lala is responsible for their wellbeing, an undertaking she holds sacred.

When listening to podcasts, the intent is simple. Lala wants to consume any and everything shocking. She wants to hear the most inhumane actions perpetrated. She wants to build her tolerance for the macabre. Why? Well, she doesn't want to be the therapist who flinches in response to a victim's story. That reaction makes survivors question their reality and can derail the healing process.

Screw that nonsense. She's here to help her clients, not harm them.

To prevent herself from recoiling during a victim's story, Lala devours horrific crime retellings. Podcasts, with their conversational style, resemble her talk-based client sessions, and she prefers them over movies or TV. Luckily there's tons to choose from. Three times a week, for hours at a time, she pops in earbuds and listens to trauma unfold. She alternates between two types of shows—ones exploring the crime and others focusing on the survivors. The different perspectives provide a 360 view and Lala's tolerance for absorbing tales of mistreatment increases episode by episode.

Her coworkers don't need to know about the hours she spends knee deep in true crime, though. Lala answers Ellen's question but doesn't divulge her obsession. "I mean, yeah, who doesn't love listening to a crime podcast every now and then?"

"I stick to romcoms personally." Ellen stretches out a sigh. "Give me a happily ever after any day."

Lala raises her eyebrows. "Can I continue?" she asks.

"Go ahead." Ellen leans back in her chair. "Sorry for commenting on your weird title."

"You know you loved it." Lala clears her throat and resumes speaking in a serious tone. "Back to Dante. He was cruel to everyone, and that included Karina. I met her once backstage at a show." She advances to the second slide. A checklist for intimate partner violence fills the screen. "I know you both have this memorized, so I'm not going to go over it, but I wanted to show you how many of the criteria I recognized from just one interaction with Karina."

Lala presses the forward button, and red check marks fly onto the slide, landing next to four bullet points. "She was extremely sensitive to polite criticism, she admitted to being socially isolated, her self-esteem was crushingly low, and I noticed a bruise on her chin. I never saw Karina and Dante interact, but Rory did, and he said it was uncomfortable. Dante was a dick to everyone but was even worse to his girlfriend. He berated her and treated her like a servant. And that was in front of people. Imagine what he did behind closed doors." She looks back and forth between her friends. "You know it got nasty."

"Yeah, slime like him usually wait until they're home before revealing their true selves," Tina says.

Ellen tilts her head. "I dunno. It sounds like Dante was a jerk wherever he was." She pauses. "There are certain celebs I wouldn't mind hanging out with—Paul Rudd or Zoe Saldana, for example. But Dante was never someone I wanted to meet. I know your stories about him have a lot to do with that opinion, Lala, but even in pictures or videos, he put off an evil vibe." She shudders and hugs herself. "It was his eyes. They were creeeeeepy."

"Agreed. And on that note, I apologize for the next slide." Lala advances forward, and a picture she borrowed from Karina's social media pops up. The image is from the couple's five-month anniversary, shortly before Dante's death. They're both facing the camera, and Karina's arm is around her boyfriend's waist. His ice-blue eyes stand out in the shot. They give spooky vibes. "This picture was posted about a week before Dante flew to Georgia to crash band practice. The dude knew he'd been kicked out of ABOS for months at this point. He knew it but still showed up where he wasn't welcome." She clicks a button and the projector zooms in on the underside of Karina's left forearm, just visible where she's hugging Dante. Faded yellow marks—small, finger-shaped—are outlined by a red circle.

Ellen inhales sharply. "Damn. I saw this picture when she posted it and didn't notice the bruises."

"Don't feel bad. I only noticed after a closer look," Lala says. "There are a few more too." She clicks through three additional photos, each containing a red circle outlining bruises in different healing phases. "It was in front of the world, and no one saw it. Not a single internet sleuth picked up on Karina's pain. Not a single friend."

The final slide contains a screenshot of Karina's confession, the last sentences in bold. "This is what she posted the day of her arrest. I'm intrigued by what she said here: 'Because of me, he's dead. I poisoned someone who loved me for who I was. I'm the person responsible for Dante's death.' What do you think she means?"

"I'm taking her at her word. It sounds like she poisoned Dante," Tina says.

"Yep. I'm going with that, too," Ellen agrees. "She put something in his drink, and he keeled over."

"But she was nowhere near him when he died. They were over two thousand miles apart." Lala places her hands on the table and leans forward. "And making it more intriguing is the fact that Dante died in a crowded room. All of ABOS was there, plus the crew. That's nine people who watched him take his final breaths after he ranted and raved for close to twenty minutes."

"What are you saying, Lala?" Tina asks, mirroring her friend's position by leaning onto the table. "Karina could have poisoned Dante right before he left. Or she could have been doing it since they met, and the dosage finally became potent enough the night he croaked."

"I'm saying that there seems to be some reasonable doubt surrounding this whole situation." Lala counts on her fingers as she makes each point. "First, Karina was battered by her boyfriend. That introduces the possibility of self-defense. Second, she wasn't in the house where Dante died. Nine other people were there, including my husband. That means she's not the only suspect. Third, Dante was yelling at everyone before he collapsed. According to Rory, he flung out some pretty damning accusations. So maybe he had a heart attack or stroke—anger plus alcoholism isn't a great combination. Or maybe, he pissed off the wrong person, and they did something to retaliate." She closes out the presentation. "So, what did you think?"

"Girl. Wow." Ellen claps for a few seconds. "You absolutely nailed that presentation."

"Your investigation skills are on point. You've one hundred percent introduced reasonable doubt and then some," Tina says.

"I wanted to show you all this because I want to intervene. Professionally. There's something weird about the whole Dante situation, and the least I can do is offer Karina some advice." Lala powers down her computer and joins her friends at the table. "Of course, I had to ask you ladies first. I'd never get LegalShe involved in something you were opposed to."

"I vote yes," Ellen says.

Tina adds, "You have a connection to this case that no one else has. Maybe you can get to the bottom of what happened." Tina grabs Lala's hand, giving it a gentle squeeze. "You've got my vote too. Go. Figure everything out."

Ellen lets out a laugh, a high-pitched sound almost as bright as her neon blouse. "And when you're done, you have to tell us everything. You know I'm a sucker for celebrity dirt."

Date: 2/15/2023 11:47:09 AM
To: Karina Belmore
From: Laverne (Lala) Ramirez

Karina,

Hi. I'm not sure if you remember me, but I wanted to reach out after hearing about your arrest. I hope you're as comfortable as you can be, given the circumstances.

When we met backstage, I know there wasn't a ton of time to chat, but I remember our conversation well. You were excited about a film idea and couldn't wait to reach out to production companies. Your enthusiasm radiated when you spoke about this dream. It was inspiring.

Since your confession, I've been thinking about you and your relationship with Dante. I've known him for a long time—since the band first formed—and he's always been…how can I say this politely? He's always been disrespectful and cruel. I'm not sure if you experienced this during the months you were together, but if so, know that I am sympathetic to what you went through. Being mistreated by a loved one is something no one should experience.

When we chatted, I mentioned my business, LegalShe Empowered, but didn't go into the details about it. Now, I'll tell you a little bit about our mission. Me and two friends, a fierce lawyer and a diligent investigator, started LegalShe because we wanted to fight against the people who harm their girlfriends, wives, or partners. We've waged war on domestic violence, and we are proud of the help we've offered to the survivors who hire us.

I spoke with my colleagues, and we thought we'd offer to assist with your case. Over the past several years, I've worked with victims who have survived the most heinous treatment, and I'm proud when these women (and some men) recapture the power their abusers stole from them. I'd like to do the same for you, if you'll have me. We can talk about what happened with Dante, and with the help of my colleagues, I can advise you on the best path forward.

Please reach out if you want to connect. I added credits to your account just in case money is a hardship right now. I know we only talked briefly, but I sensed the passion behind your words, and I would love to help you relight that fire.

Best,

Lala

Chapter 10 – Nicole

{February 16, 2023}

"Coley, can you get the door?" Jake shouts from his studio.

She barely hears him over the dogs. Penny and Bob race to the front room, toenails clicking, barks echoing off the hardwood floors. Obedience I and II hadn't cured their desire to go bananas whenever a visitor, delivery driver, or salesperson stopped at the house. Not that Nicole minds them barking at the latter. But most of the time, it's annoying. Like now.

"Bob-o, Penny-gal, will you shut your cute little mouths?" she sings to the duo. They shoot her some serious side eye and continue woofing at the person who has the audacity to invade their territory. "Okay, okay. Keep barking but move on over." She scoots their tushes off to the side, cracking the door to peek out. The person who knocks sports a blunt chestnut bob, gray cardigan, and holstered handgun. Looks like the police are here. Again.

Detective Harris notices her and gives a little wave. "Nicole, how are you? Do you have time to chat?"

Nicole suppresses a sigh. "Yes, ma'am, I do. Let me wrangle the pups, and I'll be right back."

The detective nods. "You got it."

Nicole closes the door and faces the overly excited Goldendoodles. "I bet you want a treat." The T word catches their attention, and they tilt their heads, switching from territorial to curious in less than a second. "Okay, let's go get one." She dashes to the kitchen with two furry followers close behind. Once the bacon-flavored biscuits are in hand, Penny and Bob switch gears again, this time to obedient. The pair knows treats don't get distributed unless they mind their manners.

"Bob, Penny, sit." They comply in sync. "Stay." She holds up a hand, emphasizing the command. Their intense russet eyes track her as she backs toward the rear entrance. Nicole opens the slider and steps onto the screened patio. "Okay, you're free. Come outside, my sweethearts."

They sprint her way, tails wagging, butts wiggling all over the place. She can't help laughing. "How do I have the cutest dogs in the world?" They answer with more joyful shimmies. "I could watch you dance forever, but I have to talk to the officer, which is way less fun." She lowers her voice. "Don't tell the detective I said that." Penny lets out a low whimper and fixes her mom with the saddest gaze. "I'm sorry, girl, I'm taking too long, I know." Nicole places the treats on the concrete a few feet apart. "These should last you a while. Come and get 'em."

The pups rush to their biscuits, breezing by her without a glance. While they're distracted, she heads back to the front door, this time opening it fully. "Come on in, Detective. The vicious beasts are distracted."

"They're vicious, all right." She giggles, the sound jarring. "They'll be begging for pets as soon as they finish snacking. At least, that's what happened last time."

"Yes, ma'am. And that will happen again today. Bob and Penny love a good rub down, and they learned you're a sucker for their pleading puppy dog eyes. Give them a few minutes and they'll be next to you, staring into your soul." Nicole waves her through the entry. "Coffee just finished brewing. Would you like a cup?"

"Sounds good. Thank you." Detective Harris trails her to the kitchen. "I only have a few questions, so it won't take long."

Relief floods through Nicole, but she's careful not to show it. The corners of her mouth lift a smidge. Just enough to be friendly, not enough to showcase her delight. "I'm happy to help with the investigation." She pauses.

There's a question she wants to ask, but it's probably rude. Maybe coffee will give her the courage to come out with it. "Do you take cream or sugar?" she asks the detective. "We have white or brown sugar for sweetening. And there's hazelnut and caramel creamer, plus milk or half and half."

"Nothing for me, thank you."

Nicole takes two mugs from a cabinet—a heart-covered one for the detective, a dog mom one for her—and pours dark liquid into each. Steam climbs into the air as she slides the officer's cup over the counter.

Detective Harris lifts the beverage and sips. "This coffee is marvelous, Nicole." She swigs again before getting to business. "We've spoken twice so far. Once at the station, and then again at your house. You've told me what happened the night of February 5 in painstaking detail, and I thank you for that. I think I've constructed a good timeline of Mr. Wilder's movements once he got to the BnB. The other band members helped build the narrative as well. Everything they've told me corroborates, and your point of view adds a nice out-of-the-room perspective." She tilts her chin, gazing at Nicole down her nose. "But what I don't have is any background information. I'd like to gain a more robust picture of who Mr. Wilder was and how his relationships were with the people who witnessed his final moments. Do you think you can help me with that?"

Nicole blows on her coffee, taking the seconds to construct a reply. When the detective questioned her before, she was vague on certain details. Why do the police need to know about Dante's extreme cruelty or the accusations he shouted during his final moments? It was enough for them to know he was a jerk and that he was rude before he croaked. After Karina confessed to his murder, Nicole's subtlety is even more appropriate. There's no use slinging dirt when the case is already solved.

She has a morbid fascination with true crime shows, and she's watched enough series to know that, People. Get. Dragged. Like through the mud, then the pig pen, then the swamp. The more outrageous the facts, the more viewers tune in. This means trashing the victims as well as the suspects. Being gossip-hungry is human nature, and if Nicole is being honest, she often falls prey to the urger.

But this time, it's different. This time, her friends and husband are involved.

With Dante being a celebrity of sorts, there's already enough attention focused on his murder. Social media is filled with theories about his death, ranging from political assassination to erotic asphyxiation gone wrong. If Nicole adds in his final accusations and the broken relationship with his band, there'd be a perfect storm for a viral scandal. One that would destroy everyone connected to ABOS.

For her, this means not adding fuel to the fire. She'll answer Detective Harris's questions acceptably but not fully. Avoiding too much detail will help her and her loved ones avoid disgrace.

The officer watches Nicole, her expression curious and determined but not invasive. She wants Nicole to believe that she's on her side. The detective's geniality makes sense—you catch more flies with honey than vinegar, after all—so Nicole doesn't fault her for the ruse. And she does appreciate the effort the police are making. It's nice to know that Dante's murder is receiving a full investigation. But Nicole has got to counter their probing with a smidge of evasion. She'd do anything to protect the people she cared about.

Nicole grins over the rim of her mug. "I can help you, Detective. What are you looking to find out?"

"Well, during an interview, hints were dropped about Mr. Wilder and some major disturbances he caused in the past. Do you have any idea what they were referring to? This person also mentioned your loyalty to the band. They said you hung out during the beginning of each tour, so I figured you'd have insight into any tension between Wilder and the others."

Dang it. Someone blabbed too much during their interview. Nicole's bet is on Pearl's guitar tech. He enjoys spreading gossip. Nicole keeps her expression neutral. "There's nothing much to say, Detective. More of the same nonsense I told you before. Dante would do rude things like smoke backstage or miss bus call, and the band would have a meeting to discuss it, but nothing would change. He'd do the same things over and over again." She grimaces, remembering his smug face. "That's who Dante was. A line crosser. Nothing was ever his fault, and he wouldn't dream about switching his behavior because it was everyone else's problem, not his."

"Sounds exhausting." The detective nods, maintaining her role as good cop.

"It really was. He was one of those people who sucked the joy from the room. A true energy vampire."

"Do you think he treated his girlfriend like that?" Detective Harris leans across the counter, resting her chin on her palm. "I haven't spoken with Ms. Belmore yet, but my counterparts in California say she's more timid than murderous. Is that your impression of her? Could Dante's attitude have pushed his girlfriend to retaliate?"

In the months she dated Dante, Karina had watched two concerts, the first in San Diego, the second Boston. Since the California show was during the tour's initial week, Nicole attended too, happy to send the band off on their eastward route.

Of course, Dante hadn't introduced her to his girlfriend. Nicole did it on her own during sound check. Karina sat on a chair in the dressing room's corner. Her legs were pulled up to her chest, gripped tight with her left arm. It looked like she was trying to fold into herself. Nicole could tell she was timid from just a glance. Karina was a woman who wanted to fade into the background.

She had walked over and offered the timid woman her hand. "Hi there, I'm Nicole. Jake's wife."

Karina reached up and grasped the end of her fingers, squeezing them with the barest pressure. "I'm Karina." She swiveled her head, avoiding Nicole's eyes. "I'm supposed to be here. I'm with Dante." The last word was a whisper.

"Oh, hon, there's no need to be nervous. I'm not here to kick you out."

"I'm sorry. I've never been backstage before." She lowered her head. "I'm not sure how to act."

"Like yourself, sugar." Nicole offered her hand again. "Want to grab a drink? I can show you where the band's stash is."

Karina met Nicole's gaze, and a faint smile flickered on her lips. "Yeah, that sounds great." She folded her palm into Nicole's outstretched hand and rose from the chair. "Thank you, Nicole."

"Don't mention it." They headed to the dressing room fridge. "Pick your poison," Nicole said, holding open the door.

Karina's eyes scanned the overfull shelves until she reached the can o' wine section. "One of those, please."

Nicole handed her a rosé and snagged a merlot for herself. "To your first VIP show experience. May there be many more." They clinked cans. As the first swallow trailed down their throats, the side door burst open and slammed into the wall with a booming thud.

"What the fuck is going on?" Dante's question barreled through the room as he stomped toward the women.

Karina jumped and a shriek escaped her mouth. As she moved, her drink crashed onto the cement floor. "I was just—"

"Just what? Hanging out with this bitch behind my back?" He glared Nicole's way. "Stop inserting yourself into my life. It's not cute."

"You're the only thing that's not cute here," Nicole yelled as she raced to the supply cabinet. She brought back a roll of paper towels. The wine formed a puddle around Karina's shoes, but she was oblivious to the flood. Nicole tore a few sheets off. "I'm going to mop this up, hon, but I need you to step back." Karina looked down, her eyes pools of anguish, her lips trembling. "It's okay. I can get to it just fine. You stay right there," Nicole reassured her.

Dante stomped back toward the stage entrance, shouting along the way. Although his volume was forceful, his words were emotionless. "Let her clean it up. She's the one who made the mess." When he reached the door, he pulled back his arm and launched his fist into the exit bar. Karina startled again, slipping in the puddle and crashing to the ground with a thud. Dante's laughter followed him out of the room, but his cruelty stayed put, coating the entire dressing room with its dark sheen.

For the third time, Nicole offered Karina her hand. The crying woman didn't take it. Instead, she remained on the ground, stained by rosé, drenched by tears. Nicole cleaned up the wine, careful to avoid her slumped form. Despite several attempts to cheer Karina up, she couldn't clear the heavy sadness hanging in the room.

The encounter flashes through Nicole's head as she considers Detective Harris's questions. Was Karina more murderous than timid? Could Dante's actions have pushed his girlfriend toward violence? Several of Nicole's favorite crime shows feature this exact scenario—a mistreated woman snaps, unleashing her pent-up rage on her abuser. To her, there's a certain justice in these actions. A bully can only bully for so long before their victim fights back. Perhaps that's what happened here. Dante was cruel, Karina was vulnerable. But eventually, a spark of anger grew into an inferno and consumed the person who hurt her.

People like to think they would leave an abuser if they ever found themselves in a relationship with one, but Nicole knows it's not that easy. Love, finances, children, fear—there are many reasons a person stays in a bad situation.

But sometimes, a cornered creature sees lashing out as their only option. After replaying the memory of meeting Karina, Nicole absolutely believes that's what happened. The frightened woman reached her breaking point and gave Dante a taste of his own medicine.

Like the detective, Nicole leans over the counter, closing the distance between them. She whispers her response. "I think Karina might be capable of hurting Dante, but it's only because he treated her so terribly." She straightens up, adding to her answer. "You have to understand, Dante Wilder was awful, and he burned through people like he burned through cigarettes. I saw them together once, backstage at a show. It was so uncomfortable." She frowns, regretting her inaction during the troublesome night. She should have done more to help Karina. "They say you can tell a lot about a couple by how they act in public, and if that's true, their story was really messed up. To Dante, Karina was a misbehaving child." Nicole pauses to consider the words. "Actually, he saw her as less than human. She was some plaything who needed constant correction."

Detective Harris lets out a long breath. "There are plenty of others who think that way about their partners. It's shameful to treat fellow humans like garbage."

Nicole downs the rest of her coffee, then asks the question she's been holding back. "Why do you keep coming here, Detective? Our house is a six-hour drive from your station, but this is the second time you've shown up for more questions. Is there more to this case? I thought after Karina's confession, the investigation would close."

She shakes her head. "Not necessarily, Nicole. Call these visits a way to cross my i's and dot my t's."

Nicole scrunches her brow. "Wait, don't you mean cross your t's and dot your i's?"

The detective pushes back from the counter and stands. "Nope. That's too conventional. When I run an investigation, I look at things from every angle. The who, what, where, when, and why are important to answer, of course, but the biggest question for me is 'what now?' What did this murder set in motion? Who's benefiting from it, or conversely, who lost the most?" She winks and lets out one of her high-pitched giggles. "That's why I'm here. I want to, as the great Missy Elliot said, work it. I want to figure out the details, put that information down, then flip it and reverse it. It's the best way to solve a crime."

Detective Harris hands Nicole her mug. "I must be off. Thanks again for the coffee and for welcoming me into your home, Nicole." She gestures to the patio. "Tell Bob and Penny I said hi. Maybe next time, I can stay long enough to give them some pets." After adjusting her gun belt, she gives a deep nod. "I'll let myself out."

She strides to the front door, waving before stepping outside. Nicole washes their cups and thinks about the visit. Something isn't sitting right with her, but she can't place it. After setting the mugs on the drying rack, she heads to Jake's studio and enters in a rush. He's sitting in front of the soundboard, fingers resting on two faders.

"Hon, can we talk?" she asks.

Jake rotates his chair until he's facing his wife. "Coley, I'm busy. Can't this wait?"

"I don't think it can." She gestures to the kitchen. "That nosey detective was just here, and our conversation left me feeling strange, like she's hyper-focused on me or something."

Jake's forehead wrinkles. "Did she say anything to give you that idea?"

"Not really. But sort of. She quoted Missy Elliot and said she's going to dive into the case from every possible angle." She hesitates. "What if she finds out about you and Dante?"

Jake stands, hurrying over, and she collapses into his arms. "Shhh. Shhh. It's okay, sweetheart. The police won't find out because no one is going to tell them. It's our little secret."

"I hope you're right, Jakey." She closes her eyes, nuzzling her cheek against his chest. "If Detective Harris learns about your involvement, we'll lose everything."

A Box of Stars Bassist Jake Devlin in Critical Condition After Motorcycle Accident

By Coral Wright | **Published** December 3, 2020 | Floraville Times |

Elway County, FL – Jake Devlin, the bassist for indie rock group A Box of Stars, is in critical condition after a motorcycle collision on I-95. Devlin, a 27-year-old Florida native, was traveling southbound in the right lane when he collided with a semi-truck. He was ejected from the bike and thrown onto the highway's left shoulder.

Police say that Devlin was driving above the 70 MPH speed limit and that he collided with the truck while he was trying to switch lanes.

Devlin was wearing a helmet during the incident. He was transported to Markside Mercy Hospital with critical injuries.

The Elway County Sheriff's Office, Crystal Cove Fire Department, and Daventerra Police Department assisted with this accident.

Chapter 11 – Maggie

{February 20, 2023}

Although Maggie's daughter sees her, the teenager lingers in the pickup area, flirting with a lanky brunette wearing holey jeans and a red hoodie. The unknown teen brushes hair from Danica's forehead, tucking the stick-straight strands behind her right ear. It's an intimate gesture, a sweet one, and color fills her daughter's cheeks in response. After giving Mr. Brunette an awkward hug, she darts toward the car, eyes on to the ground, arms glued to her sides.

"Well, well, well, what did I just spy?" Maggie asks as she flops into the passenger seat.

"Mom, not now. He's watching." Danica rolls down the window and waves to her dreamboat as they leave the high school.

When they're a block away, Maggie tries again. "So, who's the young gentleman that's captured your attention?"

The color on the girl's cheeks deepens to a fiery crimson, and she avoids her mother's gaze when she answers. "His name's Devon. He's into music, like me. It's not a big deal."

"Wait. Did you say you're into music? I didn't know that."

"Yeah, Mom. I'm into hardcore stuff from the nineties." She holds up her pinky and pointer to form the metal horns sign. "The scene back then was killer."

"Nineties hardcore? Like Sick of it All?" Maggie nudges her daughter's shoulder. "Many moons ago, I went to tons of shows. If there was an all-ages event, believe me, I was there."

"Mom, not to offend you…" Danica hesitates.

"Power through, sweetie."

She does. "But, judging by your lame attempts at head-banging last week, I'm guessing you were one of the people standing in the back of the crowd, not someone moshing or surfing."

"Oh, my sweet summer child, how wrong you are. Your ol' ma used to throw down with the best of them."

Danica raises her head, finally meeting Maggie's eyes. "Really?" She scans her mother's outfit—flats, skinny jeans, and a cardigan. "It's hard for me to picture you like that since you're such a mom now."

"Really truly." Maggie picks up her phone at a stop light. "Let's jam to some classics." She finds a hardcore station on her music app, and they listen to the energetic songs until they pull into the supermarket. Maggie turns to Danica. "What should we make for dinner? I was thinking tacos, but we had those a few days ago."

"Tacos always sound good. What if we use shrimp instead of beef? Does that mix things up enough?"

"Absolutely." Maggie steps out of the car, grabbing a cart from the adjacent parking spot. "Let's hustle so we can get home. I was in the middle of a mermaid board when school ended, and I want to finish the first coat of paint before it's time to cook."

Danica nods. "Challenge accepted."

At 2:30 in the afternoon, the store is dead and they're able to double-step down the aisles without bothering other shoppers. They gather ingredients for shrimp tacos, plus cookies and ice cream for dessert. As the clerk rings up their items, Maggie peeks at her watch. "That was impressively fast."

"That's what she said," the teenager behind the register mumbles.

"Good one—" Maggie eyes his nametag "—Aiden. And thanks for bagging heavy. No one ever listens when I tell them to."

"No problem." He sneaks a glimpse at Danica before announcing their total. Maggie catches him stealing another peep while she taps her card to pay. When they're in the car, she brings up the cashier's interest. "Did you notice young Aiden checking you out?"

"Gross. He's not my type at all." Danica grimaces. "His soul patch wasn't doing him any favors. Were those ever in style?"

"Is that what those hairs under his lip are called?"

"Yep."

"Fascinating."

They chat during the drive home and separate once they get inside. Danica to do her homework, Maggie to finish painting. Her studio takes up almost the entire garage, nestled inside a DIY workshop with plenty of space to spread out.

And she maximizes the square footage. Industrial shelves hold her various crafting supplies, while multi-level chests store a decent tool collection. Four by eight balsa wood sheets, some primed, some unfinished, sit upright in a huge, wheeled bin.

In the right-hand corner, a vintage overhead projector is the room's focal point. The gray plastic rectangle sits on a rolling cart next to a stack of acetate sheets and wet-erase markers. Decades ago, Maggie's mother used the machine to explain calculus to perplexed high schoolers. For some reason when her mom retired, she gifted the contraption to Maggie. Until recently, the projector stayed in the back of a closet, forgotten under a pile of winter coats. But that changed with Be Marry Boards. A few times a week, she powers up the machine and traces outlines onto smooth balsa pieces.

It's neat that a device from the eighties became her business's most valuable piece of equipment. Her mom was on to something when she handed it down. Math teachers are an intuitive bunch.

Today, her board in progress is past the tracing stage, so she won't need the projector. The wood panel leans against a ceramic-topped table that dominates the center of the studio. She painted half the image this morning, and she takes a moment to admire her work.

The board is bright. Cheery. Hilarious. It contains two merperson tails bobbing in a calm aqua ocean. The customers purchased a pearlescent paint enhancement, so jewel-toned fish scales shimmer in the studio's bright light. The sparkle is eye-catching, and she knows the buyers will be thrilled when they unbox their special delivery.

Smiling, Maggie twists her curls into a bun and dons the paint-splattered shirt hanging near the door. Danica got her in the mood for intense music during their drive. Before selecting paint colors, she connects to a speaker and blasts Agnostic Front, thankful they chose sound-deadening insulation for the walls. The blistering drums put some pep in her step. In her mind, she's a teenager again. Time to rock out.

She hums along to the beat while pulling up Debbie and Demetrius's order on her phone. The duo is buff and raven-haired, and they want their wedding board to mirror their fit physiques. Maggie squirts black, white, brown, and red hues onto her palette, grabs three brushes of varying widths, and gets started on the human halves of the mer-creatures.

Time whizzes past as she paints pecs, abs, biceps, and traps. When Agnostic Front changes to Social Distortion, she starts on the project's final details. Merman Demetrius gets a bulge, and mermaid Debbie gets a replica of her cat tattoo, a sleeping calico with its tail wrapped around her belly button. A minute later Maggie completes the last brush strokes, and steps back, checking the board for flaws.

A knock on the door interrupts her inspection. "Come in," she yells after pausing the music.

Pearl bounds into the room, face glowing with a smile. She checks out the completed wedding board, the skin on her forehead creasing as she appraises the image. "Nice package."

Maggie nods. "The bulges have been a hit."

"I'm not surprised. They add a dash of absurdity to the scene, and I'm here for it." Her gaze leaves the merman and fixes on her wife. "Did you know Danica has a boyfriend?"

"I didn't know Mr. Brunette had an official title. She said it was no big deal."

"Well, apparently, it's a very big deal. We just had a whole conversation about it. Lots of blushing, barely any eye contact." Pearl's smile widens. "And get this. Devon asked if he could take our little girl out tonight."

A squeal erupts from Maggie's mouth and she does a little jump. "Her first date? That's incredible. Where does he want to take her?"

"Some place called The Double Bass." She raises an eyebrow. "Devon's in a band, and he wants Dani to see his guitar skills in person."

"Oh man. Dating a band dude is trouble." Maggie puts a hand over her mouth. "What did I just say? I'm married to a band dude."

"You sure are." Pearl leans over, brushing her lips across Maggie's cheek. "We have no moral high ground on this issue. It looks like our girl is following in our footsteps."

"What'd you say when she asked about the date?"

"Told her I needed to discuss it with you. We have until 5:00 PM to make our decision." She checks the time on her phone. "So, about half an hour. The show starts at 7:00, and Dani needs time to get ready."

Maggie flashes back to her first date. Brett Gullrich, a wide receiver on the football team, asked her out fall of freshman year. His family owned a bowling alley, and he thought it would be fun to eat pizza and occupy a lane for a couple of hours. In theory, the activity sounded great. In practice, the evening turned out awful.

When Brett asked Maggie out, he was polite. Even a little shy. That changed the moment they sat down with their pepperoni pie. On lane 27, his true personality emerged. The real Brett was loud, rude, and handsy, and getting to second base was his primary objective. Maggie tried her best to outmaneuver his gropes, but Brett was stealthy. And flexible. The jerk stuck his hand up her shirt when she bent to grab her ball. And when she took a sip of her drink. And when she greeted friends two lanes over.

His fingers were everywhere. And, of course, he didn't listen when Maggie told him to quit. In fact, her pleas seemed to make him more determined.

It was a bowling ball to the gut that finally made him stop.

An hour into the date, Brett's movements began to repeat, and Maggie picked up on the pattern. He'd follow her to the ball return. Then up to the lane. When she squared up to roll, he'd rub his hands along her body, moaning softly as he took advantage of her passivity. To anyone else, he appeared to be helping his date bowl. Up close, he tormented her with his unwanted touches.

Eventually, Maggie had enough. Instead of shame and fear, anger surged through her chest, and she propelled the red-hot emotion into action. She strode to the ball return, grabbing his twelve-pounder instead of her eight. Her date was too busy being pervy to notice the substitute. Lucky Maggie.

Brett stayed glued to her side as she made her way up the lane, but she ignored him until he started moaning. She hated his obnoxious, disgusting moan. When he made that sound, she took a step forward, flinging her arm and the ball back. The weight nailed him in the stomach, and his lustful noises switched to shrill shrieks.

Maggie much preferred those.

The sore loser tattled to his folks, conveniently leaving out his unwelcome fondling. From the alley's front desk, they made Maggie call her parents, who picked her up within ten minutes. Mom and Dad had been nervously excited about her first date, so they asked all sorts of questions on the way home. Unfortunately, Maggie's answers confirmed their anxiety rather than their excitement. They were livid when she told them about Sir Gropes a Lot but proud of their daughter for standing up for herself.

As the terrible experience replays in her mind, she tells herself that Danica's dating life won't necessarily reflect hers. In Maggie's group of friends, some women have shared hellish stories, but others divulged perfectly normal teenage meetups. Her wife is included in the happy group. She went on a moonlit picnic with her tenth-grade crush, and had an evening free of coercion. And blunt force trauma.

"What are you thinking about, Maggie-moo?" Pearl interrupts the memory. "You've got that far-off look in your eyes."

"Not much. Just that, I hope Danica's date goes like your romantic picnic instead of my bowling horror fest." She sighs. "I'm slightly jealous of your evening under the stars. It sounds magical."

Her wife holds out her arms, and Maggie walks into the embrace. "There's no need to be jealous of something that happened ages ago, love." Pearl's lips move against her hair. "But I agree with your overall concept. I want our baby to have a good time, not have to defend herself against someone who can't keep their hands to themselves."

"Agreed." Maggie pushes back and peer into Pearl's eyes. "Aside from not letting her go, is there anything we can do to make sure she's safe?"

"I've been giving that some thought, and I have an idea."

"I am not surprised, oh brilliant one. Tell me what you came up with."

Her wife tilts her head. "What about a double date?"

Maggie bursts out laughing. "I retract my brilliant comment. Danica would never go on a date with her helicopter moms."

"Hey, give me more credit than that." Pearl laughs too, a carefree, floaty sound. "What I meant was, what if we go on a date somewhere close to The Double Bass? That way, we can drop off and pick up Danica, plus stay nearby in case anything happens."

"You're back to being brilliant." Maggie stands on tiptoe, and her lips meet Pearl's. She smiles as they kiss, and she's still grinning when she pulls away. Her wife's tousled hair and crinkled eyes radiate joy. Even after sixteen years, Pearl's beauty overwhelms Maggie. "What part of town is The Double Bass in?"

"It's on Elm Street. Right behind Taterburg and Drinking Games." Pearl's eyes sparkle as she claps her hands together. "I was thinking we could grab a burger then chill at the barcade. It's nineties night, so we'll know every song."

"Perfect. Count me in for burgers and pinball." Maggie places her hands on her hips. "You're going down, babe. *The Simpsons* machine is calling my name, so be prepared for an insanely high score."

"Riiiiiight." Pearl's sarcasm is warranted. There's no way Maggie will win a single game.

"Hopefully, Danica agrees to our plan. We think it's awesome, but who knows what a teenager will make of it," Maggie says.

"Let's go tell her."

Maggie rinses her supplies and darkens the studio. Pearl leads the way upstairs, and they knock on their daughter's bedroom door together. "Come in," Danica calls out.

Her wife opens the door, and Maggie saunters in, running her mouth. "I hear that Devon is a bigger deal than you made him out to be."

"And?" Danica asks from the center of her clothes-covered bed.

"Well, if I would have known he was my sweet princess's boyfriend, maybe I would have gotten out of the car to introduce myself," Maggie says, hoping her teasing tone is obvious.

"No freaking way." Danica doesn't pick up on the joke. Instead, she looks to Pearl for assistance. "Momma help. Tell her that's not cool."

"Your mom's kidding, sweetie." Her wife sits on the bed's edge. "But honestly, you should have told her the truth. Why withhold information? It can lead to hurt feelings."

Danica rubs the fabric of a striped tank top between her fingers. The motion calms her. She's been doing it since she was a toddler when she'd use her baby blanket to self-soothe. Now, they give her space to put words to her thoughts. Rushing their spirited child is never a good idea.

After a minute, Danica speaks up, still stroking the shirt. "I'm sorry, Mom. I should have told you."

"It's okay. I'm not upset." Maggie joins them on the bed. "So, tell me more about this date. What type of music does Devon's band play? Have you heard any of their songs?"

Danica's eyes light up, and she pulls her phone from her pocket. "Here. You can listen yourself." She opens her music app and searches for Dopamine Diver. A photo of four teenagers dressed in bloody scrubs pops up, and she clicks the image. "Pick any song. They're all really good." She hands the cell over.

Maggie reads the band's short bio—Florida-based nu-metal group— then browses their offerings, a limited selection from their first and only album. The title "Herniated Heartbreak" grabs her attention, so she presses play and listens. She's careful to maintain neutrality as overdubbed riffs and rushed drums overtake the room. It's more difficult to stay impartial when gargled vocals croon about a pair of car accident victims who fall in love, then break up while undergoing treatment for their injuries. Somehow, Maggie holds it together.

Her daughter bounces on the bed as the song plays through. When the last note fades, she faces her mom, cheeks flushing with excitement. "What did you think?"

Obviously, Maggie lies. "Wow, I didn't know high schoolers could sound that good."

"Right? And I'm dating the lead guitarist." Danica lets out a sigh. "Too bad my friends are salty about the whole thing."

"How come?" Maggie asks.

"Well—" she twirls a strand of hair "—Dopamine Driver won Battle of the Bands and got really popular, really fast. All the girls at school wanted to hook up with Marius, the singer, and when he was taken, Devon was next on the list. Unfortunately for them, he picked me because I actually liked the band before they were cool." Danica stops spinning her hair. "I'm a little bummed my besties won't talk to me right now, but that's their issue, not mine."

"I'm sorry, Dani." Pearl pats her knee. "It sucks when friends turn their back on you."

"Yeah, it does," their daughter agrees. "Maybe they'll change their mind soon."

Maggie tries to lighten the mood. "Momma and I had an idea for tonight, and we wanted to run it by you." She nudges her wife, knowing she is the more persuasive one. "Why don't you explain what we're thinking."

Pearl outlines their plan, and surprisingly Danica agrees without hesitation. "I'm down. It will be good for you two to get out of the house. You haven't done much since tour got canceled."

Ouch. The observation is brutal, but she's right. They have stayed close to home since Dante's death, Maggie catching up on Be Marry orders and Pearl working on new music. School transportation and grocery shopping are the only activities that have taken them into town. They've ordered takeout once but haven't visited a restaurant or pub in weeks, which is way outside their ordinary behavior. Usually, they visit their favorite spots every few days.

Maggie has been cooking, and her culinary skills are decent, but she misses eating meals she doesn't have to prepare. Plus, there's no way she can concoct something as delicious as the black truffle mushroom gnocchi that Tavola Cucina offers on Thursday nights. That stuff is untouchably delicious.

The day Pearl flew home from her shortened tour, they agreed to a mellow few weeks. The time would serve as a transitional period where her wife could think about ABOS's future. They thought adjusting to the band's potential demise was smart. And necessary. Who knows how fans would react to Dante's death and Pearl replacing him as singer? If her wife needed to pivot to another band, or hell, an entirely different career, then making the effort to weigh her choices was crucial.

Although judging by the hours she's spent writing ABOS-styled music, Maggie would say she wants to reunite with the dudes she's played with for almost a decade. If they do get back together, they might enjoy creating music a whole lot more. Dante drained the group. Without him, they could rise above their 2016 glory days and become the band they were always meant to be. Sucks that it took a murder to get them to a promising spot.

"Are you ready for an evening out with an average-looking thirty-six-year-old?" Maggie asks her wife.

Pearl's laugh rings out. "I'm ready to get dolled up and dominate you in pinball, if that's what you're asking."

"Let's do it." Maggie turns to Danica. "Thanks for being such an awesome kid. I can't wait to hear about the show. I bet Dopamine Diver sounds even better live than they do recorded."

Danica throws her arms around Maggie for a moment, then jumps off the bed. "It takes fifteen minutes to get to the show, so that means we need to leave at 6:45." She bounds to her closet, flinging open the door. "I have less than two hours to get ready."

"Just throw on a black shirt, jeans, and some dark eyeliner, and you'll blend right in," Pearl says.

"Momma, I don't want to blend in." Danica juts out a hip. "I want to stand out from the crowd. Devon needs to notice me while he's playing."

"Let's give her some space." Maggie stands up, offering Pearl her hand. "Plus, we also need to get dressed. I heard something about getting dolled up—" she glances down at her gray cardigan "—and what I'm wearing doesn't cut it."

"I like your sweaters, Maggie." Pearl takes the offered hand and pulls herself upright. "But I'm sure we can find something a little fancier. Let's go."

"Yes, dear." They head out, Maggie blowing Danica a kiss as they stroll. "See you at 6:45, sweetie. You're going to look beautiful no matter what."

"Thanks, Mom." Her daughter's words put a smile on her face. Gratitude is such a lovely thing.

In their room, Pearl marches to the closet and picks out a pale blue dress and silver kitten heels. "What do you think about this?"

"For you or me?"

"For you. Sky blue will accentuate your ivory skin. You'll look smashing."

"If you say so. You know I'm hopeless when it comes to that stuff." Maggie takes the outfit and lays the clothes on the bed. "I need a quick shower to wash off the paint."

"Keep the water running, please. I'll jump in after you're done."

"You got it, toots."

As Maggie waits for the water to heat up, she leans against the counter, browsing through her email. Most items relate to work—a shipping confirmation, two new orders, and a review alert—but as she scrolls, a new message comes through. It's from Pearl.

"Why'd you send me an email when we're literally twenty feet apart?" Maggie yells.

"Read it, Maggie-moo. Then tell me what you think," her wife shouts back.

She opens the message and scans the contents.

Hey all,

We just received an offer for Rage on the Waves. A band canceled last minute, so there's a spot they need to fill quickly. It's a two-show gig, and the option for meet and greets is available if you're up for it. They offered $85k, with suites and plus ones for each of you.

The boat leaves March 13 at 5PM and gets back early morning, March 19. It departs from Miami and sails to Mexico and Belize before returning to Florida.

We have until noon tomorrow to respond. What do you think?

-Dylan

After a couple of minutes, Pearl joins her in the bathroom. "Tell me, tell me, tell me," she demands like a sugared-up toddler.

"A floating concert is a cool concept. I get advertisements for them on social media, but not this one. Rage on the Waves sounds intense."

Pearl shrugs. "Yeah, we got an offer a few years ago that was nowhere near as good. We refused that one, but this one is tempting. I think the guarantee got jacked up because it's last minute." She pulls out her phone and opens the event's website. On the homepage, flashing red banners announce a waitlist. "Plus, it's already sold out, so there's a built-in audience."

"A huge crowd and eighty-five thousand dollars. That won't make up for the canceled tour, but it'll be something. A big something."

Pearl nods. "Absolutely. I'm going to say yes if that's alright with you."

Maggie reaches over and grasps her wife's hands. "Why would you need my permission? This is your career."

"Because you're going to be my plus one. Duh." Pearl bounces on her toes and does a little shimmy. "Do you want to go on a cruise with me, babe? I know we'll have the best time."

Dylan,

This cruise situation is interesting. Do we need to bring gear or is everything provided? And what about alcohol? Can we throw a few bottles on the rider?
Trev

I can ask, but I don't want to push it too much since $85k is a hell of an offer. I'll find out about the gear. I'm guessing they'll provide a backline, but I'll double check.
-D

Guys,

I'm down, but I did have a question – if we accept, how will this look in relation to Dante? Is it too soon after his death to be playing? The money is amazing, but we don't want the optics to be terrible.

Pearl

What if you guys dedicate the show to him? Not many people know you kicked him out, so it'll look legit.
-D

Whoa. That's devious. But super smart. I think it'll work.

I'm down. Let the ABOS comeback begin.
-Jake

I'm not sure dedicating the show to Dante is a good move, but if that's what everyone agrees to, then I'll go along. It'll be nice to play again though. I think our fans will be stoked that we're staying together as a four piece.
Rory

If you all agree, I'll reach out the booking agent and confirm.

What about practice? I can reserve a place outside Miami the weekend before the cruise. There are some options about half an hour from the port. Let me know asap, and I'll get everything sorted.
-D

Chapter 12 – Brandi

{February 20, 2023}

Trev's trial run was terrible.

For Brandi, at least. Her boyfriend had a blast.

During his weeklong test, the thirty-eight-year-old man-child lounged around, soaking up attention, oblivious to the extra effort Brandi showered on him. He ate all the food, drank all the drinks, and accepted all the blowjobs, and not once did he express gratitude or return the favor.

Honestly, she should thank Trev for his neglect. If he would have tossed out morsels of compassion, she might have stayed locked into their relationship, groveling for the rare attention-filled moments. Instead, her boyfriend's crappy attitude pushes her toward a straightforward decision. After five months together, it is time for them to split.

Well, close to time. To survive on her own, Brandi needs to wait for Dante's estate to disburse. That will be a huge payday. After the funds hit her account, she can leave Trev's run-down house and move on to bigger and better things. For her. And, more importantly, for the baby.

Brandi learned about her unexpected windfall from Lydia Crissik. A few days ago, when Brandi finally returned the lawyer's call, they scheduled a meeting for this morning. Lydia thought an in-person discussion would be better than a phone conversation, and she was right. The lawyer's presence grounded the surreal situation. Brandi entered the swanky law firm with limited expectations—Dante was awful with money, after all—and left with buoyant hope swirling in her chest.

True to form, Trev almost caused her to miss hearing the life-changing news. Earlier, as she rushed around the house, getting dressed and slapping on makeup, her boyfriend threw a tantrum that almost ruined the day. Brandi collided with his foul mood in the kitchen.

"Where are you going? How come you didn't make me any eggs?" he whined.

She winced at the grating sound. "That was an hour ago. You never told me you were hungry, so I never cooked."

"What the hell, Brandi? The least you can do is feed me." He crossed his arms. "You live in my house and use my WIFI for your crappy job. How about you start earning your keep? Breakfast would be a step in the right direction."

Waves of anger flooded her body, but she pushed them down. Negative emotions impacted the baby, so remaining calm was critical. Still, Trev deserved some heat. He talked to Brandi like trash, and there was no reason for the disrespect. "Did you forget about the rent checks you cash every month? Are they not hitting your account?" She pulled out her phone. "Maybe we need to call the bank. They'll clear up this misunderstanding."

"Put your phone down." Trev's whine increased in pitch, and he puckered his bottom lip. He became a toddler entering meltdown mode. "Sure, you pay rent, but I charge below market value. I'm getting shafted."

"Shafted. Right." She poked the broken kitchen counter. "Glad to hear cracked tile and peeling wallpaper land this place in the primo real estate market." She pivoted toward the front door, strode to the entry table, and donned her purse and sunglasses. "We'll talk about this later. I have to leave, or I'll get stuck in the morning rush." Five minutes mattered when it came to California traffic, and it was already dangerously close to gridlock hour.

"You never told me where you're going." He narrowed his eyes, sweeping his gaze up and down his girlfriend's body, finally noticing her suit and heels. "You're all dressed up. Are you banging some other dude?"

Brandi lowered her glasses, staring at him with her fiercest expression. A lie rolled off her tongue in an arctic tone. "I'm going to visit Karina in jail. It's time to make up with my bestie. I think she could use a friend."

The color drained from his face. "Why would you want to visit her? She's a murderer."

"And you're a jerk, yet here I am." Brandi pushed her shades back into place. "We'll talk later, like I said."

"Whatever. I don't need you to cook for me. I'll order delivery." He whipped out his cell. "Have fun with your other boyfriend."

Slamming the door was her response. Trev's lucky she released her annoyance on the wood instead of his face. A younger Brandi would have chosen violence. The more mature Brandi knew when to walk away. Also, she was in a hurry, and charging inside to smack him would waste precious seconds. She hopped into her car instead, racing off toward Lydia's office and the news of a brighter future.

Now, she is back home, sitting in the car, drumming up the motivation to survive the next three weeks while waiting for Dante's money. She still wants nothing to do with Trev, but breaking up today means starting an apartment search before she can afford something by herself. Staying in his rundown duplex would make the most sense, but can she deal with her boyfriend's infuriating behavior for an extended period?

And what about the baby? Thanks to Brandi's long torso, the pregnancy is not visible yet, but her belly could pop any day. Keeping the situation under wraps is her preference, with Trev being the last person she wants to find out. He would go crazy and either kick her out or want to claim the child. Both terrible options.

Too bad she cannot control when her little guy reveals his existence to the world. Sucking in her gut only helps so much. And while baggy shirts and leggings would conceal a growing waistband, neither will do her any good in the shower. Or if Trev requests sexy time. And if she stays at his place, she needs to resign herself to that chore.

Gross.

At least he is pleasant to look at. The dude is lucky genetics were kind to him because he would have a lot less company if he were not as hot. Trev's gorgeous face somewhat counteracts his terrible personality. It is why Brandi has hooked up with him for so long. And it's why she will be able to handle three more weeks at his house. His chiseled jaw and striking eyes are his selling features. She will focus on them while she endures the next twenty-one days.

After some deep breaths, she exits the vehicle and heads inside. The space has a vacant vibe, a deep stillness, and she confirms the emptiness after a stroll through each room. Thank God. She would much rather adjust to her new reality alone than while suffocated by Trev's idiotic presence.

Brandi's fancy clothes go on the bed, and she hops into the shower for a rinse. As the warm water runs down her back, she places a hand on her stomach. Her skin is taut, but there is no other indication of the life growing inside. At least no outward-facing evidence. Internally, there's tons going on.

A flutter stirs beneath her palm, the movement delicate, subtle. Later, his kicks will be more noticeable, painful even, but for now, she cherishes the subdued motions, delighted she is the only person who knows about them. Growing up, kids were not something she wanted, so the joy her son already provides is surprising. Her life has changed in breathtaking ways, and she is rolling with the adjustments as they come.

Five minutes in, the shower refreshes her. Even though it is noon on a Monday, she steps into sweats and a hoodie before tossing her hair into a messy bun. There is no need for business casual attire today.

Last week, when she had scheduled the meeting with Lydia, she submitted a PTO request at work. Her boss approved it without question since she rarely asked for time off. Trev was wrong when he called her job crappy. The company gives her flexibility when she needs it, and the paychecks are not the worst. She plans to stay with them even after Dante's money lands in her bank account. There is no use throwing away a steady income when she is adding another family member to her household. Plus, she can work from anywhere in the world. Her and the kiddo are definitely taking advantage of that perk. The sooner, the better.

Quiet enfolds her as she ventures to the kitchen. Yesterday was grocery day, meaning there was plenty of food in the fridge. She browses the shelves, pushing past Trev's processed junk in the front. She settles on an arugula, goat cheese, and blackened chicken salad. Healthy and yummy.

There is no way Brandi could cook this meal if her boyfriend were around. The man is almost forty, but any cheese besides American is outside his palate. He says the smell of her "stinky" varieties nauseates him, so she cannot eat anything delicious when he's at home. Annoying. It sucks that his narrow preferences dictate her menu.

But that is not the case this afternoon. After cooking the chicken, she munches the salad in peace, luxuriating in the silence, happy to be free from any judgment about her cheese selection. Trev's absence is a treat. It compounds her happiness from this morning's news.

As Brandi chews, she thinks about the meeting, which happened at a law firm nestled in the city's ritziest area. When she stepped into suite 215 five minutes before their scheduled appointment, Lydia Crissik greeted her with a firm handshake. "Welcome, Ms. Monner. It's a pleasure to meet you. Would you like any coffee?"

The lawyer was tall, easily 5'11" and her bleached blonde hair hung in a braid brushing the small of her back. Up to that point, Brandi's interactions with legal professionals were limited, so she was not sure what to expect during their interaction. Would Lydia be cold? Judgy? Mean?

Negative assumptions flowed through Brandi's head, but they vanished after their introduction. Although Lydia's voice was business-like, the lawyer's warm smile put her client at ease. She had a kind aura. Nothing shady.

Brandi's anxiety lowered, and she accepted Lydia's offer. "I would love coffee if you have decaf." After her pregnancy was confirmed, she gave up caffeine. The withdrawal headaches were killer at first, but they had faded after a week. Thank goodness. "Oh, and please call me Brandi."

"Certainly." Lydia gestured to a brown leather sofa. "Please. Make yourself comfortable."

"Thank you." Brandi strolled to the couch and got settled, purse at her feet, knees bent, ankles crossed. She wanted to appear humble. Like she was not expecting a single thing, even though excitement was brewing inside.

Lydia made her way to a chrome coffee maker near the office window. She popped open its lid and placed a decaf pod inside. "Should be ready in about a minute." She grabbed the end of her braid, twirling the processed strands. "How was the drive? I hate that 9:00 was the only time I was available. Morning rush isn't fun."

"It was fine. Although—" Brandi let out a laugh "—since I work from home, it's always a shock when I emerge into the outside world. I can't imagine dealing with all those cars twice a day."

"Tell me about it." The lawyer rolled her eyes. "That's why I moved closer to the office. My commute was way too long before." The coffee maker hissed as it shot out a line of steam. Brown liquid began pouring into the waiting mug. "Almost done."

"Thanks again for the coffee. And for reaching out. Your voicemail and letter intrigued me."

"I apologize for contacting you right after Mr. Wilder's death, but his parents insisted we wrap things up quickly." Another line of steam erupted from the machine, and the liquid flow slowed to a drip. "Let me bring this over, and we can discuss what's in Mr. Wilder's will." The lawyer waited a moment longer, until the pour completed, then carried over the coffee along with a manilla folder. "I promise it's decaf," she said as she handed the mug over, sitting on the sofa's other cushion. "The brew is just stronger than you'd expect."

For Brandi, the stronger, the better. "That sounds perfect."

"Okay." Lydia opened the folder, laying it flat on the table in front of the pair. "I asked you here because you were named in the will Mr. Wilder composed January twentieth of this year. During our appointment that day, he made adjustments to his estate in the event of his death." She handed over a document, and Brandi scanned it as she continued. "Prior to this change, you were not included as a beneficiary. Now, you are. As well as your son."

The words in Dante's will were a mix of legalese and information too good to be true. If Brandi were understanding correctly, she would inherit a huge amount, paid in sums over the next eighteen years. "This might sound awful, but did Dante really have this much money? The man I knew was not very good at life, let alone his finances."

With a serious expression, Lydia fixed her eyes on Brandi's. "He really did have that much money. His grandfather left him a substantial sum that you will take over until your son reaches the age of majority. At that point, he will become the beneficiary. You will also receive his portion of the band's royalties until your child becomes an adult." Her features softened. "Although this is good news, it can be overwhelming to hear. Do you have any questions?"

"Is this…legal?" Brandi raised her eyebrows. "Everything is happening so fast, and I thought these things took years."

"Well, Mr. Wilder had no debt, so he owes no creditors. His parents, the only other beneficiaries, want to put his death behind them, considering the circumstances under which it occurred." She leaned back into the supple leather, slinging her blonde braid over her shoulder so it wouldn't get caught. "He had no relatives to contest the will, and I made his intentions bulletproof. He unquestioningly wanted his son to inherit everything he owned, with you as the initial proxy." She pointed to the papers in Brandi's hand. "You're holding a solid legal document. Nothing about this situation is breaking any laws."

A breath escapes from Brandi's mouth. Then a laugh. "This is unbelievable." Another laugh erupted. "Like, I almost don't believe you."

"It's shocking, but it's true." The lawyer's lips lift into a smile. "I like these meetings the best. When there's a happily ever after, instead of a disgruntled relative."

"What do I even say to all this? You literally just changed my life."

Lydia shook her head. "I'm just the messenger, Brandi. Mr. Wilder is the person who changed your life."

The lawyer's words repeat in Brandi's head as she washes her lunch dishes. Dante never told her about the additions to his will. Hell, Brandi figured he was too broke to have more than a hundred bucks in his bank account. He seemed way too sleazy to oversee anything resembling an estate, but here she is, the recipient of the trashy jerk's generosity. It was an odd twist of fate.

There's no way to thank Dante for his kindness in person. Raising their son will have to do. Becoming an excellent parent was already an important goal of hers, but with the extra money, the aspiration is more attainable. Wealth does not buy happiness, but gaining middle-class status sure as hell makes everything less challenging. Without having money stress, food will be on the table, bills will be paid, and bank accounts will be full.

But the most important item she will gain is freedom. With extra deposits rolling in, Brandi will not feel forced to pick between awful days with Trev or poverty as a single mom. A third option will present itself on March 14—a cushy life featuring her and the baby. No loser dudes allowed.

A smile fills her face as Brandi leaves the kitchen. She is buoyant, carefree, untroubled, a complete one-eighty from earlier this morning. Luck shined on her when Lydia vanquished her financial woes. More sparkled when she found herself alone after the life-changing meeting. The universe knew she needed time to relax.

The contentment ends when her phone buzzes. All it takes is a text from her boyfriend and poof, instant dark mood.

TREV: b home in ten, if ur even there yet

Yuck. He is such a whiner.

Does he deserve a reply? No. But maybe if she tosses out some nice words, he will be in a decent mood when he returns. The better Trev feels, the better the next three weeks will go. Brandi clenches her jaw as she types, annoyed that catering to him is still required.

BRANDI: Hey babe, I'm home. Can't wait to see you ;)

A winky face should excite him. He will know what to expect when he gets back.

She throws her phone on the couch and heads to their room. Her lingerie is in the closet, and she digs into the chest holding the flimsy outfits. Is it a fishnet or lace kind of day? Brandi sorts through the options and pulls out a lacy crimson bodysuit with a ruffle across the belly. The detail is the perfect camouflage for her slightly stretched skin. Even though there is no pooch yet, it is never too soon for caution. Might as well get used to the habit.

Her hoodie and sweats fall to the floor, and she pulls the flimsy teddy over her body until the material is in place. A mirror hangs in the back of the closet, so she checks herself from every angle using slow pirouettes. Nothing in her reflection suggests momness, only hotness, exactly what she wants.

Brandi glances in the mirror once more. In the reflection, a stack of boxes catches her attention, a pile she had not noticed before. The containers are concealed behind Trev's hanging clothes, but their cardboard corners peek out from between two button-down shirts. She turns toward the stack and leans close. Does her boyfriend have a shoe-buying habit? The labels on the cartons hint at the possibility. According to their tags, each box contains size eleven sneakers, mostly Jordans, with a few other brands mixed in. Brandi is no footwear expert, but the stash must be worth hundreds, maybe thousands of dollars. Trev was spending money he did not have on sneakers. Cool.

The top box's lid is crooked. According to her grandmama, when something is open, a peek does not count as prying. Trev really should be more careful with his secrets.

Brandi steps forward, lifting the container from its hiding spot. The label claims Air Jordan 3s rest inside, but a rattling emits from the cardboard as she moves the box closer. She pushes the lid off and eyes the contents, which are not shoes at all. Instead, empty vape cartridges fill the interior. Rows and rows of vape cartridges.

She inspects the second box, then the third and fourth. Each contains between fifteen and twenty empty cartridges. Yuck, yuck, yuck. She had no idea Trev smoked this much. He kept the extent of his habit under wraps, probably to avoid his girlfriend's disgust. And why is he saving these useless remnants? Some sort of vape recycling program? The beginnings of a hoarding disorder?

A slamming door interrupts her thoughts. She restacks the cardboard containers then races to the living room, where she finds her boyfriend sprawled on the couch. He looks at her once with a sneer, and then he double-takes, licking his lips as he stares. "Damn Brandi. You're fine."

Oh yeah. The red lace. The cartridge collection had distracted her from her seductive plan. She responds in a low voice. "Right back atcha handsome." She moves to the couch, lowering herself between his legs. "Can I make this morning up to you? I'm sorry my attitude sucked." His eyes widen as she unbuckles his belt. "There are much better types of sucking I should be doing."

"Yes. Yes, there are." He lets out a moan. "Show me."

"Okay, babe." Brandi closes her eyes, channeling strength. And patience. The first day of her three-week sentence has begun.

Time better start flying.

From Brandi Monner

Jan 19, 2023, 3:13 PM
to Dante Wilder

Dante,

I never wanted to speak to you again, but here I am, emailing you and breaking that promise. You are a cruel, thoughtless person. A true terror. And believe me, if I could avoid you forever, I would. Unfortunately, that is not going to happen. Remember the night we met? I did my best to forget about it, but the time we spent in the dressing room has come back to haunt me. To haunt us both, I suppose.

I have attached the results of a prenatal paternity test. I'm four months pregnant with your baby. Yes, you read that right. Twenty freaking minutes of sweaty grunting turned us into parents. How awful is that? Really, really awful is the correct answer.

I guess you will want to know how I got your DNA sample. Well, a couple of weeks ago, I came over while Karina was at her boujee ketamine retreat. By the way, she should be careful about what she posts online. You never know what people will do with the information she puts out there, especially if they know you are away from home. I have heard about robberies happening during family vacations. It is a scary world out there, and you need to be more vigilant about self-preservation.

Anyways, while Karina was gone, I waited until you nodded out, then entered your house through the unlocked front door. Again, you might want to increase your security measures. You are an easy target, especially for a person who knows you tie off. Your habit certainly made my task easier. I had no trouble drawing a blood sample. You were so wasted, you did not even flinch when I pushed the needle in your arm.

I do not know what you want to do with this information. My plan is to raise the baby on my own, but it would be nice if you got your shit together and became a part of his life. If you decide not to be a father, I will pick up the slack, and our son will be just fine. I have attached termination of parental rights paperwork to the email, in case you decide to go this route.

If you are up for parenting, we can meet up and chat. You will need to show me a plan for getting clean. That is a requirement before having anything to do with the baby.

Take some time to think it over. I am not pressuring you in either direction, because regardless of your decision, the baby and I will thrive.

Get in touch when you have made up your mind.

Regards,
Brandi

Chapter 13 –Lala

{February 28, 2023}

When Lala sent the email to Karina, doubt plagued her. Was contacting someone she'd met only once the right thing to do? Lala thought so, but who knows what the person receiving her unsolicited help would think. Maybe Karina would assume Lala was out to exploit her, to feed the juicy details of her life to a gossip-hungry public. It wasn't true, but Lala wouldn't blame her for that reaction at all.

Thankfully, her uncertainty was short-lived. Karina replied to the message within hours. She remembered Lala, and she was more than willing to discuss her relationship with Dante. The pair chatted back and forth for a few days until they settled on a date two weeks in the future. They were going to meet. Lala sent the appropriate paperwork to the jail, booked her hotel and flight, and worked on her other cases until it was time to leave.

Lala's husband and coworkers supported her leading up to the California trip. They boosted her confidence with compliments, jokes, and strategy sessions. With their input, she's feeling good about tomorrow's conversation with Karina. The case may be high-profile, but the accused murderer is a person who needs assistance. Just like everyone else who employs LegalShe. There's no need to place extra importance on the situation.

Rory drives her to the airport and parks in the short-term lot. "How you feeling?" he asks as they stroll through the garage, him rolling Lala's suitcase over the concrete floor. "I'm excited, and I'm not even going with you."

"Excited is a good adjective. Nervous too." Their footsteps echo along with the strides of about twenty other travelers. The lot is busy for 6:00 AM on a Tuesday, and everyone looks exhausted. Lala's eagerness contrasts with their grim expressions. "I'm ready to see her, though. You, Ellen, and Tina have been quite the pep squad. You three really pumped me up."

He pats his wife's butt with his free hand. "That's what we're here for, mi amor."

"Thank you for your awesomeness, always and forever." She reaches over, lacing his fingers through hers. "And for waking up so early."

"For you, I'll sacrifice sleep, but not for anyone else." He pauses. "Well, maybe for my parents. But that's it."

"Probably your sister too. And your cousins and your friends—"

"Point made." He chuckles. "I'd sacrifice sleep for a lot of people."

"It's one of your most endearing qualities."

"Good thing I don't look like a zombie when I'm tired." He releases her hand and points to his right, careful to hide his movement from the person across the parking lot row. "Are you seeing your fellow travelers?" he whispers.

"Yeah." Lala's gaze follows his finger, and lands on a man with deep purple eyebags and an open-mouthed expression. "They're a rough bunch. Maybe they'll perk up after some coffee."

"One can only hope." They reach an elevator, and it opens right after they press the arrow. Purple Eyebags takes the stairs, so no one joins them inside. Still, they move to the back, away from the door. "Going down," Rory says, and they descend several floors, stopping for passengers along the way. By the time they reach ground level, the elevator is packed but silent. They disembark last, and as the doors close behind them everyone has rushed off, eager to reach their gates.

She and Rory resume their leisurely pace. "Phew. I'm glad we haven't turned into them, Lala. They look miserable."

"Me too, but I get it. Flying sucks." She shrugs. "They probably have to do it all the time, so I can understand their misery."

"You're way nicer than me." He perks up. "Oh, I meant to tell you last night. Dylan booked the pre-cruise practice space." He pulls out his phone, finds what he's looking for, and passes it over. "Look at the pictures. It's pretty awesome."

Half of Lala's attention remains on their path, and the other examines the BnB listing on Rory's screen. The title—Relax In Your Private Luxury Oasis—catches her eye. "Oasis huh? Sounds fancy." She browses the listing's description. The sentences detail an updated mansion, complete with a spa/pool combination, plus a private hiking trail. "This place is near Miami? It must be super expensive." She checks out the price, confirming her suspicion. The home is $1500 a night, and they're staying for two days. "The band can afford this?"

Rory nods. "Yep. If we got hotel rooms, they'd be just as expensive, and they wouldn't be as isolated. For practice, we need acres of space or soundproofing, and this place happens to have both. The owner confirmed it with Dylan."

"Sounds perfect." She flips through twenty images of the house. The rooms are huge and clean, the kitchen is chef quality, and the patio…well, the patio is to die for. There's a custom bar that leads into the pool's turquoise waters. Wicker cabanas line the spa, which looks big enough to fit at least ten people. Palm trees are planted in golden vases. The sky is an impossible blue. "Babe, this place is amazing. Three nights isn't enough. We need to stay an entire week."

"Right? Dylan nailed it this time. We'll definitely be ready for the cruise after lounging beside that pool."

They approach the airport's entrance, and Lala stops walking. "I feel bad for talking about this amazing vacation when I'm about to visit someone behind bars."

Rory turns toward her, resting her suitcase on the ground. "You're such a sweetheart." He opens his arms, and his wife nuzzles against his chest. "It's okay to be excited about our trip, Lala. We're going to have a good time with each other and with our friends. But I get why you're upset." He hugs her close, then lifts her off the ground. "There's a lot of bad stuff going on in the world, and it feels awful to downplay it, even for a second. But what help can you provide if you don't have something to look forward to? You'd burn out if you immersed yourself in the terribleness, never taking a break. You've got to have some sort of release, and that's what this vacation will be."

He kisses the top of her head and lowers her to the ground. "Right now, you're going to help someone accused of a crime. Yes, she's in jail and she can't travel like us. That sucks. Truly. But you're doing what you can for her with the experience and resources you have access to. I think that's pretty badass. And I think you've more than earned your stay in the luxury oasis."

"You always say the right words."

"See? That English degree comes in handy. My words are high quality."

Lala laughs and steps out of his arms. "Time to head inside, Roars."

"Want me to walk you to security check?"

"Nah. I'm good."

Rory reaches out and embraces her again. "I'll miss you. I love you. Do great things."

"I'll miss you. I love you. Write new music."

He lets her go and salutes with two fingers. "Yes, ma'am."

"See you soon handsome. I'll be doing some paperwork after I check-in, so I'll text you when I land." She grabs her suitcase and waves. "Bye. Love you."

"Love you too, Lala. Knock 'em dead." He cringes. "I take that back. Don't knock anyone dead. Knowing one murderer is enough."

"You're such a nerd." She waves again, and strolls toward the entrance's double doors. When they open, she blows Rory a kiss before scrambling inside.

This early on a weekday morning, the airport is brimming with seasoned travelers. People in suits hustle to their security lanes, most with small bags or no luggage at all. Lala doesn't hate flying—it's a necessary evil—but she does dislike contorting into uncomfortable positions for hours at a time. In her work life, air travel isn't common. The LegalShe trio goes to conferences once or twice a year, and other than that, they handle homegrown cases within a fifty-mile radius. She hates to imagine what she'd turn into if flying were a task she did often. Maybe she'd become one of the zombies trekking to their gates. There wasn't a smile in sight.

She rechecks her boarding pass, and files into the correct security line. Surprisingly, the zombies move at an efficient pace. Most people are in the express lane, but even the travelers in front of Lala breeze through security on the double. Belt and shoes off, liquids and tech out, suitcase on the conveyor. She's through the line in five minutes and finds a seat in front of her gate an hour before boarding.

Her headphones go on, and light jazz plays through the speakers. There's no other music she can work to. For some reason, the upbeat tunes kick her brain into gear and don't distract her. Plus, headphones are the international symbol for 'leave me alone,' and that's the vibe she's aiming for. Now's the time for research, not idle chit-chat.

Before she left the office yesterday, Lala printed Karina's file. Mostly, she completes tasks on the computer, but sometimes, holding a stack of papers enhances her productivity. There are fifty pages in Karina's file, and she flips through them while smooth tunes float into her ears.

Her goal today is preparedness. Reading and making notes in the margins will ensure she's ready for tomorrow's meeting. Since she only has two hours in the jail, she wants to be precise and organized.

She dives into the file. Page one is Karina's arrest affidavit. When Lala first read the document, shock flooded through her. It turns out Karina wasn't being held on a murder charge. She'd been arrested for *conspiracy to commit murder*. Big difference.

No media outlets had picked up on the altered charge. And not a single internet sleuth had gone through the steps for obtaining Karina's record. So many times, when something goes viral, the initial wave of interest dictates what information the public remembers. This is especially true in a case where the biggest events—Dante's death and Karina's arrest—were over and done with, and nothing else had occurred. In society's mind, the ABOS singer had been murdered by his girlfriend. If the case ever went to trial, the public's perception might alter, but until then, Karina was branded a killer.

Besides the conspiracy charge, there wasn't much information on the arrest affidavit. From their emails, which made up the next several pages of the file, Lala knew a bit more about Karina's criminal justice situation. Soon, Karina would be extradited to Georgia, where Dante had been killed. For now, she was being held in California, sharing a cell with three other women. The meals were terrible, the beds were uncomfortable, and one of the guards was on a constant power trip. Other than that, she was handling incarceration well enough.

Lala had talked to Karina's parents, Kitty and Teddy, and other than their adorable names, which gave her a giggle every time she said them, they provided few details about the crime. Lala gathered general information about their daughter from them—high school cheerleader, lots of volunteering, an interest in yoga and alternative medicine—but nothing stood out in Karina's background.

Just to be sure, Lala re-skims the notes from their conversation. Kitty and Teddy are concerned for their daughter, and want to bail her out of jail, but for once, Karina is assuming responsibility for her actions. Of course, they're mad about her refusal to go home, but Lala gets the sense that sadness is their primary emotion. Understandably. Karina is their only child. Wanting to help their baby but being turned down must be overwhelming.

Nothing in their words jumps out, so Lala moves on to the last section of Karina's file—articles and social media. The viral confession is printed in there first, followed by local and national news stories, and then some of the unhinged posts that make the internet so fascinating. And brutal.

Lala flips to a poem on the last page. She's read it at least twenty times but gives it another run-through in the bustling airport.

A songbird sings no more
because a Becky took him down.
The cruelty of her actions
turned our smile into a frown.
When women think they have the right
to harm a man so great,
The manosphere revolts
turning her defiance into hate.

She's not surprised the incel community supports Dante. He was a cruel man who harmed women, which fits right in with that crowd's values. Initially, Lala included the poem in Karina's file to broaden the resources. Prior to adding it, there were posts from ABOS fans, posts from ABOS haters, and posts from trolls who liked to stir the pot. In other words, the normal span of public opinion.

The poem, though, is something different. It's not just a tribute or diss. The words connect the band with an ideology, one Lala has heard about during therapy sessions at work.

At least three LegalShe clients have husbands who lost themselves down the incel rabbit hole. Each man blamed his wife for withholding sex during high-risk pregnancies, and they were furious their marital needs weren't being met. Months of no intercourse triggered them to submerge into the scarier corners of the web, where they formed bonds with other irate men. They became marcels—married men who were involuntarily celibate—and eventually, the three husbands hurt their wives in horrendous ways. Thankfully, each man was arrested, and their wives hired LegalShe while they were awaiting their abuser's trial. Based on the women's testimony, they were successful with all three cases. Long sentences and victim healing—those outcomes always make Lala's heart sing.

When she stumbled across the poem, she'd shown Rory and introduced him to the manosphere. Her husband was shocked by the hateful content and worried about a potential connection to ABOS. He brought up Pearl becoming the band's new singer. He thought a woman replacing Dante might provoke some hostility, and Lala agreed. But there aren't many preventative techniques against angry dude backlash. All the band can do is remain informed and aware.

If she has a chance during tomorrow's meeting, Lala will discuss the poem with Karina. She might know which parts of the internet Dante frequented. Although he wasn't celibate like the incels, he could have supported another brand of anti-woman malice. There are countless dark spaces on the web, and if Dante explored them, it would be good to know, for the band's sake. And maybe the information would help Karina's case.

Lala gives the poem one last glance, then flips to the beginning of the file. As she's rereading Karina's emails, the boarding announcement sounds. People rush to get in line, but Lala takes a quick trip to the restroom, followed by some pacing close by. Soon, she'll be sitting for six hours. She enjoys moving before a flight. It makes the confined trip more bearable.

When only a few people remain at the gate, she joins the boarding line. The plane isn't full, and it turns out she's sitting next to her favorite person—no one. It's Lala on the aisle, an empty seat, and an elderly man with a book by the window. Luck is shining on her today.

The flight goes smoothly, as does hotel check in. California has some gorgeous cities, but she's staying close to the jail in a town composed of strip malls and industrial parks. When Lala booked her room, she noticed there was a restaurant in the lobby. Usually, she enjoys exploring new places. Eating local fare and learning a bit of history is a great way to engage with unfamiliar surroundings. It's especially fun when there's drinking and dancing involved. She and Rory have spent many nights sipping martinis and grooving until the bars close down.

But tonight, there's no venturing out. Rest is more important than a travel buzz. Her husband and coworkers might have convinced her that Karina is just a normal client, but Lala still thinks this case is the most compelling she's ever worked on. Something about their connection, the confession, and Karina's bewildering conspiracy arrest appeals to her.

After a cobb salad in the hotel's restaurant, Lala heads to the third floor for a shower and movie. Even though it's 8:00 California time, it's 11:00 back home. That means to her body, it's wind-down time. She flips through the channels for a comedy, but true crime lures her in. She's so predictable. Instead of a movie, she watches three episodes of Marriage and Mayhem before turning off the TV and closing her eyes.

When her alarm blares at 7:30, she's amped. Finally, after weeks of preparation, she gets to talk to Karina in person. Bubbles of excitement burst in her chest as she dresses in a navy suit and flats. The bubbles turn into balloons while she eats eggs and toast. The balloons morph into the Goodyear blimp as she drives the five minutes to her destination. Her body is light, airy, and ready to launch.

Lala stashes her phone in the rental's glove box and heads out of the parking lot. Signs point visitors toward a windowless gray building. Some correctional agencies design their facilities with approachability in mind. The Clementine County Jail is not one of them. The concrete structure isn't welcoming. At all. Instead of plant life, barbed wire fences line the perimeter. Powerlines buzz overhead. The unpainted structure is grim.

On the entrance, warnings in red font tell people to leave contraband in their vehicles. Solid advice. Getting arrested for smuggling drugs or a phone is not on her to-do list today or ever. She pulls open the metal door, and the florescent-lit lobby yawns ahead. To the left, a glass booth houses a woman wearing a tan long-sleeved correctional uniform.

As Lala approaches, the guard slides out a metal box. "ID, please," she says into a microphone with a monotone voice.

Lala drops her license in the bin, and the guard rolls the container inside. While she inspects the DL, Lala scans her. The guard's nametag reads F. Bonnifaith. Her complexion is sickly, but it probably has more to do with the lighting than an illness. Lala's face probably looks just as unhealthy.

Lala smiles, trying to overcome the fluorescent's glare. "I'm here to see Karina Belmore. Do you need to see a copy of the reservation?" Internally, she cringes. The question is the same one she asked the hotel clerk yesterday. Funny how identical verbiage works in such different environments.

"No," Bonnifaith grunts. "Give me a minute." She rolls backward in her chair until she reaches a filing cabinet. From the bottom drawer, she pulls out a sheet of paper, then rolls back to the window. "Says here you need a private room. Are you a lawyer?"

"An investigator." Ellen and Tina coached her on this response. Outside therapists might be given the side-eye, but investigators are an everyday occurrence. And she's really digging into the details of Karina's crime, so the label is not a lie.

"Okay." The guard sets the paper into the metal box before rolling it Lala's way. "Sign on the bottom, with the time. And don't forget to sign out when you leave."

She nods. "Yes, Officer Bonnifaith." Lala's signature goes on the paper in swooping letters, as well as the time. "I didn't bring my phone. Is there anything else I should leave in my car?"

She doesn't look impressed with the inquiry. "Got any weapons or drugs?

"No."

"Then you should be good." Bonnifaith tilts her chin toward a door that's sliding open. "Head through there. An officer will guide you through the metal detector and escort you to your room."

Lala follows her directions and meets a tired-looking man in a scuffed white corridor. "Good morning—" she squints at his nametag "—Officer Goings."

"Morning, ma'am. Please place everything in your pockets inside this bin." He holds out a plastic rectangle. "And I'll take your bag."

A boom echoes through the hall. Lala jumps and turns to find the door latched into place. "Yikes. That would be tough to get used to."

"Been here fifteen years. It's white noise at this point." His mouth twitches into a grin under a thick brown mustache. He takes a step forward, plastic container in his outstretched arms.

Lala swaps her bag for the bin, and they both get busy—her depositing keys and lip balm into the box, him rifling through her purse. When he finishes, Officer Goings ushers Lala through the metal detector. She passes without a beep, and the guard allows her to gather her belongings.

"You ready?" he asks after she slings her bag over her shoulder.

"I am."

"Okay. Rooms are just down the hall. I'll take you to an open one, and Ms. Belmore will be there shortly after."

"Sounds good. Thank you."

He makes a call on his radio, and a door opens on the opposite side of the corridor. They hurry through the gap it makes, staying to the right side of a concrete hallway. An odor fills Lala's nose the deeper they travel inside the jail. It's a heavy scent, a combination of boiled food and housed humans. She tries breathing through her mouth, but the smell finds its way into her nostrils, coating their insides. Hopefully, she'll adapt to it soon.

After a minute of walking, they turn into an opening that leads to several glass-walled rooms. Two people occupy the one closest to the entrance. They're bent over a table, speaking with their heads bowed. When Lala and the guard breeze past the duo, they glance up for a second then get back to their conversation. None of their words leak into the corridor. The soundproofing must be top-notch.

Officer Goings leads Lala to the room behind the pair. Two wooden chairs sit on either side of a plastic table. Nothing else adorns the space. The area is sparse and compact, but it will work just fine for a discussion. She pulls out the chair on the right and lays her bag on the table. "Thank you for the escort, officer."

He nods. "My pleasure." He looks at his watch. "If I had to estimate Ms. Belmore's arrival, I'd say she'll be here in about ten minutes. Do you need anything while you wait?"

"I'm good. Thank you again."

"Alright. Someone will be here at 11:00 to bring Ms. Belmore back to her cell, and I'll collect you shortly after." With another nod, Officer Goings closes the door, leaving Lala alone to wait for Karina.

Date: 2/15/2023 13:45:11 PM
To: Laverne (Lala) Ramirez
From: Karina Belmore

Lala,
Of course, I remember you! You, Maggie, and Nicole were so nice to me at the ABOS shows. I never felt comfortable backstage. I had some weird hang-up about not really belonging there, but the three of you welcomed me without hesitation. Which was nice. Especially since I was there with someone who couldn't care less about me.

Is it weird that I never considered how terrible Dante was until I was in jail? Outside, there was always something to distract me from his cruelty, but here, there's no escaping my thoughts. He was abusive. There, I put it in writing. The man was abusive, and he hurt me hours after our first date.

I was raised by good parents, who taught me independence and how to think critically. In other words, I never saw myself being hurt by some guy. And I'm sorry to say that my view on domestic violence was horribly skewed before it happened to me. I thought it was a terrible crime, but I also placed burdens on the victim. Instead of saying "How can we stop people from harming their loved ones?" I asked "Why would she stay with such an awful man? She should just leave."

Now, I know that's not the truth. Leaving isn't easy. In my situation, I deluded myself. I was a rich girl from SoCal, and there was no way my relationship could be labeled abusive. So what if Dante twisted my words and isolated me? So what if he pinched hard enough to leave bruises? I was dating a celebrity, and those were the things you put up with. Or so I rationalized. I never asked you or Maggie or Nicole about your significant others. Did they hurt you too? My guess is no because they're decent partners. Unlike Dante.

I'd love to chat more. That is, if this email didn't push you away. Maybe we can arrange for you to come out here. A visit would be nice. I bet you can support me while I process my experiences with Dante. Although my cellmates are great, you and I have a connection that might help me decipher everything that happened before his death. Why did I let him treat me like trash? Why did I kill him? I would love to answer those questions, with your help, if you're up for it.

TTYS, Karina

Chapter 14 – Karina

{February 28, 2023}

Karina prepared for Lala's visit all last week. When Karina heard from the psychologist, she wasn't sure how their reunion would go, especially after she revealed her previous beliefs about domestic violence. Her past attitude was ignorant. And shameful. Seriously, how can she have put so much blame on the victim? Growing up, Karina thought of herself as a fair person, but once she started analyzing her opinions in jail, she realized that isn't always true. She can be a jerk.

Facing her viewpoints is brutal, but Karina forces herself to confront the dumb ideas every day. Cici guides her through the process, and her mental load is shrinking as they deep dive into the past. Her cellmate also shares her history, and Cici's perspective grounds her. Her bunkie's early life was rough, but she's learned to move forward with her traumas, not forgetting them but not letting them weigh her down either. Karina is awestruck. And grateful. Cici owes her nothing, yet she's already given more than any friend Karina had on the outside.

Cici is why she was honest with Lala. Her bunkmate advised transparency, and Karina followed her guidance. If she were to accept the psychologist's help, Karina wanted her to know what she was getting into. It was only fair. Sure, Karina's former boyfriend abused her, but she used to be blasé about people who found themselves in the same situation. Does she really deserve assistance? Karina left it up to Lala to decide.

Luckily, Lala took her thoughts in stride and even told her that victim blaming happens among the clients at LegalShe. From the hundreds of sessions Lala has conducted, every once in a while a sexual assault survivor will judge another woman's clothing, calling an outfit too provocative or revealing. Or they'll shame a victim when a make-out session turns violent, calling them teases who got what they wanted. During therapy, Lala works to reverse these clients' negative stereotypes, encouraging supportive behavior rather than destructive misconceptions aimed at other women.

Lala's reassurance calmed Karina, and after a few back-and-forth emails, they chose a date for her visit. February 28.

Today.

The State of Georgia plans to extradite Karina late next month, so she wanted to leave plenty of time for a second meeting before her trip across the country to the new jail. That's if their first meetup goes well, of course. And she'll know how it turns out soon enough. After breakfast and an hour of tutoring her fellow inmates.

It's Tuesday, so the morning meal is scrambled eggs, a bran muffin, and a cup of Orange Sunrise, a Sunny D knockoff. An undrinkable knockoff, in Karina's opinion. She passes her cup to Cici, who happily swallows the extra juice while giving out advice.

"Today is important, K." She sips the beverage without wincing. "You can't be too eager. That's a bad look."

"Don't worry. I can hold it together." Karina pauses, giving thought to what Cici said. Can she really keep cool during the meeting? Besides her parents, Lala is the only person who's visited Karina or even reached out at all, and she's excited. Very. Despite the friendships she's formed in jail, she longs for glimpses of her old life, and Lala will provide that lens. But controlling her anticipation is crucial. Karina doesn't want to scare an outside connection away. "On second thought, maybe you're right about appearing too eager. I'm bursting right now. What can I do to chill?"

"How 'bout some yoga? I used to think it was bullshit, but those poses you showed me actually work," Cici says.

"Yeah. Good idea. We can stretch before my shift."

Karina forces herself to eat the eggs and muffin. They're tasteless but healthy. At least according to the nutritional information posted on the mess hall's bulletin board. She doesn't put much faith in the data's accuracy, but it would be stupid to waste away. Her body doesn't react well to restricting calories—fasting had been a disaster—so she consumes enough food to stay strong. And alert. There are many nice women behind bars, but others are cruel. Tangling with them would be trouble, even more so on an empty stomach.

After they finish breakfast, Karina and Cici head back to their cell, where they move through three sun salutations. Although Karina's heart rate perks up after the sequence, less nervous energy flows through her body. "That was just what I needed. You're always right."

"Don't I know it." Cici flops onto her bed and laughs as she picks up her toiletry bag. She squirts lotion onto her fingertips, then dabs the product under her eyes. "You'd think a person who's always right would avoid ending up here."

"You got caught up in something, that's all." Karina grabs a brush and runs it through her blonde locks. "Anyways, you'll be out soon. Judge Winrock is going to free you during your next court date. No doubt. One hundred million percent."

"Now, I hope you're right."

"Mark my words. You'll be home by Friday. And it sounds like your mom is taking good care of your apartment, so it'll be like you never left," Karina says while twisting her hair into a loose braid. When she checks her reflection in the cell's cracked mirror, she looks tired but not haggard. Good enough. "I'm off. Wish me luck."

"You got this, girl. Good luck with your friend." Cici flashes a smile and bounces off her bunk. "Gimme a hug."

Karina wraps her arms around the smaller woman while closing her eyes. A deep breath steadies her. "Thanks, Cici. See you at lunch." She releases her friend and heads to the library.

Every morning and afternoon, Karina helps women study for their GED. It's been her job since the guards found out she had a college degree. The achievement put her in a small minority at the jail, although many of the women in her cellblock were unbelievably smart, especially considering the not-so-great upbringings they lived through. They create poetry and art that blow her away. They have thesis-level opinions on the criminal justice system, backed by lived experience and research. They concoct culinary masterpieces with food purchased from the canteen. Talent is widespread inside the jail.

Tutoring has put Karina in contact with women she probably wouldn't have met in her pampered outside life. A few are single moms who want to earn their diploma and kickstart a better life for their families. Some students are former sex workers who are ready to do something for themselves rather than a pimp or john. And more frequently, there are women close to Karina's age, who struggle with addiction or mental health or violent partners, and all they want to do is interrupt the cycle dragging them down.

During this morning's shift, Karina walks two women through a passage from The Secret Garden. She convinced her cellmate Eve to enroll in the GED program, and Eve brought her friend Carmine, as well. The women read through the paragraphs, and then answer questions.

"Okay, what did the author mean when she said, 'Everything was strange and silent and she seemed to be hundreds of miles away from anyone, but somehow she did not feel lonely at all?' How can a person be alone, but not lonely?" Karina asks.

"I know this one," Eve answers, her eyes lighting up. "Whenever I drive to the wildflower field in Marmouth, I go to the center and sit for twenty minutes or so, just zoning out. I always get there early, before the loud crowds show up to take selfies no one cares about. But when I'm sitting there, the most calming sense of peace overtakes me. I feel connected to nature or some shit like that." Her mouth bends into a smile. "The flower field is the opposite of this place. There, you're by yourself, but you feel at ease."

"Yes, Eve. That's beautiful," Karina says. "Anything come to mind for you, Carmine?"

Her forehead creases. "Does driving my car count?" She gestures to Eve. "It's not as pretty as her story, but when I'm in my car, sometimes I turn the radio off and go into a sort of trace. You ever done that?" she asks her teacher.

"Yeah." Karina nods. "When I need to think, a quiet car ride helps."

"There's something soothing about the road noise. I dunno…it makes me feel like everything is going to be okay." Carmine frowns. "I wish I could take a ride now."

"Me too." Karina pauses. "That would be nice."

Eve and Carmine distract her with their enthusiasm. The trio flies through the first passage, then gets through another two before Officer Allen interrupts their session. "Belmore, let's get moving. You got a visitor. I heard it's an investigator." She smirks and lets out a cruel laugh. "You think there's a chance you'll get out of here? That's hilarious."

Karina ignores her and cleans up the printouts she'd used. The library has limited copies, and keeping track of them is a big part of the tutoring job. Just last week, a student lost a GED prep guide, devastating the librarian and the women who were waiting to check it out. The mishap caused restrictions to tighten around reference items. Photocopies were now used instead of the books themselves.

After Karina places everything inside a folder, Allen's still sneering. Ugh. The guard is awful, but pretending she's not is part of the game. "I'm ready, officer," Karina says, voice saccharine sweet.

"Arms behind your back." Karina complies, and the guard cuffs her, too tight like always. "Now hustle." She shoves her captive toward the door.

If inmates behave well, they're rarely restrained, but the warden makes an exception for visitors. He doesn't want his jail to look soft on crime, so the guards cuff inmates up when delivering them to family, friends, or lawyers. Officer Allen seems to take pleasure in the practice. Whenever she restrains Karina, the guard forces her wrists into the steel bracelets, clicking them into place a notch past bearable.

Today, Karina's arms throb as they travel between the library and the meeting rooms. She waits for numbness, but the distance isn't long enough for her limbs to stop hurting. Instead, sharp pain rockets through her body when Allen pushes her through the visitor's hallway. "Hurry up. I don't have all day."

Karina moves faster until they reach the second room, but when she sees Lala sitting inside the glass walls, she stops, barely believing the psychologist is there. Officer Allen steps around her and unlocks the door. "Don't just stand there, Belmore. Get inside." Karina rushes in, and Allen grips her shoulder, rotating her body until her forehead presses against the closest glass panel. The guard uses her key to release the handcuffs. "I'll be back in two hours. Be ready for me," and with those words, she speeds off, slamming the door behind her.

Karina's wrists sting, and she rubs them while turning to Lala. Her visitor stands with a huge grin lighting up her face. "You came. I almost can't believe it," Karina says.

"Believe it, lady. I'm here." Lala strides over and throws her arms around Karina. "How are you? You look surprisingly well, considering where you've been living the past two weeks."

Karina pulls her close, breathing in her lilac scent. "It's so good to see you. Like, beyond good." After one more squeeze, she lets Lala go. "This place is terrible, but they do feed me. And I have a few friends who keep me sane."

"Awesome. Friends can make all the difference." Lala starts back toward her chair. "Let's sit down and catch up. I bet you have a lot to tell me."

"More than you probably want to know."

"I doubt it. Ever since we set up this meeting, I've been dying to hear your side of the story." Lala sits, waving her over. "Let's do this."

Karina settles into the chair across the table and leans onto the sticky laminate surface. "I've rehashed this with my cellmate, Cici, a few times. She's been helping me come to terms with a lot of things. Like, my relationship with Dante and why I put myself in such an awful position."

"Cici sounds very insightful. That's one of the concepts I work on with my clients." Lala leans on the table to match Karina. "It's true what they say about domestic violence—it's a vicious cycle. And when experts say that, they're not just referring to the honeymoon, build-up, and abuse phases. They're talking about the fact that once a person finds themselves in an abusive relationship, they're more likely to repeat the pattern in their next relationship. Helping them escape the quicksand is part of what I do."

Karina nods. "Quicksand. That's pretty accurate. Being with him made me feel like I was being sucked into an abyss."

"Being hurt by someone you love is the ultimate betrayal."

"I can't imagine Rory hurting you in any way."

"Oh no, he would never." Lala blinks hard, then frowns. "But I did have a boyfriend in high school who put his hands on me, so I understand how crushing a violent relationship can be. And how draining. I remember being so, so tired. Not just from his abuse, but from trying to rationalize his actions while trying to hide everything from my parents."

"It is exhausting," Karina agrees. "What made you leave him?"

"A therapist. They helped me see that his actions weren't acceptable." A grin creeps onto her face, and she pumps her fist in the air. "I broke up with him and told our high school counselor about his cruelty. The asshole got arrested, and his promising baseball career was derailed before it even began."

Karina's eyes widen. "Wow. That's a happy ending."

"It is."

"Do you think I'll ever be able to have one of those?" Karina waves her hand at Lala. "A happy ending like you." She slowly lowers her hand to the table. "I feel like my life is over.".

"How about we talk through what happened with Dante. I have some questions, and I think your answers will help me determine the probability of a happily ever after for your situation."

"Ask me anything. I have nothing to hide."

Lala reaches into her bag and brings out a manilla folder with Karina's name printed on the tab. The psychologist opens it up and brings out the top piece of paper. "Have you seen this?"

Karina takes the page and looks it over. The title says arrest affidavit, and it contains her demographics and the crime she's in jail for. She knows her age, gender, and race, of course, and she assumed she knew her arrest information.

But she was wrong.

In the offense box, she doesn't see a charge of murder. She reads something entirely different: conspiracy to commit a crime. "What is this conspiracy nonsense? I thought it only applied to like, spies or the government."

"It means that you and someone else talked about committing a crime, and you undertook one or more actions to make that crime happen. So, if you were planning to off me by using an assassin, and you got into contact with that assassin and paid them a deposit, you'd be guilty of conspiracy even if I was never killed."

Karina lays the paper on the table, furrowing her brow. "But in my case, Dante did die, so why isn't it murder?"

"Did you actually kill him?" Lala points at her. "Did *your* actions cause his death?"

Karina contemplates her question. The last time she'd seen Dante had been on the way to the airport. During the drive, her boyfriend hadn't uttered a word; he'd only typed frantically on his phone, making sure to tilt the screen away from her view. The cell was on silent, but Karina heard buzz after buzz during the hour drive.

At the terminal, Dante jumped from the car, gathering his suitcase while avoiding her gaze. She called out his name from the front seat, but he ignored her and slammed the trunk before merging into the LAX departures crowd, never looking back, never slowing down. Despite the honking behind her, Karina waited until he disappeared before pulling away from the curb.

As she drove home, the thoughts dominating her mind weren't about missing him or regretting the part she played in his anger. They were simple. She wanted to know if he'd carry out their plan. Would Dante follow her instructions? Would he be able to pull off his role in her documentary?

And now she has another question to consider, the one Lala asked. Did Karina's actions cause Dante's death? Lala gives her space to work through the matter. Karina's visitor sits in silence as she considers exactly what occurred during her boyfriend's final hours. She played a part in what went down, but it wasn't her who pulled the trigger. Or poured the poison in Dante's case. That's how she answers. "My actions weren't the direct cause of his death. My crazy idea just put it into motion."

"Yes. And that's why you weren't charged with murder." Lala places the arrest affidavit back into the folder. "Your lawyer should have explained the charge to you, but it sounds like they dropped the ball. Do you remember hearing about it during your first appearance?"

"Honestly, it was a blur. I blocked everything out except my plea. Which was guilty." Karina leans back in her chair. "Was I right to do that?"

"We'll discuss your plea in a minute. First, I need more details. Tell me about your idea. What were you planning with Dante?"

Warmth floods her cheeks. "Promise you won't think I'm dumb?" Karina asks.

Lala reaches over and gives her hand a squeeze. "Not at all. I just want to hear your side of the story. People online churned out some off the wall theories, but I have an idea what really happened isn't as wild as what I've read."

"It might be as bad." Karina cringes, knowing her scheme was plenty stupid. "I'll let you be the judge of that."

"Shoot. Let me have it."

"In the first email you sent me, you mentioned how excited I was about a film idea. Remember that?" Lala nods, and Karina continues. "Well, the plan with Dante had to do with that film idea. For some reason, I came up with a pitch that played off Romeo and Juliet but with a modern flare. I was going to have Dante eat enough deadly nightshade to go into a catatonic state, and he was going to do it in front of the band. The idea was to record everything, including Dante's sudden sickness, how the band reacted, and then Dante's ultimate recovery. It was going to be my path into Hollywood."

Lala jerks back in her chair. "Jesus, Karina. You're right. That's not the best idea I've ever heard." Her expression is pinched, and her next words come out higher-pitched than normal. "Why would you do that to the other band members? Even though Dante was awful, witnessing him sink into a coma isn't something they'd want to see."

Karina lowers her head in shame. "Yeah. I know. It was so incredibly stupid. And selfish." She raises her eyes to meet Lala's, hoping for understanding. "Now that I've had time to reflect, I realize how messed up my perception was. I was willing to traumatize people to break into the film industry. How fucked up is that?"

"Honestly, it's super fucked." Lala draws in a deep breath, then slowly releasees the air. "But I'm not here to judge you based on an idea you had. I'm here to help detangle what actually occurred."

"What do you mean?"

"Well, did you end up buying the poison?"

"No. We were supposed to pick it up on the way to the airport, but Dante and I got into a fight, and we never stopped." Karina slumps into her chair. "He never told me he was kicked out of the band. I only knew because I checked his phone and saw a text from Dylan warning him to stay away from practice. That was right before we left for the airport."

Lala's reply is almost a growl. "Dante was a serial abuser, and his arrest in November was the final straw. He deserved to get kicked out."

"Oh, I agree. ABOS is better off without him." Karina perks up, raising her chin and throwing her shoulders back. "But I never bought the poison, and until now, I assumed he grabbed it after he landed in Atlanta. But what if he didn't?"

Lala snaps her fingers. "Now, that's the question we need to answer. The tox reports should be back in a couple of weeks, and we'll for sure know at that point." She shakes her head. "I think the police arrested you too soon. Like you, they're also making an assumption—a pretty big one—and they pinned the crime on the most convenient suspect. The one who confessed."

"Are you saying I might not be guilty?" Karina asks.

"Exactly," Lala says. She pulls out a notebook and pen. "Now, let's go over everything you remember. We need all the evidence we can get."

Clemons Police Department Record of Interrogation
February 12, 2023
Karina Belmore re: Murder of Dante Wilder

Det. C: We hope your break was refreshing, Ms. Belmore. Are you ready to begin?

KB: I am.

Det. C: Okay, so you told us about a Romeo and Juliet idea. What exactly did you mean by that?

KB: So, you know how Juliet took a poison to pretend like she was dead? Well, that was my idea. Dante was going to take enough poison to get sick, but it wouldn't be enough to kill him. We were going to record the band's reaction and show it to the world. Kind of like a reality TV show.

Det. B: You do know Romeo and Juliet is a tragedy, right?

KB: Yes, but only because Romeo was impatient. And out of the loop. He didn't know about Juliet's plan. Dante and I both knew about the poison, and we knew he wasn't going to actually die from the dosage he was taking.

Det. B: What poison did you use?

KB: Deadly nightshade. We were going to pick some up on the way to the airport, and he was going to add it to his whisky during practice.

Det. C: How'd you figure out the dosage? Seems like something you'd want to be precise about, since taking too much can be fatal.

KB: There's this cool calculator online. It's for people who make their own herbal remedies. You enter a person's age, weight, and height, and it will calculate the dosage you need for all sorts of medical needs.

Det. C: You used an online calculator to determine the amount of poison that would make a person sick but wouldn't kill them?

KB: Yes. But apparently there was a mix-up, and Dante took a higher dose than he was supposed to.

Det. B: He took a lethal dose instead.

KB: It was an accident. None of this was supposed to happen. I didn't mean to kill him.

Det. C: Would you be willing to sign an official confession? We'd type it up for you, and it would talk about your plan and how it went too far. All you'd have to do is put your signature on it.

KB: Yes. I can do that. I want to make everything right.

Chapter 15 – Maggie

{March 3, 2023}

Between Dante's murder and the upcoming cruise, Pearl and Maggie considered rescheduling their Joshua Tree trip. Tons of reviews claimed the park was still cool enough in late spring, so they figured a May trip would be just as good as a March one, maybe better. If they moved the vacation after Rage on the Waves, they'd have a month and a half buffer to chill at home. The downtime would revitalize them when they finally headed to the national park.

But when they discussed the postponement with Danica, she protested. "No way." She shook her head, then aimed a glare at Pearl and Maggie. "Mom, Momma, I've been looking forward to this trip for months. Can't we just follow our original plan? Are you seriously going to let that idiot Dante ruin our fun?"

Maggie winced. Teenagers don't hold back. "Sweetheart, it isn't nice to talk ill of the dead."

"Even if he was gross?" she asked, not masking the disgust in her voice.

"Yes, even if he was gross." Maggie cocked her head. "I figured you'd be okay with pushing it back since you have a boyfriend now. You guys can rack up some more dates before we leave town for a week."

"Seriously, Mom? I know people think fifteen-year-olds go gaga when they're in a relationship, but it's not always true." Danica points at Maggie first, then Pearl. "You two taught me that space is important. Devon and I have interests outside each other. We don't need to cling."

"Holy crap. You sound way too mature, Dani," Pearl said.

"Whatever," she rolled her eyes. "Can we just keep our vacation how we planned it?"

"You got it, toots." Maggie raised her hands into the air. "Joshua Tree or bust."

So, on Wednesday, they boarded a plane to California and set off to explore their sixth national park. After picking up a rental car, they drove to an adorable cottage outfitted with a hot tub and desert-facing backyard. As soon as they parked, Danica carried her suitcase into the smaller room, threw on her bathing suit, and jumped into the spa. She rested her head on the wooden deck and closed her eyes while she soaked in the bubbling water. The khaki and bronze desert background framed her perfectly. Maggie's sweet girl was in her element.

Two days of hiking had shown them the beauty of the Mojave. On previous trips, they'd explored green forests, glaciers, and geysers, all gorgeous in their own ways. But there was something magical about the rock formations and twisted foliage here. Standing in the vast landscape was humbling.

The morning after their UFO tour, Pearl agrees. "I'm glad we came, Maggie-moo. The stars last night were amazing." She blows on her coffee. "I can't believe we lose so much to light pollution. Logically, I know there are countless planets and stars, but you don't grasp that concept when you only see a constellation or two." She sips from her mug and leans back in her chair. "How many constellations do you think we saw last night? A thousand? Two?"

"Closer to a million. Probably more. I'm still in awe," Maggie answers. "The guide took us to the perfect spot. I can't imagine a better view."

Danica's voice pipes up behind her mom. "We didn't see a single alien though."

"You're right. A million stars. Zero UFOs." Maggie pulls out the chair next to her and her daughter drops into it. "Smart move bringing a tripod last night. You got some amazing pictures."

"When I was researching tour companies, that was a suggestion from one of the reviewers. And they were totally right," Danica says. "Even though I didn't discover any little green men, I did get some decent shots of the sky."

"We'll have to frame your favorite." Pearl swivels her gaze to her wife. "I think you should add an alien board to Be Marry's offerings. I can picture the UFO-themed weddings already."

"Um, yes, please." Maggie reaches across the table and gives Pearl's hand a squeeze. "This is why I married you. You're brilliant."

Danica groans. "Moooommm, it's too early for that. I need at least a cup of coffee before you two get lovey-dovey."

"You need one cup, period." Maggie heads to the kitchen and returns with a peach-flowered mug brimming with steaming liquid. "Here you go. The coffee's strong, but some cream and sugar will tone it down."

"Thanks, Mom."

"Welcome." She plops back into her seat. "Would it be okay if we did some arts and crafts today?"

Danica stirs a spoon full of sugar into her brew. "What kind of craft?"

"There's a cute shop in town called Encircled, and you make custom rings there." Maggie whips out her phone and pulls up the business's website. "Look. We can forge our own bands." She passes the cell to Danica.

She scrolls through the page, reading descriptions and swiping through images. Her smile is wide when she looks up from the screen. "Yep. I'm in."

"Lemme see." Pearl holds out her hand, and Danica gives her the phone. After a minute, she's also grinning. "I second that yep. Let's do it."

"We have an appointment at noon. I knew you gals would love it," Maggie says.

Danica raises her mug. "I'll drink to that." She takes a swallow, then glances back and forth between her moms. "Aren't you glad we didn't cancel our trip?"

"Super glad," Maggie concedes. "Listening to you was the right move."

"Agreed." Pearl clinks her cup against their daughter's before draining the liquid. "You're smart."

"She gets it from her momma," Maggie says.

"No. From her mom." Pearl laughs and wiggles her shoulders, causing her wife to crack up.

"Ughhh. I'm still not done with my coffee." Danica rolls her eyes. "You two are too much."

Maggie stands, flourishing a hand. "Shall we venture to the patio? The young lady seems annoyed with our antics."

"It would be an honor to join you." Pearl laces her fingers through her wife's and pushes back from the table. "Don't miss us too much." She gets to her feet. "Love you, Dani. Join us when you're ready."

"Okay, Momma. Love you both."

Pearl tugs Maggie toward the French doors leading to the backyard. They giggle as they walk onto the patio. The sun is low in the sky, and the evening's coolness hangs on the air. Maggie hugs her sweatshirt against her body and settles into her favorite spot at the rental—a teal and navy striped hammock. The seat is secured to driftwood beams facing the backyard desert's serenity.

Pearl drags a lounge chair close and sits with her long legs pulled to her chest. Without speaking, the couple observes the movements around them. Twittering birds hop from cactus to cactus. Lizards race around, sunning on rocks. In the distance, two people ride a pair of chestnut horses. The animals travel across the hard-packed sand, stepping almost in sync.

"Where'd you find the ring place?" Pearl's voice breaks the silence.

"Don't judge me, but it was from a social media ad." Maggie sighs. "I can't come up with ideas anymore. My phone does the work for me."

"Think about it this way—" Pearl holds up her cell "—this computer has access to billions of data points. Your brain has access to far less. Using your phone as a resource is smart. You can find way more information with the right tools." She pauses to bite her lip. "Speaking of phones, I made a recording the day Dante died."

"Wait. You did what?" Maggie raises her eyebrows, shocked by the change of subject. "Did you tell the police?"

"Yeah. I mentioned it to the detective who interviewed me, but she didn't seem too interested. She had me email the file, and other than that, nothing."

"Why didn't you tell me, Pearl? I know you were upset, but this seems important," Maggie says.

"I'm not sure." Her mouth drops into a frown. "I really hated him, you know? Once ABOS got big, he did everything in his power to push me out of the band. Trev was almost as bad, but he'd shut up if I confronted him. Not Dante. He was persistent. The jerk never gave it a rest."

When A Box of Stars was formed, Trev and Dante made an occasional sexist remark during practice. Nothing too toxic. Barely enough to catch her wife's attention. Pearl would respond like a typical people-pleaser—by laughing off their comments and bringing the focus back to the band. Rory and Jake defended her, but they weren't always around. Sometimes it was just Pearl alone with the misogynists, and she'd be subjected to their effed-up viewpoints without a buffer. Thankfully, in the first two years, this rarely happened.

Although Pearl hated the gender-bashing, she stuck around because she loved what ABOS was doing. Women are scarce in the harder musical genres, especially Black women, so when she saw an opportunity to squeeze into a group, she took it. When she was on stage, Maggie's wife radiated confidence, and their daughter adored watching her play. Thousands more women and girls felt the same way. Pearl became a role model for a lot of indie rock fans.

Through the unease with Trev and Dante, Maggie was there for her wife. On the bad days, they'd discuss the jerks' newest tirade over a glass of wine. The awful topics ranged from 'reverse rape' to 'body counts' to 'hitting the wall.' The couple was baffled by the animosity, especially because it came from two good-looking, successful men. These dudes were getting laid left and right, yet they detested the women they slept with. Called them whores. Used up. Easy. But the attention was never focused on their own promiscuity. It was always the women—the young women, never a hag past twenty-five—who were at fault.

Over the years, as the duo's behavior worsened, wine and venting became less effective weapons. Pearl's mental health took a dive, and she seriously considered leaving ABOS. Rory and Jake begged her to stay, promised her the awfulness would stop. And it did for a while. The bigots kept to themselves, and instead of talking crap in front of Pearl, they left whenever she entered the room. Despite the tension, ABOS booked and played shows, selling out venues and their merch tables. Everything was okay.

But okay changed to volatile when the band's third album released. Dante received huge backlash for his awful vocals, and he took it out on the band's most vulnerable member—Maggie's wife. When they were on tour, he followed Pearl around, taunting her with insults. When she was home, he'd stalk her on social media, creating burner accounts to leave disgusting comments on her posts.

Pearl went into hiding. She refused to go anywhere with Dante, and the band had to cancel their summer festival tour in Europe. Pearl also wiped her online presence, deleting years of content in hours. Her goal was to eliminate any web-based or physical environments that made her a target, and she did. Pearl was outside Dante's reach.

Not that he didn't try circumventing her efforts. The weasel texted Maggie, and even Danica, to get to Pearl. They blocked his number and sent everything to the band's manager. Saving evidence of the harassment was crucial because they never wanted it to come to a he-said-she-said situation. Solid proof was their friend.

It took legal action to make things right. Rory brought in his wife's lawyer friend, and she mopped the floor with Dante. She let him know his actions were cause for a civil suit and that he'd be paying Pearl tons of money if he didn't knock it off.

Maggie took SO much pleasure in the fact that the lawyer was a woman. And that she wore head-to-toe pink when she confronted Dante. Amazing.

The expression on the creep's face must have been satisfying. Maggie is sorry she missed it. The thirdhand account Lala gave her was pretty epic though. Apparently, Dante started sweating halfway through the meeting. Literally dripping sweat onto the table. And he wouldn't look her in the eye. He'd stare at his hands or the ceiling, but he wouldn't meet the lawyer's gaze.

For a man who talked crap about women, he sure seemed intimidated when one brought the heat. Maggie guesses even sexist jerks wanted to avoid legal issues. Perhaps he had one brain cell kicking around in his head, but that's probably being generous.

After the lawyer scare, Dante behaved. To Pearl, at least. He left his bandmate alone and instead directed his rage at his fling of the moment. In November, his toxic attitude built up to his domestic violence arrest, which was the catalyst for his removal from ABOS. Firing him meant Pearl was free.

They celebrated that day. After the band made the decision to reject Dante, Pearl and Maggie splurged on a truffle and wine-tasting event where they toasted his downfall. Justice tasted divine alongside their delicious pairings. It was nice when an awful person got what they deserved, because a fair outcome is never guaranteed.

At the tasting, Maggie's wife got tipsy and let loose for the first time in almost two years. Seeing her throw her head back in laughter meant Pearl was back. She'd lost a one-hundred-and-ninety-pound burden and was feeling alive.

Last month, when she texted Maggie at practice, letting her know Dante had shown up uninvited, Maggie feared the worst. She knew Pearl was fragile, and the bully's sudden appearance might crush her reclaimed joy. Why couldn't he just stay away? No one wanted him back.

Pearl was happy to take over as lead vocalist, but nerves still rattled her on occasion. With Dante's unexpected appearance, Maggie wasn't sure her wife would be able to claim her new role. The jerk's presence might paralyze her, and she may not feel comfortable fronting the band. He could derail her career.

Instead, he died. And Pearl was free from him again, this time permanently.

Now, Pearl is bringing up a recording of Dante's final tirade, a literal reminder of the bully's cruelty. Why would she hide this from Maggie? The motives can't be malicious. Her wife is loving and trusting, and she wouldn't use deception to cause pain.

Maybe a trauma response is to blame. Dante put Pearl through a lot, and a desire to dismiss anything related to him is understandable. Maybe she wasn't ready to bring up the recording before. Maybe she's finally gathered enough courage.

If Maggie can help her wife process what happened, it might be the first step toward healing. She asks about the recording again. "I know you hated him, babe. He absolutely deserved it too. But why wouldn't you tell me about this huge thing? Hatred alone doesn't explain why you kept it hidden." She smiles and reaches over to brush a piece of hair behind Pearl's ear. "We used to talk shit about Dante all the time, so I know you aren't holding back his last words for his benefit."

"You're right about that. Nothing I do is for him. Would it be mean to say I do things to spite him?"

"Nah. Spite is an excellent motivator."

Pearl pushes her lips together and stares into the distance. Maggie gives her space to think and shifts her own eyes to the desert backyard. Her wife might have to work through some thoughts to untangle her rationale. Three minutes pass in silence. Finally, she's ready.

With a sigh, Pearl begins, "I told you that Dante was really nasty before he died. He really went to town on everyone in the room, not just me. I think I kept the recording to myself because I was afraid to let you in on the band's secrets." She pauses, biting her lip. "It was never about keeping anything from you, Maggie-moo. We have a relationship where honesty is valued, and we both stay well within the bounds of that promise. But I think some things should stay between friends and outside our marriage. As long as a secret doesn't harm either one of us, if my gut tells me I don't need to share with you, then I won't. Especially if it feels like I'm gossiping, which you know I hate."

Maggie nods. "Okay. I can accept that. We don't need to know every single thing about each other, and I certainly don't need to know everything that happens with your bandmates. That would be information overload."

Pearl rises from her lounger and leans toward Maggie's spot on the hammock. She brings her mouth to her wife's and gently slides her tongue inside Maggie's parted lips. The seconds suspend as they stay locked in their kiss. Luckily, Maggie is sitting. Her wife's love makes her knees weak.

When Pearl pulls back, her eyes are filled with a dreamy haze. "That's why I love you," she says.

"Because I'm a good kisser?"

"No. Because you're the most understanding person in the world. How many partners would be okay with their wives withholding information? Not many, me thinks."

Maggie wiggles her eyebrows. "And I'm a good kisser?"

Pearl bursts out laughing. "Fine. You kiss like a dream." She gives her a peck on the cheek and returns to her seat. "Do you want to listen to the recording? It's long and super cringy at points, but it'll give you more insight into what I dealt with for so long."

"I'd like to listen." Maggie adjusts her position and faces her wife. "My question for you is, can you handle hearing it again? That day was traumatic. The audio might be triggering."

"Now that it's been a month, I'm pretty sure I'll be okay."

"Well, we can stop at any time. Remember that." Maggie drains her coffee. "Let me refill my cup and let Danica know we need some privacy."

She meanders to the kitchen. Her daughter is at the table scrolling through her phone. "Whatcha looking at?" Maggie asks.

"Devon sent me a band to check out. They dress up as cats, and the bassist's guitar is set to the purr frequency, whatever that means." She tilts her phone. "Look, Mom. Aren't you glad Momma doesn't have to wear a costume when she plays?"

Maggie tops off her mug, then walks to Danica. Her daughter passes over the phone. On the screen, she skims a band's social media profile for Real Fine Feline, a rock trio that wears giant cat masks onstage. There's a calico and two tabbies, and they all have wide yellow eyes with slim pupils. In the picture Danica enlarged, the singer holds a microphone with one hand

and claws at a scratching post with the other. The drummer and bassist aren't even playing their instruments. Instead, they're tossing a ball of yarn between them, the thread unraveling across the plywood stage. I swipe through more images, and the cat band continues their shenanigans in each shot.

Maggie returns the phone to her daughter. "That's one way to get fans. People love a gimmick."

"Ew." Danica scrunches her face. "They're degrading the integrity of the music."

"Yes, they're being silly. But if they can actually play, I'm okay with some antics. I'd rather watch a few goofballs than a band who takes themselves too seriously."

"Whatever you say, Mom."

"That's the spirit. Your parents are always right."

Danica rewards her with an eye-roll. "Should I join you outside? I'd hate to miss any of your valuable insights."

"Actually, Momma and I are going to have an adult conversation. I'll come grab you when we're done."

"Sure. I'll take a shower while you're talking."

"Perfect." Maggie picks up her steaming mug. "See you soon, love bug."

When she returns to the patio, Pearl is staring at the hot tub with a frown on her face. "What did the hot tub ever do to you?" Maggie asks.

A grin replaces her frown. "Why haven't we taken a dip yet?"

"We're slackers."

"Let's change that tonight. We can admire our custom rings amongst the bubbles," Pearl says.

"It's a date." Maggie resumes her place on the hammock. "Okay. I'm ready to listen."

Pearl takes a deep breath as she cues up the recording. Then, she gives her wife a wink. "I bring you the closing scene in the life and times of Dante Wilder." And with those words, she presses play.

Right away, Dante's hostility leaps from the audio. "Hey, assholes. Bet you didn't expect to see me." A loud boom echoes out. It sounds like a kick to the bass drum. "You thought you could keep this location secret? That's funny...hilarious. You can't keep me away. I'm the reason this band happened. Why it exists. You're nothing without me."

Another noise, this time its cymbals crashing around. "I'm here to get us on the right track. Before the night ends, you'll be asking me...begging me to come back."

His voice is angry, contempt-filled, and garbled. After several minutes, Maggie asks her wife about the verbal stumbling. "Why is he talking like that?"

Pearl pauses the recording. "Well, he might be drunk or high or both. Take your pick."

"What kind of high?"

"He was fond of chasing the dragon. I think that's the right phrase. Started with pills and eventually moved to the needle. His arm was a wreck right before his arrest. He stopped trying to hide it by then."

"Damn. I knew he was an alcoholic, but opioids are a whole new level." Maggie shakes her head. "Not that his substance abuse excuses anything, but it might explain some of his erratic behavior."

"Yeah. The drugs weren't doing him any favors." Pearl's chin sinks, and she hugs herself, squeezing tight. "At first, I didn't know where he was getting his supply. Figured it was some random dealer he knew in whatever cities we happened to tour through. But early last year, I found out who it was." She lowers her voice almost to a whisper. "One night on the bus, I woke up super late to pee. I shuffled to the bathroom, and saw Dante passed out in the front lounge. He was snoring—loud—so I knew he was zonked.

Thankfully, 'cause I didn't want to deal with him. Even though he stopped cussing me out, he'd glare at me with his creeptastic eyes when he wanted to get under my skin." She pauses to shudder. "Anyways, I did my business, then approached him, expecting him to wake up any second, but he never did. Even when I peeked at the pill bottle clutched in his hand."

"What did the bottle say, Pearl?"

"It was a prescription for oxys from some online pharmacy. And it was made out to Jake Devlin." A tear slips down her cheek, and she wipes it away with the back of her hand. "I knew Jake had a problem, but I didn't know he was supplying Dante. When I begged him to stop, he refused to listen. He kept feeding Dante drugs like it was candy."

"This doesn't make sense. Why would Jake risk his career for someone like Dante?" Maggie asks.

"Extortion." Pearl's eyes grow, and her hands ball into fists. "I think Dante was holding something over Jake's head. I don't have any proof, just a feeling, but from what I saw, there had to be bad blood between the two of them. My guess is that Dante knew a nasty secret, and Jake was doing what he could to keep it from getting out." She perks up. "Wait. Dante said something right before he died about Jake hooking up with other dudes. I thought he was just being a jerk, but maybe that was the secret. I couldn't care less if he's bisexual, but that's me. Maybe other people would."

"You might be onto something, babe. How about we put our feelers out next week when we're all together in Miami," Maggie suggests.

"Yes. Let's do that." Pearl reaches over and gives her wife's knee a squeeze. "We can put on our detective hats and try to get to the bottom of this mess."

Jake Devlin, A Box of Stars Bassist, Checks Himself into Rehab

By Coral Wright | **Published** February 30, 2022 | Floraville Times |

Elway County, FL – After suffering major injuries from a 2020 motorcycle accident, Jake Devlin developed an addiction to prescription opioids. Devlin went public with this information after a show was canceled due to an overdose. He apologized to fans and promised he would seek help to overcome his addiction.

He followed through on that promise this morning when he checked himself into Nu You, a luxury treatment facility outside Asheville, NC. Devlin's wife Nicole said he's scheduled for a three-month stay. "We're hopeful that Nu You can help Jake become the person he was before opioids dimmed his light."

ABOS will resume touring with their guitar tech, Andrew Greene, filling in for Devlin. The band will use profits from the concerts to fund Devlin's stay at Nu You. They released the following statement on their website:

"We're rooting for Jake. He's taken the brave step of entering treatment, and we know he'll use strength to beat his addiction. Sending love and light."

We're rooting for you at the Floraville Times, too. Good luck, Jake.

Chapter 16 – Nicole

{March 10, 2023}

An SUV swerves in front of Nicole and Jake, coming within a foot of their bumper. Nicole sees the driver holding up his phone, blocking his sightline. A video plays on the screen. Something colorful. Cartoony. Obnoxious. Seems like an idiot is threatening her life so he can catch the latest episode of *Family Guy*. That's exactly the way she wants to leave the world.

Not.

They'd hit the road less than six hours ago, but she already missed their little town. Fewer people harassed her with their vehicles in her neck of the woods. "Traffic down here is awful. No one can drive." Nicole gestures to the man who cut them off. "And most people aren't even paying attention. They're focused on their stupid phones."

"We're almost there, Coley. We get off at the next exit, and then it's fifteen minutes west." Jake gives her a grin while keeping his eyes on the road. "After that, it's relaxation. We're not practicing until 6:00, so there's plenty of time to float in the pool."

"Yes. You're right, hon. If we survive this drive, the pool will feel amazing." She leans back in the passenger seat and scrolls through her phone. For the past week, ABOS has been filling their social media accounts with cruise hype. Whatever they post, Nicole shares and her page is flooded with comments from friends. It ranges from "Whoa, I didn't know there were music cruises" to "Can I sneak onboard in your suitcase?" People are curious about the boat. And about the band's future.

To her, accepting the gig was smart. Public interest has been swirling since Rage on the Waves added ABOS to the lineup, and none of it has to do with Dante's murder. Fans are excited about Pearl taking over as singer, and thousands of posts have asked when their next tour will be. It seems like a rebound isn't just possible. A comeback is going to happen and soon.

She's relieved the naysayers were drowned out. Some grumbled about the cruise's timeline—two or three posters thought it was too soon after losing Dante—but the complainers were in the teensiest minority.

Jake never saw the negative comments. Since leaving rehab, he refuses to read anything concerning the band, and honestly, his mental health has improved since ditching social media. Nicole shares posts with him when something big happens, but only the positive stuff. Yesterday she showed him a bunch of comments from ABOS fans, all declaring anticipation about the band's return. Since then, he's been smiling big and humming under his breath. His enthusiasm thrills his wife. After ABOS's third album, he lost his passion for music, and his disappointment was the biggest factor driving his addiction.

But that world is behind the couple now. Jake is sober, and Dante won't be demanding another pill ever again. Her husband can focus on the band, and she can focus on reentering the workforce to shrink their debt. Her worries have simplified. She'd rather face overdue bills than addiction, hands down.

They finish the rest of the ride without wrecking, and, at 3:00, pull into their home for the weekend. When Dylan first brought up practice before the cruise, Nicole was skeptical about Miami's offerings. She grew up in a town of several thousand, not several hundred thousand, and logically when you have more people, the distance between them shrinks. She figured Miami was all condos and smaller houses, with nothing big enough to host a band, their crew, and their significant others. But she was wrong. There are areas outside the city—fancy suburbs with giant houses—and that's where they were staying until the cruise launches. Dylan rented a sprawling compound, and there was more than enough space for everyone to spread out.

After they grab their bags, Dylan bursts through the front door and jogs toward them. "You guys made it. Excellent." He hugs Jake with his right arm and Nicole with his left. "Last time I hugged you like this, the day ended terribly. Let's not have a repeat."

"Agreed," Nicole says. "Let's make it through the weekend without a murder."

"Whoa. Too soon." When she fires a glare at Dylan, he grins. "I'm just kidding, Coley. You know I have a soft spot for morbid humor."

"Well, I wasn't really joking." She continues to glare.

Dylan lets the couple go and holds up his hands. "Sorry. I didn't mean to make it weird."

A laugh bursts from her throat. "Dylan, of course I'm joking." She nudges his shoulder. "You guys are working this weekend, but I'm here on vacation. Bring on the fun. And the adult beverages."

"Yes, ma'am. Right this way." He scoops up her suitcase. "Let me show you around your lovely vacation home. Then we can stop in the kitchen for a frosty drink."

The trio chats as they stroll through the massive house. Dylan has been busy contacting managers and booking agents, who connect him with bands who need openers for upcoming tours. He's also got press lined up before the cruise launches. Pearl and Rory are going to talk with a metal mag about ABOS. They'll be talking about the band's vision for the future, which includes concerts and a new album in 2024.

So far, the inquiries have received nibbles from two big-name bands. Jake is stoked. "I'd love to tour with either one of them. Opening for Steel Damsel or Dark Sunday would give us a huge built-in audience."

Dylan nods. "Don't worry, I'll keep bugging them. Things are looking up for you guys, and I think the cruise will be the beginning of a massive comeback."

Nicole curls her hand into an invisible microphone and speaks into it. "Dylan Tynall, manager for A Box of Stars, predicts an epic ABOS comeback. You heard it here first, folks."

"You can quote me on it," he replies.

While they talk, Dylan leads them through a library, a ten-person movie theater, and a wine cellar stocked to the ceiling. He points out the pool as they pass the towering French doors leading outside. The water is impossibly blue, and it sparkles in the afternoon sun, luring passersby. Instead of heading to the patio, Dylan takes them underneath an ornate archway and into the biggest kitchen she's ever seen.

"Goodness. Look at this, hon. Green cabinets with a blue backsplash. And the island is huge." Nicole runs her hand along the white marble countertops. "It's like they took my dream kitchen and made it a reality."

"Maybe next year we can remodel 'cause this is nice." Jake circles around the room. "I wouldn't be mad if our house looked like this."

"We definitely need an ABOS comeback to afford this big of an upgrade." She swivels her gaze to Dylan. "But I heard from a reliable source that a massive rebound is on the horizon."

"Yep." The manager ambles to the refrigerator and opens it up. "A beer is even closer on the horizon. IPA, lager, or sour?"

"Sour for me," she answers.

"And I'll take an IPA," Jake says. "The strongest one you got."

Dylan grabs three cans from the fridge and brings them over. "Here you go, my friends." When everyone opens their drinks, he toasts. "To Jake, Rory, Trev, and Pearl. By the end of the year, you guys are going to have more fans than ever. And you're going to make boatloads of money. Cheers to that."

They raise their cans and clink them together. Nicole gulps her sour, but Dylan and Jake swallow their drinks in a single chug. Boys. They have no self-control. "You two drink faster than a hot knife through butter."

"You know it, Coley." Jake reaches out his hand. "Let's change into our swimsuits and go for a dip."

"Yes, please." She threads her fingers through his and follows him through the maze of rooms, giggling as he weaves between couches and chairs. When they reach their 1920s-themed quarters, they close the door and disrobe. Nicole tosses Jake his trunks and digs her bikini from the suitcase. As she pulls the turquoise two-piece on, she studies the mural behind the bed, a gorgeous painting covering the entire wall.

The scene is split in half. On the right side, bruised colors show an alleyway where a couple leans against a wooden door. Heavy-lidded eyes peek out from a small open panel, and the woman outside is cupping her mouth, whispering something to the hidden doorman.

On the left, what's behind the wooden barrier is revealed. Bright paint highlights the inside of a swinging jazz club. Women in flapper dresses party to music played by a quintet on an elevated stage. Men in pinstripe suits hold whiskey-filled glasses and try to keep up with their partners on the dance floor. Everyone is smiling. Everything seems delightful.

Nicole sighs. "This house is dreamy."

"How much money do you think it takes to build a compound with decade-themed guest rooms?" Jake asks.

"All the money." She laughs. "Way more than we'll ever have."

"Well, let's pretend that it's our place then. So, we can see how it feels to be loaded."

"Excellent idea." She heads to the bathroom and picks up two striped towels. "Ready to sit by our pool?" she asks.

"Yep. Let's get a beer on the way out." He takes his towel, and they retrace their steps to the kitchen. Jake grabs a beverage for both of them. He rustles in the drawers until he finds the koozie stash and shoves our cans into a matching maroon pair. "We're all set now. It's time to par-tay." He raises his arms above his head and pumps them twice. Then he darts to the French doors. "Last one in the pool is a rotten egg," he yells over his shoulder.

"No fair. You got a head start." Nicole scampers after him, and when she gets outside, he's already draping his towel over a lounger.

Jake pats the chair next to him. "I saved you a seat, babe."

"You're the best. But I'm not in the mood for sitting." She chucks her towel at his hand. "How about a cannonball contest to kick our vacation off?"

"I'm down," Jake says. "But who's going to judge?"

"Me," a voice calls out.

"Me too," a second voice chimes in.

Nicole turns to find Lala and Rory emerging from the house, both wearing green swimsuits and huge smiles. "You're here." She squeals and runs to Lala, throwing her arms around her friend in a hug. "When's the last time we saw each other? Dylan's wedding in Austin?"

Lala squeezes her tight. "Yep. And six months is way too long." She steps back. "You look great, girl. I love that suit."

Nicole pivots and spins, ending the rotation with her hands on her hips. "Thank you, thank you. I got it for this trip." Despite the sunshine, a breeze moves through the air, chilling her. Goosebumps emerge over her body, and she hugs herself. "Brrrr. If it feels like this, I won't be swimming much on the cruise. Why is it still cold in March?"

"You call this cold?" Lala asks. "It's seventy-five out. When we left Jersey, it was in the forties."

"No thank you. I'll never understand why you guys left Florida." Nicole turns toward the pool. "Luckily, this thing is heated, so it'll be warmer in the water." She moves to the deep end and steps back a few feet from the edge. "Here goes nothing." She crouches down, then propels herself toward the ledge, leaping at the last second. "Cannonball!" Her knees go to her chest, and she hits the surface at full velocity.

Immediately, the water warms her. She holds her breath as long as possible, enjoying the cocoon-like environment. From the bottom of the pool, the world is sparkly, serene, soundless.

The quiet ends when she floats back up.

Rory yells out her score. "I give it a seven. You had good form, Nicole, but your splash didn't impress me." He smacks Jake on the shoulder. "This lug is going to smoke you."

"You're such a nerd." Lala shakes her head. "I think your splash was marvelous, Coley. I'm gonna go with a nine-point-five."

"Cheater," Rory says. He laughs at the scowl from his wife. "I love you, baby. You can cheat all you want."

Without warning, Jake charges toward the pool, turning a front flip on the way into the water. Nicole covers her face as he slips below the surface, trying to keep the rocketing droplets out of her eyes. She's just in time, too. The splash rains across the patio, and waves ripple from his point of impact.

After the spray settles, Nicole lowers her hands. "Damn him and his gymnastics skills." She looks at Rory. "Lemme guess. You're gonna give him a ten."

"You know it. My man rocked that dive." When Jake emerges, Rory meets him at the ladder for a high five. "You win, bro. Hands down."

"In your face, Coley," her husband says as he pulls himself out of the water.

"Whatever." She swims to the pool's edge. "How about a chicken fight? Girls vs. boys?"

"You're on," Rory says. He jumps in next to Nicole, and Jake and Lala follow. They get through two matches before Pearl and Maggie show up wearing sunhats and sarongs over vintage styled swimsuits. They look amazing.

During the two hours before practice, the group switches from beer to margaritas. There aren't any more cannonballs or chicken fights, but everyone finds a float, and they laze in the middle of the water, sipping drinks, laughing nonstop. Nicole missed her ABOS family. They make her heart happy.

And they're lifesavers. She owes them the world.

Nicole thinks back to the night before Jake's overdose, and gratitude forms a tight ball in her chest. Pearl saved her husband. She was there when it mattered most, and Nicole will never forget the value of her presence.

The overdose happened during tour. One night, near the end of the run, Nicole noticed Jake acting weird when they talked on the phone. After every few words, her husband would become silent, staying quiet for longer and longer periods. The silences weren't the comfortable type. They were the kind that suggested the conversation was one-sided, that the person on the other end had fallen asleep or faded into another dimension.

She tried to get his attention. "Hon." She paused, waiting for a response. Ten seconds passed. Twenty. "Hon, are you there?"

A sharp intake of breath answered, followed by a single word. "Who?"

"Jake, it's me. Nicole." She answered calmly, although all she wanted to do was scream. Something was wrong, horrifyingly so.

"Coley? How are you, babe…sweetie? I…I miss you." His tempo was sluggish, his pitch low, almost monotone. And he was repeating himself. When they started the conversation ten minutes prior, he'd said the same thing.

"Will you put Pearl on the phone, darlin'? There's something I need to tell her." Nicole stayed upbeat, hoping he wouldn't notice her panic.

Jake doesn't answer. Instead, Pearl's voice flows into the receiver. "Hey, Nicole. What's up?"

With the guitarist, Nicole wasn't afraid to let her terror leak out. "He's using, Pearl. I know it. Will you watch him extra close? I'll get there as soon as I can. Probably tomorrow."

"Shit," she says. "We're going on stage in an hour. I'll see what I can do to wake him up."

"Thank you for helping him. I love you." A sob escaped Nicole's throat.

"I love you too. A lot." Peal pauses, her breath slow and steady. "Everything is going to be okay. He'll make it through this, I promise."

Pearl hung up and monitored Jake until the show. He made it through the set. Barely. He wasn't so lucky the following day. Nicole's flight arrived at 4:00 PM. He overdosed at 4:15, right as her cab pulled away from the airport. Minutes before she arrived at the concert venue, Jake was riding in an ambulance, breathing normally after receiving three naloxone injections.

When Nicole's cab arrived at the venue, Pearl jumped in, and the women rushed to the hospital, staying silent, tearful, scared, during the drive. His bandmate stayed in the waiting room for hours, only leaving after Jake's vitals steadied. Nicole stayed by his side as long as possible, putting up with the lumpy guest cot and no sleep because it was the only option. There's no way she'd leave her man.

Earlier, right as the paramedics rushed backstage to help him, Jake's heart stopped beating. Her husband—her sweet, silly, talented husband— could no longer breathe. He floated between the living and the dead, brought back from the brink by a triple dose of medicine.

Nicole came so close to losing him that night. To losing her everything.

For months after, every time she thought about Jake and his non-beating heart, heavy sorrow surged through her chest. In sympathy, she held her breath, waiting for the lack of oxygen to transform into pain. What did he feel in those moments? Hopefully, nothing. It was the only time she prayed the opioids did their job and made him numb to the world.

When Jake was released from the hospital, the couple traveled to North Carolina, where she checked him into Nu You. The program boasted a 60% success rate, a number astonishingly high in the opioid recovery realm. Nicole's hopes were pinned on that statistic. He needed big help, and apparently Nu You delivered.

Jake's addiction began in a legitimate way. After his motorcycle accident, a painkiller prescription was his gateway to drug dependence. He went from 5mg to 30mg pills three times a day and still wanted more. Once his injuries healed, Jake played up his residual pain for an increased dosage, which his doctors reluctantly agreed to.

He got high that way for a while, but eventually, he turned to the streets when he was denied a prescription refill. Dealers were loaded with blues at the time, and he was able to purchase potent oxys on the cheap. And he did. He bought bottles and bottles of the drug, yet somehow, he remained a functioning addict. There were signs looking back, but while he was in the worst of his addiction, Nicole was blissfully unaware of Jake's decline.

It was Dante who changed that. The singer was the one who introduced him to another way of buying drugs—online pharmacies.

Weeks before his overdose, in a moment of desperation, Nicole's husband confided in Dante about his struggles with opioids. Jake poured out his agony only to encounter manipulation from the singer. There were no caring words shared, no friendly pats on the back. Dante insulted Jake, telling him he was terrible in every way imaginable. He ended the berating with a proposition. The singer would be willing to mentor Jake, to elevate him above his flaws and toward the person he wanted to be, for a cost. And the cost was her sweet man's fragile grip on the world. Dante wanted someone to supply him with drugs, someone who would assume the risk of getting arrested. With Jake, he found the perfect mark.

Online, there were countless pill mill websites, and the chance of purchasers getting caught was incredibly small. These odds worked to the pill pusher's advantage. There were fewer tech-savvy cops than illegal sites, and if the good guys raided one page, another could be built within hours.

Jake uploaded his expired prescriptions, edited to reflect a current date, and he received hundreds of oxys from overseas. The shady businesses he found, with names like ezpills.fun or bogopharmacy.net, didn't care how legitimate his paperwork was. Or about the chemicals in their products. All they cared about was cash.

This was Jake's downfall. He ingested pills with no idea what was inside them. Unknown to him, fentanyl traveled up his nose and through his body, delivering a huge high, while overwhelming his nervous system. His overdose was almost fatal. Thankfully, when he crashed, Pearl was nearby, and she called 911 within seconds of finding him sprawled backstage.

Now, a year later, Jake feels revived. He embraces the days and removes himself from difficult situations before they bring him down. They live by his triggers. Avoiding them at least. Dante was the biggest one, but his death eliminated that threat. Kicking the singer out of ABOS hadn't been enough. His murder became the only way to keep him away. For good.

Nicole glances down at her empty drink and then at her friends. Pearl, Rory, and Jake were inside for practice, but Lala and Maggie stayed outside for extra hang time. They'd switched from bathing suits to sweatpants, and she's glad for the added warmth. Once the sun set, the temperature dipped into the sixties, which chills her Florida bones. But she'll deal with the cold because she's there with a sober husband, surrounded by people she loves. And that's enough warmth to carry her through anything.

"Anyone need a refill?" She shakes her cup, and ice tinkles against the side. Both women raise their hands, and Nicole picks up their glasses. "Be right back."

The French doors are propped open, so the kitchen is as cold as the outdoors. She shivers while whipping up three margaritas, going easy on the pour. My buzz is low key and pleasant. Keeping it going is the goal. She doesn't want to push it too far.

She arranges their drinks on a cocktail tray, adding salsa and tortilla chips to the spread. Even though she'd devoured dinner, her stomach growls. The drunk munchies are surging through her hard, and she needs to calm them down. The girls will probably appreciate the snack too.

Nicole picks up the tray, and a quick turn points her toward the patio. She starts that way, balancing the food and drinks with both hands.

"Save some chips for me. You don't need the whole bag," a voice behind her says.

Nicole whirls around, coming face to face with a pale brunette. The other woman is tiny, not much taller than five feet, and even at her average 5'4" Nicole towers over her. The stranger's eyes squint in surprise. Or anger.

"Who are you?" Nicole asks, puzzled by her presence.

"Why does it matter?" The brunette's lips raise into a sneer, and all attractiveness abandons her face. She's definitely mad now. There's no mistaking that expression. "I'm supposed to be here. That's all you need to know."

"Aren't you a peach." Nicole rotates toward the patio again, calling out over her shoulder as she rushes away. "Don't worry, mysterious figure. I'll save you some chips."

"You better," she says.

The words slip into Nicole's ears right before she slams the French doors shut, leaving the grumpy stranger by herself.

She'll ask Jake about the brunette later. For now, snacking is all she wants to do.

Therapy Notes

Autumn Brooks
Nu You
4345 First Dawn Blvd.
Mills Bend, NC 28799

Patient: Jake Devlin
DOB: 02/13/1989
Diagnosis: F11.2, Opioid Dependence, Uncomplicated
Secondary Diagnosis: F.30, Major Depressive Disorder, Recurrent, Mild

Date: 03/06/2022
Start Time: 02:10 PM
End Time: 03:00 PM

This is my fourth session with Mr. Devlin, and so far, he's made tremendous progress. When the patient came to Nu You, he was experiencing noticeable symptoms of opioid withdrawal. With medical care, his tremors and sweating have subsided, and he reports no nausea, and improved sleep patterns.

Mr. Devlin's drug tests during treatment have been negative, but he still experiences strong cravings for opioids. During group sessions, he is an active participant and encourages other patients to contribute in a helpful manner. His willingness to share his own experiences leads me to believe he is aware of the impacts of his drug dependence and is willing to confront them.

Mr. Devlin claims he "doesn't want to turn to drugs again" and that he "never expected to overdose." He is aware of his depression diagnosis and has attended therapy in the past to address it. Patient denies suicide ideation. When speaking about his triggers, he stated "when he feels like he let others down, he spirals."

Client's goals: Mr. Devlin stated he wants to "get better, so he can go home to his wife and music."

Chapter 17 – Maggie

{March 12, 2023}

"Did you call Danica this morning?" Pearl asks her wife. Jars of lotion lay open on the bathroom counter, and she massages their contents into her skin while she talks. Pearl's beauty regimen is complex, but it works. Her face shines, glassy, poreless, and healthy. She looks exactly the same as the day the couple met—smoking hot.

Maggie does not. Lines and freckles have given her face the veneer of middle age, but she's not mad. Her experiences display clearly on her features for everyone to see, but she's into that look. Plus, Pearl digs it too. Lucky her.

"Yep. I called her while I was out by the pool, drinking my coffee. Was about an hour ago." Maggie answers. "She was cranky and rushed. You know, her typical before-school attitude."

"That's our girl." Pearl shakes her head while she rubs cream from a gold container on her forehead. "I'm a little sad we're missing her spring break. But that makes me extra happy we listened to her and went to Joshua Tree. Even though she's grouchy, she's got brains."

"She gets it from her moms." Maggie rises from the bench at the bed's end and turns toward the headboard, in awe at the artwork that spans from floor to ceiling. "I still can't get over this mural. Whoever painted this has some serious talent." Their room was fifties-inspired, and the picture on the wall was a scene from an old-timey television show. A group of teenagers dressed in retro clothing dances in front of a camera and a live audience. From their positions, she'd guess they were doing the jitterbug or the lindy bop. Whatever style it is, the teens are having a blast. Smiles and laughter radiate from their faces, and their bodies display the carefree comfort of those letting loose and living in the moment. "Why don't we do stuff like this anymore?" Maggie points to the painting. "I bet people would be friendlier to each other if they danced together. They'd get those happy endorphins flowing and forget why they're angry at their neighbors and everybody else."

Pearl raises an eyebrow. "This coming from the person who can't keep a beat?"

"Sure is. I know a good thing when I see it. Our world needs an activity that creates joy. Dancing definitely makes that happen. And I bet if there were more opportunities to practice, I'd be spinning and dipping you in no time." Maggie glances at her watch. "What time is band practice today?"

"Eleven. We're going to play through the cruise sets twice, so we should finish up around two."

"Cool. I'm about halfway done with my book. That'll give me enough time to finish."

"How many have you read this weekend?" Pearl dots on foundation, transitioning from skincare to makeup. For a practice day, she'll go light. For a show day, she's full slap. She never knows where her pictures will be featured, so she always looks her best.

"I'm on the third one. It's pretty spicy. Like, loads of ghost sex." Maggie goes over to her bag and rummages around until she finds her current novel. "Look at this cover. It's brilliant."

Pearl pauses her routine and comes over, squinting at the book. "Oh my God. Is that a library filled with ghosts you can check out?"

"Nailed it. How freaking awesome is that concept? You can rent a ghost for two weeks, return it, then get another one after. Every ghost doesn't let you bang, of course. Even in the supernatural realm, consent matters. But some of them will give you a history lecture because they were alive during

these pivotal moments, like the Roman Empire or the Salem Witch Trials."
Maggie lowers the novel. "I'm pretty excited about finishing it."

"You're a nerd, Maggie-moo." Pearl leans over and plants a kiss on
her forehead. "The cutest nerd ever." She turns to the vanity, then back to her
wife. "Don't feel like you need to wait for me to finish. Go on and get
reading. I'll be out in ten minutes or so."

"Perfect. See you in ten." Maggie throws on a sweater, grabs her
book, then zips to the patio. It's early, and no one is outside yet. Exactly what
she was hoping for. The quiet welcomes her as she finds a lounge chair and
her place in *Spectral Collection.*

Between hang sessions, she's been cramming in as many pages as
possible. The two stories she's already finished were joyous. They were less
ghostly and more fantasy, unlike the current tale, which is full-on phantom
erotica. For the cruise, she packed a book for each day, and so far, the pace
she's set will get her through them all.

When Maggie is out in public, she makes sure to hide what she's
reading from prying eyes. People get weird about romance, especially the
smuttier varieties, and she'd rather avoid any judgy stares. Here, no one cares
about her genre selection. When Lala saw her second book, *Deirdre's
Dwarven Delight*, she squealed. After Maggie gave her friend a rundown of
the plot, she asked to borrow the paperback when Maggie was done, and
yesterday, she handed it over. Hours later, she saw Lala dive into the novel,
her face amused while she paged through. Clearly, she's in good company.
Maggie's friends get her taste.

The sun warms her skin as she flips through *Spectral Selection.* A
breeze rushes through the screened patio and offsets the heat from the
sunbeams, creating the ideal temperature. The morning couldn't be more
beautiful.

She flies through the words, getting deeper into the story, juicy scene
by juicy scene. She's digging into a good one—a professor checks out

Freud's ghost, and they're about to test some of his theories in the bedroom—when a voice breaks her concentration.

"Mind if I join you?"

She looks up to find Brandi standing outside the French doors. The petite brunette is wearing black joggers with a long-sleeved tunic.

And a faint smile.

Compared to the first evening, when Brandi nearly argued with Nicole over some tortilla chips, her current mood is exuberant. Over the past two days, during chats here and there, Maggie has gotten to know Brandi, which helped calm her prickly attitude a notch. Even with this improvement, the younger woman isn't the most welcoming person, but Maggie understands the defensive attitude. If Pearl took her to a place where she was a stranger and everyone else was friends, she'd be hesitant to jump into the festivities too.

Maggie waves her over. "Grab a seat. There are plenty."

Brandi picks one close to the pool. "Thanks, Maggie." She leans back into the chair, settling into the cushion. "Don't worry, I won't interrupt your reading. I'm just here for a little sunbathing. The weather makes me want to curl up like a cat." She closes her eyes and tilts her head toward the sunshine.

"Enjoy," Maggie says before reentering the Freud chapter. In real life, the man and his theories were problematic, but in this book, she's invested. She needs to discover what happens. Does Freud's ghost allow his id to overpower his superego for some freaky deaky fun? Judging by the steamy setup, she says yes.

As she's getting to the meat of the plot, another voice rings out, drawing her attention away from the page. "Ready for breakfast?" Pearl chirps as she steps onto the porch, stopping when she reaches her wife's lounger. "I am so, so hungry, babe. I'm pretty sure I can eat a dozen eggs, plus toast and fruit, and maybe some yogurt too. Come cook with me." She pokes out her bottom lip and bats her eyelashes. "Pretty please."

"My poor, sweet hungry wife. Of course, I'll help you cook." Maggie places a bookmark in her paperback and lays it down on the chair between her legs, leaving it there for when she returns. She rotates toward Brandi. "Want some eggs? We can make extra. It wouldn't be a problem at all."

Brandi's eyes flutter open, and she focuses on Maggie. "That would be awesome. Thank you." She flashes a grin before resuming her relaxed position.

"You got it. Scrambled eggs coming right up." Maggie stands and takes hold of Pearl's hand. "Let's get you fed. We can't have your hunger morph into hanger."

The couple heads to the kitchen, and Maggie opens the fridge to search for ingredients while Pearl shuffles around for cookware. There's still food on the shelves, but the supply is dwindling after multiple people have raided it for two days. Thankfully, Dylan stocked up on eggs, cheese, and produce, so there's plenty to make a triple serving of breakfast. Maggie pulls out what she needs, then closes the door.

Her wife is still rummaging when she finishes, but Pearl has already placed a mixing bowl, a pan, and a whisk, next to each other on the counter. Maggie rinses the veggies, plopping the food next to the utensils after it's clean. "Ready to get started?"

Pearl spins her way, holding a knife and cutting board. "Yep. Let's do this." She sets the board down and grabs a red pepper. Her chopping is measured. Smooth. Her face isn't. Pearl grimaces as she presses the blade through the bright vegetable.

"What's up, buttercup? You look pissed," Maggie says.

Pearl lets out her breath in a huff. "How come you offered to cook breakfast for that chick? She's been nothing but a bitch the entire weekend.

And Trev has been in a Mood, with a capital M. His normal crankiness is amplified by at least a thousand. She seems to bring out his worst qualities." Pearl lays down the knife and squints at her wife. "I'm annoyed by her too. Do you know how many times she interrupted practice yesterday?"

"Do you really want me to guess?" Pearl nods her head. "Okay. Did she interrupt you twice?" Maggie asks.

"Four times." Pearl's eyes widen. "She disturbed us four times, Mags. And there wasn't anything the matter with her. She just wanted Trev's attention. It was painful to watch. I felt so uncomfortable seeing them argue." Her jaw clenches. "And mad, too."

Maggie places her hand over her wife's and caresses the skin with her thumb. After a moment, Pearl's mouth relaxes. "I'm sorry, babe. I had no idea she was such a pain. Honestly, she's been somewhat nice to me. We chatted about clothes and vacations, nothing too important, but they were pleasant conversations. She didn't give off evil vibes while we were talking," Maggie says.

"Lucky you. She must think you're worthy of her friendly side." Pearl rolls her eyes. "The band must be on her shit list. Maybe because we're associated with the boyfriend she clearly hates."

Maggie nods. "You might be onto something. Trev is a part of ABOS, and so are you. That's a pretty big connection. Not that it justifies rudeness, of course."

"Cool. I love when I'm judged for nonsense reasons." Pearl picks up the knife and gets back to prepping. Her chopping is quicker but still precise. "You know what else is annoying? Trev has been pitching ideas for new music. They're terrible because he's an awful songwriter, but that's not what irks me the most." She finishes slicing the pepper and moves on to the mushrooms, cutting each portabella into strips and then quarters. "We're here for one reason—to prepare for the cruise. New songs aren't part of our prep. Getting into the groove as a four-piece is. Nothing more. So, he's wasting the limited practice time we have with idiotic pitches for songs identical to the ones from our third album. The one that tanked. Smart right?" She takes her eyes off the food, and stares at Maggie, eyebrows raised, lips pressed into a line.

Even though Pearl is frustrated, beauty radiates from her face. Her wife is a knockout. Her rich tan skin, her deep brown eyes, her wavy hair. Everything about her is perfection. She feels the same about Maggie, thankfully, and their relationship's foundation is mutual respect and passion. Maggie leans into these characteristics when she responds. "You know Trev better than I do. Your instincts about him are always spot on." She leans over and brushes a kiss across Pearl's cheek. "What is your gut saying? Why would he be pushing new music so hard?"

"I think…" She pauses and taps her chin, a cute habit that means she's thinking. After a few seconds she continues, her voice snappy. "It's stupid, but I think he's gunning for the band leader position now that Dante's dead. He's trying to establish that he's in charge. But the thing is, Rory, Jake, and I never considered Dante as our leader. It was all in his egotistical mind. Every decision we made, we voted on." Her jaw clenches again. "The only item he bullied us into was the musical direction for *Deviance Driven*, and we see how that turned out. Low sales and lower reviews." Pearl releases a long breath and picks up the last vegetable, a yellow onion. "Trev was always Dante's shadow, copying everything he did, so it makes sense that he'd be putting himself out there right now. The idiot thinks we need him to lead us into ABOS's next phase when his guidance is the last thing we need."

"How are some people so clueless? Trev is lucky you haven't replaced him as drummer, yet here is thinking he's got the brains to oversee the band." Maggie raises her left hand, lifting the pinkie up. "You have more talent in your little finger than Trev has in his entire body. Try not to let him get to you, babe. He's not worth it."

"I know. I know." She lays down the knife and reaches up to massage her jawline. "I'm letting the jerk give me a headache. What nonsense."

"How about I keep Brandi occupied today? That way, she won't bother you during practice," Maggie says.

"What about your book? Weren't you going to finish it this afternoon?"

"I can finish later. I'd much rather help you avoid someone who's making your life hell." She picks up the knife and nudges her wife over. "Let me finish all this, and I'll bring your plate to our room. You can eat on the balcony. You can see the canal from there."

"Yes. That sounds perfect." Pearl hugs her from the side. "Love you, Maggie-moo. Thanks for wrangling the annoying interrupter. It'll be nice to run through both sets without any distractions." She squeezes Maggie before letting go. "I'll take extra cheese on my eggs. You're the best." Pearl leaves, waving over her shoulder until she rounds the first corner.

While Maggie finishes cooking, the salsa tempo runs through her head, and she gives into the rhythm, moving her feet on each count. Practice has paid off. This morning, her body lands in the correct position 80% of the time. Pearl's birthday is right after the cruise. By then, she'll marvel at Maggie's dancing skills. Or she won't laugh at them, at least.

After the veggies soften, she throws the eggs into the pan. The mixture heats up quickly, and with some flicks of the spatula, everything scrambles nicely. She switches the burner off, and portions out Pearl's breakfast, topping the eggs with a palmful of cheddar. She rushes the plate to her love, taking sweeping steps on the way to their room. The movement stretches her hips, and warm pulses travel down her leg.

Her wife is on the balcony when she enters their suite. Pearl beams when Maggie sets her plate down on the fancy marble table. "Breakfast is served. Hope that's enough cheese," Maggie says.

"Well, there's never enough cheese, but this will do." Pearl picks up her fork. "Thank you, most beautiful woman in the whole entire world."

Warmth heats her cheeks. Gah. Maggie's wife still makes her blush after so many years. "Anything for you." She bends down and kisses the top of Pearl's head. "Let me get back to babysitting duty. See you after practice."

Maggie rushes off as her wife digs into her food. In the kitchen, she plates the remaining eggs and on a whim, grabs two apples to round out the meal. Coffee is the final addition. On a tray, she brings everything to the patio, choosing to land on a mosaic-topped table. "Come and get it," she calls out.

Brandi opens her eyes. "I thought you forgot about me. But I'm so glad you didn't. I am starving." She stands and shuffles over. "Wow. This looks amazing, Maggie. Thank you." She flops into a seat, reaches onto the tray for her plate, and sets to it, shoveling food into her mouth at an impressive pace.

Her speed shocks Maggie. When she's halfway done with her eggs, Brandi consumes the last bite of her scramble. Her apple disappears in five giant bites, and she's eyeing the second red delicious next to Maggie's plate. She offers it to the ravenous woman. "You look hungry. Take it."

She snatches the fruit and devours it, eating every edible morsel before tossing the core on the tray. She reaches for the coffee but drops her hands into her lap. "Is this decaf?"

"Nope. It's caffeinated. In fact, I'd call it rocket fuel. I'm heavy-handed when I add the grounds. A cup gives me enough zip to get through the morning." Maggie gulps her own coffee, loving the mocha afternotes. As she swallows the mouthful, she notices an odd expression on Brandi's face. Her lips are puckered, her eyes narrowed. "Everything okay?"

"I guess so," she answers, her tone more acidic than the coffee. "It would be nice if you considered alternative diets, though."

Panic floods through Maggie. Holy crap. Did she serve something harmful? "Brandi, do you have any allergies? I didn't even think to ask."

"No allergies. But I'm not drinking caffeine right now, so this is a waste." She picks up her mug and hustles to the edge of the porch. A flick of the wrist upends her coffee into the grass. Steam wafts up from the puddle. "There. Now there's nothing to tempt me." She approaches the table but pauses when she sees Maggie's open mouth. "I hope that didn't look too unhinged. A few months ago, I would have been drinking multiple glasses with you, but now, I have to avoid it. Out of sight, out of mind is best for me, which is why I dumped it." She offers a smile. "No offense, Maggie. I'm sure it tasted great."

She pulls her face into what she hopes is a neutral expression. "None taken. And now I know for next time—no caffeine for Brandi. Noted."

"Well, the restriction is temporary, so maybe I can try a cup in the future." She slides back into her chair and leans onto the table. "Thanks again for breakfast. And for being nice to me." Her mouth settles into a frown. "No one else has even tried getting to know me. I hate being an outsider."

Excellent. She's given Maggie the perfect in. "How about we get to know each other better today? We could take the car and go shopping. I don't know about you, but I could use another vacation outfit. Fans probably expect a band member's wife to look decent." She glances down at her holey jeans and scuffed flats. "My wardrobe could use a cool infusion, and you're young enough to know what's hip."

Brandi lets out a low-pitched laugh, the sound deeper than Maggie expected. "Well, I'm not the most fashionable, but even I know the word hip went out of style a while ago. You want to look snatched." She claps her hands together and bounces in her seat. "Let's do it. I'll meet you at the front door in ten."

While Brandi gets ready, Maggie returns to her room to let Pearl know what's going on. Her wife is impressed with her quick thinking and asks her to grab a sun hat at the mall. Maggie agrees, then hunts down the rental car's keys. They're near the front entrance, resting on top of a sticky note containing a single sentence written in jagged letters.

Text me if you take the keys.
-Dylan

She shoots him a message, then rushes to the kitchen to clean up the breakfast mess. Right at ten minutes, she places the last dish on the drying rack and strolls to the front door. Brandi, now wearing a flowy skirt and cropped sweater, is already there. Her hands rest on her hips, and she taps her right foot in a quick pattern. *Tap-tap.* Pause. *Tap-tap.*

Out of curiosity, Maggie observes her for a minute, tucking into a dark spot in the adjacent living room. As the seconds tick by, Brandi's movements grow. Her feet no longer sound expectant; they sound furious. *Tap-tap-tap-tap-tap.* The rhythm accelerates into a blast beat, hitting faster than the double bass in any ABOS song. Her hand joins the discord. With a fingernail, she thumps the same hastened pace on her front tooth, making a hollow thud with each hit.

As Maggie takes a step forward, not wanting to see any more of her unsettling behavior, Brandi stops tapping. In robotic jerks, she swings her body toward the entrance table, snatching up the note from Dylan. She reads the words with a smirk, and, without warning, rips the yellow paper into shreds.

The next part is weird. And haunting. Brandi balls up the pieces, rubbing the bits between her left thumb and pointer over and over again. When she's satisfied with the shape, she pops the sphere into her mouth, swallowing it down with a gulp.

Maggie can see her eyes the entire time. They're fixed somewhere above Maggie's head, staring into the empty room. From the little she knows of Brandi, she isn't a very expressive person. Smiles are muted. Laughs restrained. She gives few clues about how she's feeling.

But the brunette acts differently during the paper-eating episode. Here, her emotions are on full display. Even from a room away, there's no mistaking the hostility blazing from her. Her pupils are pinpricks. Her teeth gnash into her bottom lip. Her hands ball into fists. Brandi is furious.

Maggie hopes it's not at her. Shopping would be a lot less fun if her companion hated her guts. But she's on a mission, and she must brave this odd person's anger for her wife. Maggie promised to keep Brandi occupied, and that's what she's going to do.

After a few deep breaths, she ducks into the kitchen, careful to stay in the shadows on the way. Once there, she shakes out her limbs. The motion eases the tension in her shoulders and erases the rigidity in her posture. She doesn't want Brandi knowing she witnessed the creepy outburst. Acting natural is key.

So, Maggie does. She pinches her cheeks for color, then saunters into the front room, announcing her presence with a jolly voice. "Sorry I'm late. The dishes held me up." She stops walking and faces the last place she saw Brandi. The other woman is still standing there, watching Maggie's approach. Thankfully, her scariness has retreated inside, and Brandi displays an indifferent exterior. Maggie might have lost her cool if any menace still showed. "Are you ready to go?" she asks.

"Yes, I am. We're going to have so much fun," Brandi answers. In contrast to her words, her monotone doesn't convey excitement. If anything, she sounds bored. Uninterested.

Maggie fills her voice with enough jolliness to compensate for the detachment. "Let's get this adventure started," she says. Brandi opens the front door, and Maggie squeezes past, avoiding contact without being obvious. "I'll drive. You sit back and relax," she says over her shoulder.

Brandi nods and follows her to the SUV. As the brunette gets into the passenger seat, Maggie fires off a text to Pearl, facing away from the car so Brandi won't notice.

MAGGIE: Wish me luck. I'm going to need it.
PEARL: love you babe
PEARL: you got this
PEARL: don't let the weirdo get you down
MAGGIE: I won't, but you owe me. This chick has some serious issues.
PEARL: can't wait to hear all about them
PEARL: gotta run to practice now. love you. ttyl

And with Pearl's vote of confidence, she climbs into the vehicle and drives off with someone who may or may not despise her. At the very least, her shopping partner's mood swings are something to be wary of.

And wary of them she is.

1 more day until Rage on the Waves

Hey, Ragers! Are you ready to set sail with your favorite bands? We've been preparing for months to bring you the perfect blend of music and mayhem, and we can't wait to show you what's in store. Check-in begins at 1:00 PM, and once you're on the Rage Ride the party begins.

Launch day kicks off with booze and a buffet. After the sun sets, Sans Dong and Downtonal will melt your face off with their thrash metal beats. DJ Flaunty Fresh will hit the stage after them, so don't forget to pack your dancing shoes.

During our first day at sea, Gigging for Love, Blood Bonders, and Feed the Brethren will be kicking things off during the daylight hours. And when the moon comes out, so do the big bands. At 7:00 PM, we're welcoming A Box of Stars to our lineup for the first time, and they'll be followed by Sword of Thy Lady's Vengeance. It's going to be a night to remember.

So, get to the Port of Miami, and get ready to rock! See you tomorrow, Ragers.

Chapter 18 – Lala

{March 13, 2023}

During their stay in the swanky rental house, they were tucked away, hidden in the South Florida suburbs among giant houses and zero crowds. It was quiet there. Subdued. Exactly the right environment for winding down and transitioning to their weeklong cruise.

This morning, in downtown Miami, the atmosphere is the opposite. On the way to breakfast, they're immersed in the vibrant city's life force as they navigate people and traffic. The nonstop activity energizes Lala.

"Take the next right. Then it's another block," Rory says from behind.

"Got it." She follows a group across the street and turns right at the corner. "What's the name of the restaurant again? I don't want to miss it."

"Gertrude's." Rory catches up, snagging her hand and twining his fingers with hers. "And you absolutely won't miss it. There's a giant rooster out front."

"Sweet." She glances over her shoulder, frowning when she doesn't recognize the people behind them. "Did we lose everyone?"

"Nah, I told them where we'd be. After we dropped off our luggage, they got distracted by an art exhibit in the park and wanted to take selfies." He shrugs. "What are you going to do? They're on vacation. If they want to take pictures, they can."

"For me, food comes before pictures." Lala's stomach growls right on cue. "Let's hurry. We can order an appetizer while we wait for them to catch up."

After a few steps down the block, the rooster comes into view. After about twenty more steps, she can make out the design painted on its exterior. With thick lines and a rust-toned palette, a steampunk version of *The Starry Night* adorns the ten-foot-tall bird. When they get closer, she notices that each of the painting's stars is composed of small portraits. Lala approaches the statue, inspecting the pictures, trying to recognize who the men are. Thirty seconds of staring leaves her with no guesses. She asks Rory for help. "Babe, who are the dudes on the rooster?"

"They're the Heat and the Dolphins players. The owner is a huge fan." He tugs on his wife's hand. "Come on. Let's get inside, La. My stomach is growling too."

The couple walks through glass double doors and the aroma of bacon and coffee slaps Lala in the face. She almost drools while the host puts together a table for eight, and by the time she sits them, Lala. Is. Ready. Rory orders croissants and café con leche, and she adds a side of turkey sausage to their pre-breakfast snack.

When the food arrives, she digs in, making a sandwich with the sausage and flaky pastry. She follows each mouthful with sips of espresso. The buttery, milky goodness boosts her happiness tenfold. Her noisy stomach stills. "Oh my God, this is delicious," she gets out between bites.

"Gertrude knows what's up. I eat here whenever we're down this way." The bell on the entrance chimes, and Rory turns his head toward the door. A smile lights up his face. "Looks like everyone made it." He narrows his eyes. "Well, almost everyone. Trev's not with them, but that's nothing tragic."

Lala shoves the last bit of croissant into her mouth and watches the group file in and tromp over. Their cheeks are sun-kissed from afternoons around the pool, and laughter floats between each person. The luxury oasis had done everyone well. Other than some weirdness with Brandi and Trev, the weekend had been lovely. Catching up with Maggie and Nicole was the highlight of the trip, but the show the band gave them yesterday also ranked pretty high.

Last night at dinner, Nicole asked if there was any way the wives could hear a song or two from the ABOS four piece. The question made Maggie and Lala cheer. They whooped and whistled, feeding off each other's enthusiasm. Even Brandi added a smattering of applause. None of them had heard what the new lineup sounded like, and they were dying for a listen.

Pearl, Rory, Jake, and Trev were enthusiastic about the idea, and luckily the crew hadn't packed their gear yet. When they finished their salmon burgers, everyone barreled into the practice space and settled into their respective spots—the players with their instruments, and the wives perched on chairs in front.

From the first note, Lala could tell that the band felt good about their arrangement. Their faces were calm, their poses comfortable, their vibe synced. Before seeing them perform, she'd been worried about Trev's awkwardness, and how it would impact the rest of the band. Rory had filled her in on the drummer's strange relationship with Brandi, and her uncanny ability to disrupt practice during pivotal moments. But the last day at the oasis, thanks to Maggie's ingenious intervention, the band was able to get down with their music. And each other.

Uninterrupted, they played through their cruise sets twice, and had a successful meeting after. Each of the four members shared their ideas for ABOS's future. They discussed how often they wanted to tour, and when they anticipated their next album release. The conversation was done without yelling, bullying, or drinking, something that hadn't happened in years. To Lala, the last factor was the most crucial. Everyone was sober, which led to zero drama and tons of productivity. If the band maintained this pace, they would soon bypass their 2016 greatness.

Last night, Lala went to bed hopeful, delighted that Rory's decision to stick with ABOS seemed promising. Her man loves music, and he adores playing with Jake and Pearl. She knew this and supported his choice to stay after Dante's death. But underneath her support, there was a small part of her that thought the band was tainted by the ex-singer's cruel legacy. What if the group was cursed?

The four remaining members diminished this notion when they slayed their impromptu concert. She hadn't witnessed such harmony, both musically and person wise, since the band's early days. It was nice to have them back. When ABOS was good, they were untouchable, and if they kept playing like they did in the practice spot, they'd have no trouble impressing fans.

While they went through their songs, tears welled in Lala's eyes, and her heart surged with joy. Listening to great music is magical, and the tunes coming from their instruments transported her to a euphoric place. Apparently, her worries about them were misplaced. This band was going places, with Rage on the Waves marking the beginning of their comeback.

But that serenity doesn't last long. Her panic reignites over Trev's absence this morning. Why didn't he show up to the restaurant? Breakfast is the last group activity before they board the cruise and everyone else is here as planned. He's a jerk for picking the morning of their big gig to skip out on his team.

Someone must know where he went. She waits for everyone to settle before asking about the missing drummer. "Guys, the food here is amazing. The café con leche too." She points to the empty chair. "Do we need to wait for Trev? Did he get lost?"

"He got sidetracked. By a tattoo shop." Pearl rolls her eyes. "We told him that band check-in begins at 10:00, which is only an hour from now, but the dude insisted on staying."

"I mean, he's getting something to honor Dante, so maybe cut him some slack," Brandi says, leveling an icy glare at Pearl.

"Tell me more. What's this tattoo all about?" Lala tilts her head, curiosity piqued. Trev honoring Dante? That is rich. Those two shared a lot of the same beliefs and addictions, but they were more frenemies than pals.

Brandi shifts her gaze to Lala. "He's getting a whisky bottle with a microphone and the date of Dante's murder on the label. I think it's nice." She huffs, and stares at Pearl again. "Unlike some people."

Yikes. Lala reminds herself to never get on Brandi's bad side. The girl is mean. "Interesting. Hopefully the tattoo artist finishes on time. We don't want Trev missing the boat." While everyone else explores the menu, she pauses to think about Brandi's words. *Dante's murder.* Why is the phrase bothering her?

In a flash, the reason pops into her brain. Results! LegalShe was supposed to get a copy of Dante's toxicology report today. The piece of evidence would either seal Karina's fate in prison or mark the beginning of her freedom. Since the autopsy and lab work were handled by the prosecution, the LegalShe team had to put in a discovery request to access the document. Lucky for them, Ellen knew who to contact and what forms to fill out.

After Lala's meeting with Karina late last month, she hired LegalShe to investigate the case pending against her. Their main job is compiling research for Karina's attorney in Georgia. Her Georgia team will use everything LegalShe gathers during her trial, if the case gets to that point. Hopefully the toxicology results will disprove Karina's involvement in Dante's death, and the prosecutor will drop the conspiracy charge.

Lala's intuition tells her the case will get dropped. From what she knows of Dante, he wasn't one to follow through on anything, especially a favor for a woman. On top of that, Karina's plan would have made him sick, and he was a wuss when it came to illness. According to Rory, every sniffle Dante had would become the man flu, and he'd whine from his bunk, begging the rest of the band to buy him medicine or chicken noodle soup.

She'd bet half her savings on a clean tox report. There's no way the singer would have willingly consumed poison. He wasn't the type.

Lala scans her email but doesn't see a message from Ellen. Bummer. The medical examiner must not have sent it yet. Lala shoots her colleague a text just in case she forgot about the evidence coming her way.

LALA: Hey lady, I know you're probably busy, but please please please send me the Wilder tox report when it hits your inbox. I have a good feeling about it.
ELLEN: Girl. Why are you texting me about work while you're on vacation? Stoppppp. And don't worry. I'm on it.
ELLEN: I'm in court all day, but I'm checking my phone every chance I get. That's why I answered you so quick.
LALA: xoxoxox you're the best.
ELLEN: Don't forget it.
ELLEN: Bring me a souvenir to show me how much you appreciate my awesomeness.
LALA: Noted. Love you Ellie-belly.
ELLEN: Love you too, La.

She tucks her phone inside her purse, and tunes into the conversation. Rory is telling everyone about his last visit to the restaurant. "We finished our show at 11:00, and I started slamming IPAs in the dressing room, and I kept going at the hotel. A local brewery had dropped off two twenty-four packs, and me and Jake drank most of them in a couple of hours."

Jake grimaces. "We did. And then regretted it the next day."

"Maybe you did, but that's only 'cause you didn't hit up Gertrude's. When I stumbled in at 1:00 AM, the overnight chef fixed me home fries and a breakfast burrito, and after I wolfed everything down, I felt amazing." Rory looks from person to person. "The food here performs miracles. I didn't have a hangover the next day. No headache, no dry mouth, no upset stomach. Nothing."

"I feel a little rough from last night's margaritas, so hopefully the food will get rid of my queasiness," Maggie says.

"Guaranteed, Mags. You'll be feeling better after a few bites." Rory turns to his wife. "Everything okay? You looked serious when you were firing off those texts."

She smiles. "Everything is good, handsome. Just some work-related stuff. No big deal."

"Lala, you're supposed to be letting loose. No work allowed," Pearl says.

"Well, you might make an exception for this particular task." She leans in, huddling close to the middle of the table. "There's an important piece of evidence coming in today, and it has to do with Dante's case."

Pearl's eyes grow. "What is it?"

"His toxicology report. We'll have a better idea about his cause of death after we review it." Lala lowers her voice more. "This evidence might make or break Karina's case."

Brandi slams her fist on the table, startling everyone. "Don't say that bitch's name in front of me."

"Whoa. No freaking way." Rory holds up a hand and stares hard at Brandi. "There's no need to be rude. Karina is my wife's client, and when you say nasty things, Lala might take it as a personal attack." His voice lowers to a growl. "I'm not cool with that."

Lala's pulse pounds, and a tightness gathers in her stomach. Brandi's words shock her, but she doesn't take them personally. She's focused on the fact that Brandi knows Karina. "Do you two have a history?" she asks, pushing through her physical unease at the other woman's attitude.

"Yeah, you could say that." Brandi's cheeks flush. "We used to be friends, but that changed when she stole the guy I was interested in. She did it on purpose too. Wore some skank outfit and waltzed by him with her tits hanging out. What man can resist that?"

Rory's mouth opens like he's about to answer. Without thinking, Lala reaches under the table and pinches his knee. Her man's leg flinches under her hand, but his upper half remains unfazed. He's smart, so he gets the hint. Instead of lashing out at Brandi, he grabs his coffee and downs a mouthful, giving Lala major side eye as he drinks.

If she wants to get the dirt from Brandi, it's time for some serious acting. She cranks up the wattage of her smile and leans toward the grumpy woman. "No man can resist a good-looking woman. Not even my hubby and he's practically a saint." She giggles and restrains herself from cringing at the ridiculous sound. "Fake friends who do that type of nonsense are the worst. What if the guy you were eyeing was your prince charming? Does that mean Karina stole your happily ever after? That would be crushing." She widens her eyes and pushes out her lower lip.

Lala's over-the-top performance hasn't repelled Brandi. Her face is rapt, and she tilts even further over the table, inching as close to Lala as possible. The psycho is hooked, and she wants to talk. "The guy was a hundred percent not my prince charming. He's actually dead now. And Karina is locked up for his murder. They got the justice they both deserved."

No one at the table makes a sound. Their eyes lock on Lala as they wait for her reply to the explosive tidbit. She's thrown off by the revelation, but she recovers before Brandi senses her shock. And revulsion. "Oh wow. I'd say you made out the best in the situation."

Our server stops by, interrupting the conversation. After ordering a Monte Cristo, Lala spends time regrouping. Should she pump Brandi for more information? The glint in the brunette's eyes frightens her, but she wants to know more about the connection between Karina and Dante. Maybe Brandi could provide details that would help the case.

After the last person orders, Lala goes for it. "So, where did you meet Dante?"

She gets a far-off look in her eyes. "I was a runner, at a club in Los Angeles. The Wishmaster's Sanctum. It was a gig I did on the weekends to supplement my income, but I didn't make much money, so I don't know why I kept doing it." She laughs, a bitter, jagged sound. "Oh yeah. Maybe it was the games I played that made it worthwhile." Glee replaces the wistfulness in her expression. She's thrilled to be sharing. "Most of the time, it was mixing up orders. Like if someone ordered a burger and fries, I'd get them a chicken sandwich and slaw. Stupid stuff like that. I'd time the delivery so it was close to showtime, and it was impossible to fit in a second run. The band members could either live with my mistakes or go hungry. The majority just shoveled the food down and didn't ask me for anything else the rest of the night, which I count as a win."

Brandi pauses to drink some water. She dabs the corners of her mouth with a napkin when she's done, then gets back to her story. "Special diets were the best. Not allergies, because I didn't want to kill anyone, but I loved the vegan and gluten-free people. I'd have so much fun messing with their food, giving them small bits of meat or cheese or bread. Whatever I could camouflage in their order. And while I watched them chow down, I'd imagine their reactions if they found out. The vegans would have a meltdown, of course, yelling at me about animal cruelty and the toxic food industry. Blah, blah, blah. And the gluten-free idiots would probably just pout because they have no idea what gluten is or the actual impact the protein has on their bodies." She leans back and crosses her arms, looking pleased with herself. "But I knew, no matter what, that all of them would get the shits later that night. And since number two isn't allowed on the bus, they'd be in big, uncomfortable, smelly trouble."

This time Lala can't mask her distress, and she winces at the revelation. "What the hell, Brandi? You could have done major damage. Why would you do something like that?"

"Because I could. And because a lot of the band members were arrogant, and I wanted to put them in their place. Someone had to do it, so why not me?" she asks.

Ugh. Way to victim blame. Lala shakes her head to refocus, and gross images of gastrointestinal distress fade from her thoughts. Thank goodness. There was no way she could have concentrated with those disgusting visions clogging her brain. She draws in a deep breath and releases it. Her exhale trembles the slightest bit. Brandi is really getting to her. She needs to pull it together.

As if sensing her fragility, Rory places a hand on Lala's back, stroking between her shoulder blades with his thumb. He makes a circular pattern. The gentle motion soothes her, and she draws strength from the contact. His touch reminds her of the good in the world. The compassion. Not every human is as mean-spirited as the pallid brunette sitting across from her. She's an anomaly, not the norm.

Lala glances at her friends, their faces reflecting the horror that still surged through her body, despite Rory's touch. Should she stop questioning Brandi? Maybe she'd gone too far. Karina's case is important, but not at the expense of the people Lala loves. Who knows what Brandi will reveal next. Depending on how terrible her words were, they could cause actual trauma to everyone listening.

"How about we change subjects? This is getting too intense for me," Lala says, hoping Brandi listens.

"Agreed," Maggie adds. Her voice is forceful, but her expression is not. Her drawn eyebrows and pinched mouth display the loathing she must feel.

"But I didn't answer Lala's question. She wanted to know how I met Dante, and I haven't gotten to that part yet." Brandi's arms clutch her torso tighter. "I promise to keep it short. And less disgusting."

Lala lifts her chin. "No. I'm fine without knowing. How about everyone else?" Heads nod around the table. "Maybe you can tell us another day. Drop it for now."

"Fine. Whatever. I'm just trying to be friendly." Brandi rises from her seat and strikes her fists against her thighs. "Sorry I'm not cool enough to be a tour wife. I thought you guys would be more welcoming, but you're just as snobby as I thought." She turns on her heel and stomps toward the entrance, nearly knocking into another customer on their way from the restroom. She whips around to shoot the group a menacing glare, then storms out of the restaurant, the bells hanging on the door tinkling behind her.

A lot happens in the next hour—the server brings their food, they eat, they pay, they walk to the port—but the six of them stay quiet, other than mumbling answers to questions about their meals or payment preferences. As they queue up to present their boarding credentials, Maggie breaks the silence. "Are we really going to let her ruin our fun? She's an awful person and we have to deal with her for the next week, but I think we should keep being ourselves, and doing our thing. She's not worth it."

Pearl beams a huge smile at her. "You're totally right, babe. Let's go back to being our goofy selves."

"Agreed," Lala says. "We just have to make sure she doesn't go near any of our meals."

Everyone laughs, and the elevated mood carries them up to the check-in window. By couple, they present their IDs and receive laminates, boat maps, and drink cards after the receptionist locates their names on the band list.

"Looks like Trev got some free drinks after all," Jake says as they head down the gangplank to board the boat.

"Too bad he's not here to get them." Rory checks the time on his phone. "Pretty soon, they'll open the terminal to general boarding. The idiot will have to wait in a super long line."

"Dude, as long as he's onboard before the ship leaves, we're good." Pearl shifts her backpack. "I definitely over-packed. This thing is heavy."

"Let's hurry to our room so you can drop it off. Then we can wander around and explore," Maggie says.

"Alright, let's get moving." Lala picks up the pace, and they reach the boat's entrance in less than a minute. They check in with their laminates. After that, each couple leaves to find their rooms. Jake and Nicole are on a separate deck, but Pearl and Maggie are on the seventh deck with Rory and Lala. They find their room first.

"See you in a few." Maggie waves and closes the door behind them.

Rory and Lala find number 7927, and he scans an app on his phone to enter. The space is small, of course, but there's a window. The light shining through gives the room a cheery air. "I'm glad we don't have an internal room. Looking out the window will be nice," Lala says.

"Arrrr. Don't you mean porthole?" Rory drops his carry-on and slides over to his wife. He wraps her in his arms. "I'm happy we're here together, mi amor. This should be fun."

"It will be fun. But only because the world's best husband is my cruise partner." She rises on her toes until their lips meet. They press into each other, and Lala melts into his kiss.

After a few seconds, he pushes back. His voice is deep. Sexy. Wanting. "You're hot. Do you think we have time for a quickie?"

"You're hot too, babe." She kisses the tip of his nose. "But we promised to meet everyone in five minutes." She looks at her watch. "And two of those minutes have already passed. Do you think we can get naked, plow, then get dressed in less than three minutes?"

"Yep," he takes her hand and shows her how.

Remarkably, they beat the clock, and they're above deck as the others emerge. Rory is a little flushed, and Lala's hair is rumpled, but everyone else shows hints of naughty time too. Guess they all had the same idea. The cruise seems to be going off with a bang.

Maggie scans their surroundings and points to the left. "Looks like a bar over there. Shall we start drinking?"

No one answers. They don't have to because the group strolls in the direction she pointed without words. They snag a table close to the railing, and Jake and Rory head to the bar to order the first round.

While Lala waits, she pulls out her phone for a quick check. It's lit up with notifications—four texts and an email. She opens the messages first. They're all from Ellen, sent while she and Rory were having their quickie.

ELLEN: It came!
ELLEN: forwarding the email your way. You're going to like what's on the report.
ELLEN: La! Where are you? Tell me what you think?
ELLEN: Hurry up and read it!!!!!!!!!

Her hands shake as she opens her email. The unread message is at the top.

Fwd: Wilder, Dante – Preliminary Toxicology Report

Oh my God, oh my God, oh my God. The report is finally here. Lala clicks the subject and the medical examiner's letter pops onto the screen. It's all formalities. Nothing worth spending time on. The attachment is what's important. She downloads the document and inhales the results with her eyes. The findings are unbelievable.

Lala's breath catches in her throat. Her heart beats a frenzied staccato. This can't be real.

A slower readthrough verifies what she saw the first time. There wasn't any deadly nightshade in Dante's blood. Other things were found, but the poison wasn't one of them.

She goes back to her texts and sends Ellen a reply.

LALA: She didn't do it!

ELLEN: Yep. This should clear her conspiracy charge since she didn't take any action to further the crime. Talking about something isn't enough.

ELLEN: I've already reached out to the prosecutor. Hopefully he'll be rational and just drop the charges. But there's a lot of pressure to solve this crime, so he might be a jerk and take this to court if he thinks the police can find something else to pin on Karina.

LALA: Ughhhhhh. That would be awful. Do your best, lady. You've got more than enough skills to turn this in Karina's favor.

ELLEN: I'm on it! Now, go enjoy your cruise.

LALA: Thank youuuuuuu

ELLEN: Oh, I did have another thought. If Karina's poison didn't kill Dante, who and what did? He had plenty of chemicals in his blood, so it may be self-induced...but La, what if it's another band member? You're on a boat with everyone who was in the room with him when he died.

ELLEN: It's just something to think about.

ELLEN: Be careful out there. Love you.

4 C's Reference Laboratory
62 Lily Lane
Collierville, GA 30159

Patient: Wilder, Dante   Age: 35   Sex: M

Physician: Philips, Aubree   Case #: 632488   Client: District 38 Medical Examiner

---

PRELIMINARY TOXICOLOGY
Specimen Collected: 02/07/2023

Test Name	Result	Units	Cutoff/Reporting Limit

VOLATILE PANEL

SPECIMEN TYPE: HEART BLOOD

Test Name	Result	Units	Cutoff/Reporting Limit
Ethanol	0.181	g/dL	0.010
Acetone	None Detected	mg/dL	7.5
Methanol	None Detected	mg/dL	15.0

BLOOD IMMUNOASSAY SCREEN

Test Name	Result	Units	Cutoff/Reporting Limit
Amphetamines	NEGATIVE	mg/L	0.100
Nightshade	NEGATIVE	mg/L	0.005
Barbiturates	NEGATIVE	mg/L	0.100
Cannabinoids	NEGATIVE	mg/L	0.050
Cocaine Metabolite	NEGATIVE	mg/L	0.050
Fentanyl	DETECTED *	mg/L	0.001
Nicotine Metabolite	DETECTED *	mg/L	0.075
Opiates	DETECTED *	mg/L	0.050

*Screening result suggests the need for further testing

Note: Preliminary results require confirmation testing. Specimens were intact upon receipt. Chain of custody has been maintained.

Reviewed by: Velma Aticas, MD | Date: 03/09/2023

Chapter 19 – Brandi

{March 13, 2023}

When Brandi reaches the tattoo studio, she calls Trev from the sidewalk, but the idiot does not pick up his phone. After a text is met with the same non-response, she barges into the shop, slamming the door on the way in. A blue-haired artist crouches over Trev's calf. His eyes follow her as she strides his way. "Can I help you?"

"No. But the idiot you're tattooing can." She slips past the half wall separating the lounge from the workstations. Trev faces away from the entrance, sitting backward in the leather chair. She stands where he can see her, less than a foot away. He cannot ignore her now. "Why didn't you answer your phone?"

He gestures to Blue Hair, who is still mean mugging her. "'Cause Brodie is laying down some ink. I think that's pretty obvious."

"Not good enough. Your arms and ears are free, so you could have answered my call without interrupting him. Or, at the very least, you could have sent a text." Brandi stomps her foot. "You left me with your friends, and they were total assholes. I was completely embarrassed, and I want you to do something about it."

Trev scoffs. "Brandi, you're not the nicest person to be around. I'm sure you acted crazy in front of them. Like you're doing right now."

"I am not acting crazy. But I'm about to." She steps out of his view and edges closer to Blue Hair. Small containers of ink rest on the table next to him, and before the guy can stop her, she picks up the red and white ones and spatters them onto Trev's hair. When the act is done, his black locks resemble a knockoff Jackson Pollok painting. "There. That's crazy." Both men stare at Brandi, mouths agape. Blue Hair pushes his feet on the ground, rolling his chair away.

He is afraid of her. Excellent. Maybe now she will get some respect. "Okay. Are you ready to listen?"

Trev's mouth slams shut. When he answers, his words are stilted. "Sure. I'll listen. Whatever will get you to leave the quickest."

Good enough for her. Brandi circles back around, planting herself in his sightline again. Her pointer finger jabs his chest. "Your friends treated me like garbage. They asked me a question and didn't give me a chance to answer. Who does that?" She moves her gaze between Trev and Blue Hair. Their eyes almost bug out. "I'll tell you who does that. Losers. Washed-up has-beens. Zeroes."

Trev shrinks from her touch. His voice is a full-on whine this time. "What do you want me to do, Brandi? I have to play with them on the boat, and I won't do anything to mess up our shows."

"Well, you don't have to play with Lala, Nicole, or Maggie." She lifts her eyebrows. "A little scare might teach them a lesson."

Trev's whine hits a higher octave. "Can we talk about this on the boat? Please. I want to help you, but I also need Brodie to finish this tattoo." He offers Brandi a grin, and he looks adorable—almost puppylike—but if he thinks his charm will win her over, he is wrong. She needs his support, not his worthless facial expressions.

But she must be logical. It would be smarter to discuss her revenge on the boat instead of inside the tattoo shop. Blue Hair seems like he might bolt at any second, and she bets he would run straight to the cops. She would rather not get arrested. Plus, there is one detail she needs to verify during check-in. Alone.

Brandi returns Trev's smile. "You're right. Let's talk about this later." She bends down and kisses his forehead. Her lips land next to a splash of red. "Sorry about the paint. Hope you both can forgive my outburst."

"Forgiven," Trev says. "See you in an hour."

She lets the boys get back to playtime and strolls to the port. When she steps into the cruise line's massive terminal, three people wait in line to check in. By the time she winds through the zig-zagging queue, one of the three has gone up to the counter. Thank goodness she beat the general admission rush. The baby is using her bladder as a punching bag, and she needs the restroom soon.

Two minutes pass, and the couple in front of her finishes. She scurries to the receptionist. "Checking in for Brandi Monner. I'm with A Box of Stars."

The worker smiles. "Welcome to Rage on the Waves. May I see your ID?" He takes the passport she slides under his window and types something into his computer. "I see you're sharing a room with Trev Devlin. Is that correct?"

"Yes. We traveled separately, though. He'll be here soon." She peeks at the receptionist's name tag. "Thanks, Bradley."

"You're welcome, Ms. Monner." Bradley's fingers fly across the keyboard. "Do you have a credit card for onboard charges? The band gets four drinks comped a day, but anything above that amount will need to be covered personally."

"Oh, I won't be drinking."

"Well, ma'am, I'll still need a card for any extras." He flashes a smile. "But if you don't purchase anything, you won't be charged."

Brandi reaches into her purse and removes her debit card. Tomorrow, she will have access to loads of money, but this morning, her available balance is less than $500. Since she found out about Dante's estate, she's burned through her salary preparing for the start of her post-Trev life.

For the past three weeks, every time she made a purchase for her future, jolts of bliss zipped through her body. It was fun buying things for herself. And even more fun getting stuff for the baby. Her son is already spoiled.

But the receptionist does not need to know any of that. He just wants an account for incidentals. She lifts the plastic rectangle where he can see it. "Is a debit card okay?"

"Sure is. We put a hold on it for $100 but release the funds as soon as the boat returns to Miami." Bradley reaches for the card, and she places it into his hand. "Thank you." He swipes the plastic and returns it. "Do you have any questions, Ms. Monner?"

"Just one. About my early departure. Is everything set?"

Bradley punches a few keys, then nods. "You're good to go." He shuffles through a plastic box and pulls out a small manilla envelope with her name typed on the front. "In here, you'll find your laminate, a ship map, and your drink card. Download the Rage on the Wave app and use the information on the back of your laminate to log in. You'll use the app for your room key and when you check on and off the boat at any ports." He prints something from the computer and folds it into the envelope. "This paper contains the information for your early disembarkation. Bring it with you when we reach your final destination. The crew at the port of entry will know what to do." He hands the packet over.

"You're awesome." She removes each item from the envelope, giving them a once over. Everything is in order. "Thank you again."

"My pleasure. Have fun on the cruise. Don't be afraid to get your rage on!" He throws up metal horns, and she returns the gesture. "Rock on, Ms. Monner."

"You too, Bradley."

With her carry-on and purse in hand, she leaves the terminal and exits onto the sidewalk leading to the ship's gangplank. The vessel is ginormous, dwarfing the others around it. How many people can fit on a boat that size? Probably four or five thousand, which is way too many.

Normally, a crowd that big would push Brandi's anxiety to the max. But not today. This cruise marks the beginning of her future, and even sharing space with thousands is not going to bring her down. Only positive thoughts from here on out. Good vibes all the way, even though that means ditching her plans for revenge. Lala, Maggie, and Nicole are lucky she changed her mind. She does not want bad karma ruining her future.

At the ship's entry, she takes out her laminate. A tatted-up crew member scans her in and delivers a breakdown of the evening's events. "Welcome aboard. There's a buffet and cocktails on the Lido deck until 5:00. The Set Sail Party kicks off after that, and the first concert begins at 7:00. Sans Dong will be playing, followed by Downtonal. Should be rocking."

"Sounds great," she says while hurrying through the entrance. The urge to pee had faded during check-in, but now, it was demanding attention. An arrow points to a staircase on the right, and she ascends the steps to an elevator bank. After checking the app, she takes a lift to the fifth floor, squirming the whole way. The doors open to loud carpeting and a hallway that stretches for days. Getting lost here would be scary.

Signage tells her to head to the left, so she speeds along the yellow and green carpet until room 5536 comes into view. The app lets her inside, and she races to the bathroom, yanking her leggings down during the sprint. The bathroom is tiny, barely larger than a closet, but it has enough space for her to relieve herself. And good lord, it feels amazing.

While the liquid drains from her body, she prods her belly. "Take it easy on my bladder, little guy. Practice your roundhouses on another organ next time, okay?" Her skin presses outward. It is the first time she's seen his movement. How freaking cool.

And dangerous.

If Trev notices her pregnancy before they reach Belize, she is in big trouble. He would freak. Like absolutely lose his mind. And who knows how big his reaction would be. It could be something as annoying as a tantrum or he could go the violent route. Would he hurt Brandi or the baby? She is not sure and does not want to find out.

Her voice is calm when she speaks to her son again. "Hey, little man, can you take it easy for a few more days? Mommy's going to take us on a nice vacation, but you have to stay hidden until we get off the boat." Again, he pushes on her skin, but after the nudge, he stills. "Yes, stay quiet. Or at least kick softer."

She finishes on the toilet and washes her hands in the miniature sink. A peek in the mirror makes her cringe. Brandi's paleness stands out in the bathroom lighting, the harsh glow offsetting every bit of tan she gained over the weekend. Gross. How come she looks so sick? She rummages through her carry on, remove her tattered makeup bag for some TLC.

A swipe of blush gives her cheeks the color they need. Strokes of bronzer repair her suntan. Now, she's presentable. She tucks her carry-on away after snagging her beach bag from inside. Time to head to the Lido deck. The pool is calling her name.

The colorful flooring leads her to the elevator, and she takes a car up several floors. Wind tousles her hair as soon as she steps onto the deck. Tropical music floats on the breeze. People roam around, drinks in hand. The party has begun.

After passing under a towering arch, the pool comes into view. Navy loungers line up in rows around the gigantic rectangle. Since only the bands are on board right now, the majority are empty. Brandi gravitates toward an isolated one away from the action. The chair is wedged into a corner, tucked away from any prying eyes. Knowing the others, she guesses that they are already enjoying drinks, exchanging stories, maybe talking smack about her. They are somewhere on this deck, most likely by the bar, and evading their company is Brandi's main goal until she gets off the boat. Running into Lala or Maggie or Nicole would kill the good vibes she had promised herself, and day one is way too early for that to happen.

Towel on the chair, hat on her head, phone in her hand. Brandi props the top half of the lounger at an angle and sits with her legs stretched out, soaking up the sun. Currently, her favorite pastime is scrolling through real estate listings, daydreaming about fancy houses she can't afford. She still wasn't sure where she would end up after her son was born. California was out.

Twenty-five years there was too much.

She has researched Washington and Vermont, and both states seem family oriented. She has also read about other countries. Sweden and Spain top that list. Her age and income made her a good candidate for citizenship, but is moving that far away smart? She is no contact with her family, and she has zero friends since Karina betrayed her. People are not keeping her tethered to the states.

Maybe two months in Belize will open her mind to living outside the United States. Brandi paid for a rental, a beautiful beach house in Ambergris Caye, and she foresees existing on a mellow wavelength until it's time to return home and deliver the baby. Days spent walking along the beach will be the best type of therapy. The waves will decompress her anxious mind.

There are only three days until she leaves the boat, earlier than everyone else. Three days until she reaches her personal slice of paradise.

At poolside, she browses mansions in Burlington and Seattle, hearting the ones with big backyards and quality school districts. Even though the giant houses would break her budget, it's nice to have examples for the future. And who knows? Maybe she will get a raise at work. Or maybe the investments she makes with Dante's money will elevate her to upper-middle class. A lot could go right.

There are sounds around her—water frolics and the low hum of conversation—but they fade into white noise. After an hour, her focus is broken. An angry shout rings out from the bar. Then the scraping of chairs. When she looks up, she recognizes the person yelling. It is Trev. Of course, her boyfriend is causing the chaos. Why does he have to make a scene?

From what she can tell, Trev's shouts are directed at his bandmates and their wives. Five of the group sit around a cocktail table, but Jake stands chest to chest with Brandi's boyfriend, and neither one of them is backing down. Was Trev defending her? Although she had pushed thoughts of revenge aside, her boyfriend might be acting on his own against the ABOS brats. Pleasure surges through her at the thought. Someone is finally sticking up for her.

She needs a closer look.

Without drawing attention to herself, she tugs her hat lower and tears toward the bar. Her feet barely skim the boat's surface, just her tippy toes in a fast, silent run. Thank you, third-grade ballet class. Knowing how to sneak gracefully is a valuable skill.

Brandi spots a turquoise column next to the group's table. There's room behind it, and she can reach the obscure alcove without being spotted. A few more tiptoes bring her to the hiding place. Once she is concealed in the shadows, a peek around the curved barrier reveals her view. Yes. It's the perfect perspective. Her breaths become excited huffs as the action unfolds.

Jake, face red and sweaty, pushes his chest against Trev's. "You need to back down bro."

"And what if I don't?" Trev asks.

"We'll play without you tomorrow." Jake glances at the others. "Everyone else cool with that? I guarantee we can find someone on this boat who can substitute. Your drum parts aren't that difficult." Pearl and Rory nod in answer. "Alright. It's decided. Either sit your ass down, or we'll replace you."

Trev's shoulders droop. "I can't believe you're trying to pull a Dante on me. First you kick him out, and he gets killed, and now you're threatening me with the same." He backs into a chair. "Whatever."

"Dude, seriously?" Rory shakes his head while boring his eyes into the drummer. "We had nothing to do with Dante's murder. And why are you even bringing that up? We're focusing on the scene you're causing, not our former singer. Stop trying to shift the attention off yourself."

"Tell us why you came shouting out of nowhere," Jake says as he drops back into his seat. "We were enjoying ourselves, but we're not anymore."

This is where Trev is going to tell them he is defending Brandi's honor. She holds her breath in anticipation. She does not want to miss a word.

"How come you put me in the shittiest room? Everyone got a window except me. You left me in the dark," Trev says in his patented whine. "We need to make this right. I should take priority over most of these people. They can downgrade a guest or someone from a less popular band."

He is not protecting Brandi. He is trying to weasel his way into a room upgrade. She squeezes her eyes shut and bites her lip. His selfishness shouldn't be a surprise, yet here she is, upset that he put his needs before hers. Again. When would she learn?

Before Trev makes her angrier, Brandi opens her eyes and runs toward the elevator bank, dodging people and buffet tables. More guests have boarded the boat, so it takes minutes for a free car to open. When one does, she rushes in and presses the close door button, hoping to move off before anyone joins her. But she's too late.

An arm shoots through the door when the gap is a few inches. After the metal slides open, Trev steps into the cart. "Why were you running away?"

A lie falls from her mouth. "Bathroom. I need to go."

"There are some up here." He gestures to the Lido deck as the doors slide shut.

"I was going to change out of my pool clothes too." She peers down at her sundress. "Wouldn't something dressier be better for the launch party?"

"I guess." He leans against the side of the elevator. "Don't expect anything formal from me. I have an image to keep up. Fans expect a certain look."

The sarcasm slips out before she can stop it. "I bet they do."

"What's that supposed to mean?" His brow creases. "I have plenty of fans, you know."

"Uh-huh. Tons and tons." The elevator dings, and as soon as the door opens, Brandi steps into the hall. Trev follows close behind. Her phone unlocks their room, but her boyfriend pushes past her before she can cross the threshold. "What's going on? You have a major attitude," Brandi accuses.

"You psycho, don't you remember embarrassing me in the tattoo shop? I really had to sweet talk Brodie. He was set on calling the police and filing a report against you." Trev pushes her shoulder and lowers his face into hers. "Maybe I should have let him. Then you and your best friend Karina would have another thing in common. Besides banging Dante."

He's always throwing Dante in her face. Brandi narrows her eyes. "Well, Karina might be getting out soon, smart guy. Lala mentioned something at breakfast."

The color drains from his face. "What did she say?"

"I don't know. She mentioned a lab report. Why don't you ask her?"

"Maybe I will." Trev's eyes dart around, until they reach the bathroom. "Think you can clean up after yourself? There's already makeup on the sink, and we haven't even set sail yet. I hate living with such a slob. It's nasty."

"Yeah. Let me clean up my mess." She takes the few steps toward her makeup bag and yanks it from the counter. "See? That was easy." She twirls to face him. "You're really going to call me a slob when you wear the same socks two days in a row? And how about the seventy-five vape cartridges in your closet? Saving trash like that is something a hoarder would do. You're disgusting."

Trev leaps forward, pushing Brandi against the wall. "Stay out of my stuff, you nosey bitch." His breath is hot and shallow. The dark brown of his irises is not visible, only his pupils. His fury radiates onto her skin.

She has been wary of her boyfriend but never afraid. His sudden anger changes this. In the confined space, she is terrified—for her and for her child. The situation requires a change of tactic. No more sarcasm or irritation. It is time to enter placate mode.

Brandi's voice is a whisper. "Trev, I'm sorry. I never should have snooped. That was wrong." She bats her lashes and lowers her dress straps. "How can I make it up to you?"

Usually, he is a sucker for flirting, but not today. "Leave me alone, Brandi. That's all I want from you. Some peace and quiet."

He presses her into the wall. Hard. Her chest tightens, and the edge of her vision darkens. She is going to pass out. Fighting will not work too well. Her position puts her at a disadvantage. Any kicks would land on his thighs, not his more sensitive bits. So, she gives in and closes her eyes for the inevitable. Hopefully, he will leave her alone when she loses consciousness. This is his first time being violent. She is not sure what to expect from him.

Instead of taking it further, Trev releases her. "I'm going upstairs for a drink. Don't bother joining." He storms to his carry-on and rummages around until he pulls out his vape. He tucks the orange rectangle into his pocket on his way out of the room.

When the door slams, Brandi rushes to the mirror to check for bruises. Her skin is pink where Trev's hands squeezed, but the marks look like they will fade. Relief floods through her body. That could have been so much worse. He could have hurt her, and no one would have known. She could be lying on the floor right now, bleeding and broken, gasping her last breaths.

Brandi's relief is replaced by fatigue. Her limbs become heavy, so she crawls into the bed, pulling the covers up to her neck. A quick nap will revive her. Gruesome could-have-beens will fade from her brain after some sleep. She uses a remote to switch off the lights. She closes her eyes and pushes the dark thoughts away. It takes time, but eventually, blankness replaces the negativity, and she drifts into a deep slumber.

***

There are no windows in their room, so she wakes hours later in a pitch-black cavern. The nap has calmed her nerves, the cruelness Trev displayed a faded memory. Her mind must be in protective mode.

When she fell asleep, the boat was still docked, but now there was a gentle motion underfoot. They must have set sail while she was passed out. A glance at her phone tells her it is 7:30. She not only missed the launch party but also the beginning of the first show. Trev's violence shut her down big time, but the nap helped her reboot. Now, she is ready for music. Some good songs will put her on the road to normal.

She throws a sweater over her sundress and pulls on gold sandals. Hopefully, there is still time left in Sans Dong's set. An all-chick thrash metal band sounds amazing and just the type to lift her spirits. A little dose of girl power. Trev will be watching from backstage, so she should be good if she joins the general crowd. He is now part of her "to-be avoided list." Bedtime will be an issue, but she will figure that out before the evening ends.

Her purse goes on her shoulder, and she heads out the door. The carpet is even brighter after a four-hour nap. She squints and strolls to the elevators. By the time she reaches the bank, her eyes have adjusted to the electric colors.

Everyone's upstairs partying, so a car comes within seconds. She steps in and presses the button for the Lido deck. Excited bubbles swirl in her stomach. It is finally time to enjoy herself. Thank goodness.

She makes it two floors before the elevator stops. The doors slide open, and Lala is waiting with a glass in her hand. Her cheeks are flushed. "Oh hey, Brandi. Mind if I join you?" Lala doesn't wait for a reply. She barges into the car and stands close enough for Brandi to smell the alcohol she's drinking.

Lala holds out her cup. "Want some? It's a hurricane, and it's really strong."

"I'll pass." Brandi backs away from the spicy scent of the rum. Her nose has gotten more sensitive during pregnancy. Overpowering smells are nauseating. "You weren't very nice to me at breakfast. Why would you offer me your drink?"

"'Cause I'm tipsy." She laughs. "But seriously, we'll be on the boat together for the next week. Everything will be better if we get along."

"I guess so." They reach deck 11. "Where are you watching the show?"

"There's a balcony over there." Lala points to a spot to the left of the stage, right over the pool. "Wanna join?" Lala frowns. "Unless you're going to watch with Trev."

"I'd rather not be near him right now." A surge of panic startles her. Brandi thought she was over Trev's outburst, but apparently it still bothers her.

Lala looks Brandi up and down, pausing when she gets to her eyes. "Are you okay? It looks like you were crying."

Warmth replaces the panic, and tears almost spill from her eyes. It is nice to be asked about. Trev had not paid attention to her mood in forever. He was always too lost in his own happenings. Brandi blinks back the tears. "I'm fine. But I've been better."

Out of nowhere, Lala pulls her into a hug. "We might not get along, but I still don't want you to get hurt. Keep that in mind." She heads in the direction she pointed. A few steps away she turns toward Brandi yelling over the music. "You coming?"

Does Brandi want to hang with them? They made her feel terrible this morning, but Maggie had been nice to her on their shopping trip yesterday. And Lala was being sweet right now. Maybe they were not so bad. She has heard pregnancy hormones can mess with a woman's emotions. What if she overreacted at breakfast? It would be nice to watch the concert with people she knows instead of strangers crowding her personal space.

"Yes. I'm coming." She trails after Lala until they reach a spiral staircase. She points at it and then up, and Brandi climbs the steps behind her. At the top, scarlet patio furniture is arranged in an arc pointed at the stage. Besides Trev, everyone from ABOS is on the balcony, sitting in the cushy seats. Maggie and Nicole do a double take when they notice Lala's guest, but they quickly replace their shock with grins. Brandi finds an empty chair and leans back to enjoy the music. The sound up here is great.

She catches thirty minutes of Sans Dong, who is amazing, and Downtonal's entire set. A cocktail waiter pops up to the balcony every twenty minutes, and on his second trip, she orders a virgin daiquiri. As the chilly deliciousness slides down her throat, she is overcome with happiness. Life is beautiful. She will not let Trev ruin her future.

On the water, the stars shimmer brighter than they do at home. Brandi turns her head left and right. There is nothing but ocean as far as she can see. Floating on the ocean is serene. The music drifting on the breeze adds a surreal element to the evening. This is perfection.

Right before the last song, the waiter strides over, drink in hand. "Ms. Monner?" She nods. "A gentleman sent this to you. Enjoy." He sets the glass, a tall one topped with a pineapple garnish, on the table next to her chair. When he leaves, Brandi grabs the cup and inspects its contents.

It is frozen like her other drink, but it is definitely not virgin. The overpowering scent of alcohol is her first clue. There is also a layer of dark liquid topping the daiquiri. Probably an extra shot. It looks like someone ordered Brandi a grown-up drink with lots of rum. Before pregnancy, she would have downed this in a heartbeat. But not now. She is staying sober until after the baby is born.

Trashing the daiquiri would be wasteful, so she stands and brings the beverage to Lala. "Someone bought this for me, but I'm not drinking right now. Do you want it?"

"Someone bought this for you?" She raises her eyebrows. "Specifically, you?"

"Yeah. Our server brought it up."

"Weird. Have you talked to anyone else besides us since you got on the boat?"

Brandi shakes her head. "No. Just you guys. And Trev."

Lala grabs the drink. "Let's use a screening strip on this sucker. It will test for GHB and Ketamine." She takes a small package from her purse and rips into the plastic wrapper. She removes a small white card. "I've carried these since college after I caught a guy trying to drug my roommate's beer." Lala dips her finger in the daiquiri, then drops liquid on the card's two sensors. "Just need to let this dry."

"What are you guys doing?" Maggie asks from behind. Brandi sidesteps to give her a better view. Maggie slides into the space.

"Yeah. What's going on?" Nicole wedges herself on Maggie's other side.

"An unknown person ordered a drink for Brandi. We're testing it to make sure it's not spiked with something." Lala stares at the card. "The strip will darken if there's anything bad in the drink."

They stare at the sensors as the evening breeze dries the card. After a minute, Lala smiles. "Looks like there's nothing in the daiquiri besides booze. Who wants it?"

"Wait." Nicole reaches into her purse. She brings something out, concealed in her fist. "Let's test for one more thing." She opens her hand, and a small plastic container rests on her palm. "Jake isn't using anymore, but I still keep these with me. Force of habit, I guess." She removes a thin strip. "Stick this in the drink, wavy side down. Let it sit for fifteen seconds."

Lala does as she's instructed. When she removes the strip from the drink, a single pink line shows. "What's that mean, Nicole?"

Her eyes are huge when she answers. "It means there's fentanyl in that drink, La. You might want to throw it away."

Wednesday, March, 8 • 12:34 PM

DYLAN: Anyone have any questions about the cruise? Everything performance wise is all set. Trev, you just need to bring your cymbals.

DYLAN: But other than that, do you have any questions about the boat or the meet and greet Wednesday?

PEARL: all good here. excited to play again

RORY: How much can we pack? Is there a bag limit? The wife wants to bring a lot of clothes, but I want to make sure it's cool first.

DYLAN: Two suitcases and one carry on per person.

RORY: I'll let Lala know.

TREV: will they be searching our bags? was thinking of sneaking some booze on board. Maybe some party fuel too

DYLAN: They search random suitcases and x-ray the carry-ons, so it's not worth the risk dude. We got 4 drink coupons, which is more than most bands. Don't sneak anything on. If you get caught, we're all screwed.

TREV: maybe i won't

JAKE: No questions here, D-man! See you guys on Friday. Practice is going to be killer.

Chapter 20 – Nicole

{March 13, 2023}

Maggie, Lala, and Brandi stare at Nicole when she tells them what the results mean. She can read their thoughts. *Her husband was addicted to opioids. He must be the one who sent the tainted drink.*

Nicole doesn't blame them for what they're thinking, but it's not true. Jake hasn't used in over a year. He still takes weekly drug tests to ease his wife's mind, although she's told him it wasn't necessary. So, he's clean. Without a doubt.

That meant someone else was responsible for Brandi's almost-poisoning. Someone on the boat. "Who brought you the drink? Was it the server who's been checking on us all night?" she asks, hoping to jolt everyone into motion.

Brandi nods. "Yes. He said a gentleman sent it to me."

"Let's ask him if he knows who the gentleman is," Nicole says.

"Let me tell Pearl where I'll be. And to keep an eye out for anything suspicious." Maggie shivers and hugs her gray cardigan against her. "I can't believe someone tried to hurt you, Brandi."

"Kill," Lala says. "Brandi would have died if she drank the daiquiri." She picks up the glass with the fentanyl inside. "I'm not going to throw this out. I'm going to have Rory guard it. This is evidence."

Everyone breaks off to tell their spouses what's happening. Except Brandi. She stands in place, looking frightened. And cold. Her sweater and dress aren't enough to block the ocean chill.

Nicole pulls her eyes away from Brandi and heads Jake's way. He's lounging in a chair facing the stage. "Hon, listen. This is going to sound bonkers, but I swear it's true."

He takes a swig of beer. "What's up?"

"Someone tried to poison Brandi. And—"

"Stop." He sets his bottle down and stands in front of her. "Coley, are you serious?"

"I am."

Jake's eyes widen. "We need to report this to the captain or the boat police, or whoever is in charge on a cruise." He reaches out, placing his hands on her shoulders. "If there's a dangerous person onboard, we have to let someone know."

"But I don't want them questioning you." Nicole runs a hand through his wavy blond hair and tries to keep her voice steady. "It was fentanyl, hon, and you have a history with the drug. They'd see that as suspicious."

He narrows his eyes. "They can question me all they want. I had nothing to do with poisoning Brandi. This is the first I'm hearing of it."

"I know that. But the police won't. They'll need to interrogate you before they clear you, and that'll waste time." She removes his right hand from her shoulder and brings it to her lips. "Let me and the wives investigate a little bit. That way, we'll have a direction to send the police."

His shoulders sag. "Okay, but promise you'll be safe. And turn your location tracking on." He drops his hands and opens his arms. Nicole steps into them as he lowers his head for a kiss, a sweet, soft kiss. Her body melts into his.

When he pulls away, his eyes are dark. "I hate this, Coley. If anything happens to you, I don't know what I'd do."

"Nothing is going to happen, hon. We're just going to ask our server some questions and do some surveilling. Lala does this all the time at work," she fibs, praying he doesn't know she's a psychologist and not an investigator.

"Hurry back. I'll stay here with Rory, Pearl, and the crew. We'll keep our eyes open from above."

She plants a kiss on his cheek. "See you soon. I love you."

"Love you too, Coley."

His face is so sad that she almost stays with him. But then she glances at Brandi and sees her shivering. The brunette isn't a nice person. In fact, she's meaner than a two-headed snake. But that doesn't mean she deserves to be murdered. Helping her is the right thing to do. And it will take the heat off Nicole's husband.

She waves to Jake and heads toward Brandi. Maggie and Lala join them within a minute. The group huddles together to work through their plan. Lala takes the lead. "Step one, we need to question the waiter. I'll do the talking. Step two will be determined by what he says. Hopefully, he'll remember who sent the drink." She takes a deep breath. "You ladies ready?" She looks at each of them and they nod in turn. "Let's do this."

As a group they traipse down the stairs, with Nicole and Lala in front, and Brandi and Maggie behind them. The main deck is crowded. Too crowded. After the bands played, a DJ took over and there were flailing couples all over the dance floor. The four women weave between the pairs, locating their server near the bar. He's hustling and carrying a bucket of beer and a bottle of champagne. They wait until after he delivers the booze to corner him.

Lala nudges Brandi in front of the server. "Hi there. Do you remember taking this lovely lady a drink?"

He squints at Brandi's face. "Maybe, but it's been crazy busy all night. My memory might be off."

Lala snags a twenty-dollar bill from her purse. "I forgot to tip you during your last trip upstairs. Sorry about that"—she leans close to his name badge—"Connor." She tucks the money into his shirt pocket.

Connor takes another look at Brandi. He studies her features, squinting at her face. Finally, he nods. "Yeah, I brought her a drink. A strawberry daiquiri."

"Do you remember who ordered it for her?" Lala asks.

"It was a dude. With dark hair. That's all I remember." He glances at the bar, where the drinks have started to pile up. "I need to go. I'm working fifteen tables tonight, and three of their orders just came up."

"Wait." Lala reaches into her purse again, this time coming out with a hot pink business card. "If you think of anything else, text my cell."

Connor takes the offered card and slips it into the pocket with the twenty. He salutes with two fingers. "Got it. Now excuse me, ladies." He hustles to the bar and transfers a dozen beers and cocktails onto his tray.

Nicole steps in front of the group, eyes wide. "I hate to accuse anyone, but what about Trev? He definitely has dark hair, plus he has a temper. I've seen it on tour before." She turns to Brandi. "Did anything happen between you two today? Anything that might have made him angry?"

She hesitates before answering. "Well, we had a fight in our room. And he held me against the wall. He's yelled at me before, but this was the first time he's put his hands on me." Brandi lowers her head and her voice. "I didn't fight back."

"It's okay, Brandi. You have nothing to be ashamed of. Most people freeze when they're facing violence." Nicole reaches over and takes her hand. "Did he say anything before he hurt you? Or during?"

"He was talking about how messy I was, and I threw some of his gross habits back at him. Like how he wears socks for two days in a row. And how he hoards empty vape cartridges." She grimaces. "I hate the habit so much, but I put up with it because he usually goes outside to smoke. But having like, fifty used cartridges in our closet is too much. I can't stand it."

"According to Jake, he uses his vape like a pacifier," Nicole says.

"Yeah. He's not exaggerating. The disgusting thing goes everywhere with him." Brandi raises her eyebrows. "When I said Trev smokes outside, that doesn't include the last month and a half. Ever since Dante died, he uses the thing constantly. I have to pry it out of his hand before bed. What a turn-off."

"Do you think your argument made him mad enough to murder?" Maggie gags. "Asking that makes me want to take a shower."

Nicole glances at Lala, but she seems lost in thought. Usually, she's a talker, and is even chattier when the topic is domestic violence, her specialty. But now, she's quietly peering at her phone. This is way outside her norm. Nicole wonders what she's thinking about.

She tunes back into Brandi. The younger woman's coppery eyes brim with tears. "I've never seen him as mad as he was earlier. But was he angry enough to kill? I don't know. That level has to be different for everyone, right?" She bites her lip. "He was furious, though. And he said he was going to get a drink, which probably got him even angrier. Alcohol is not his friend."

"Let's find Trev. Then we can question him." Nicole gestures at the three women. "There are four of us and only one of him, so it's not like he could hurt us all. We'd be safe. The numbers are on our side."

Maggie nods. "I'm in."

"Me too," Brandi says. "If he did this to me, I want to know.

"Lala? Are you alright?" Nicole nudges her shoulder, and Lala's eyes refocus.

Her tone is spacey, like she's still lost in thought. "Sorry…there's an idea dancing just outside my perception, and I'm trying to catch it." She looks from Nicole to Maggie to Brandi. "I'm in, ladies. Let's find this creep."

Their first stop is the bar. Brandi pulls up a photo of Trev on her phone and asks the bartender if he was there. "Have you seen my husband? It's time to take his medicine, but I can't find him."

After a moment, the bartender answers. "Yeah. He downed a few shots and took off about ten minutes ago." She points to a door marked Employees Only. "I'm assuming he's with one of the bands since he went through there. Regular guests aren't allowed to use the crew corridors."

"Did he order a drink for me? I asked him to grab me a daiquiri, but he hasn't brought it to me yet." Brandi leans onto the bar and rolls her eyes. She's the picture of an annoyed wife.

"Most times, when a husband says he's going to do something for his wife, he gets distracted and forgets. But your man didn't. He ordered the drink and took it with him when he left." The bartender throws back her head and laughs. "Seems like he forgot the most important part, though. Bringing it to you. He was so close to getting it right, yet still so far away."

"Yep. That's Trev. Always forgetting something." Brandi backs away from the bar. "Thanks for your help. Hope you make all the tips tonight."

"Thanks. And good luck finding him. This ship is huge, so it won't be an easy task," she says before turning to a waving customer.

Lala motions the group to a quiet spot behind a turquoise pillar. "I thought of the thing that was bothering me. There's no subtle way to say this, so I'll just say it." She inhales, then releases the breath. "I think Trev killed Dante."

"Wait. Weren't they friends?" Brandi asks.

"Frenemies is a better term. But when you mentioned the empty vape cartridges in your closet, something sparked in my brain." Lala pulls out her phone and lights up the screen. "I got Dante's lab results today. I just reread them, and the hit for nicotine metabolite jumped out this time. According to the tox report, it was found in huge quantities. Way more than you'd see in a smoker's blood." She thrusts the phone out. "Take a look."

They lean close, peering at the screen. Nicole sees the nicotine level, but there's also numbers for fentanyl and opioids. "What about the other drugs?"

Brandi answers. "Dante was probably drunk and high when he showed up to practice. The man loved his whisky and downers."

"We'll have to wait for confirmation testing to see if the other drugs were fatal. The screening test is extra sensitive, so it picks up casual use too." She darkens her phone. "But not for nicotine. The levels here are toxic. It's more than enough to kill."

"Should we tell the others?" Maggie asks.

"Text them as we go. The bartender pointed us in the right direction, and I'd hate to lose the trail." Lala heads toward the employee door. She unlocks her phone again, finds the cruise app, then holds it to the sensor. When the light blinks green, she pushes the door open. "Thank goodness they gave us access."

Nicole enters the corridor first, followed by Brandi, then Maggie. Lala closes the door behind them. They take a moment to acclimate to their new environment. The hallway is huge, at least ten feet wide, and who knows how long. Lights and white walls add to the size. The brightness contrasts with the evening they just left. Nicole's eyes adjust slowly to the sudden glow.

Ahead of them, at an intersection, a trio of uniformed men pass by. They're talking animatedly and don't notice the four women huddled at the entrance. After their voices fade, Lala steps forward. "I have no idea how we'll find him, but we might as well start searching."

"Do you think there's a crew bar somewhere?" Brandi asks. "I feel like he'd try hiding somewhere with alcohol."

"Good thinking. Since he already started drinking, he'll want to keep it going." Lala runs after the men who passed by. "Excuse me. Excuse me, guys," she shouts.

She sprints ahead and turns right at the intersection. She's out of view, but they can hear voices discussing something. When she trots back, she's grinning. "There are three crew bars and the first is up ahead. We go down this hallway, and take the first staircase we see, down two flights, and voila, a bar." She looks at Brandi. "A smoker's bar."

They race down the corridor, scanning the walls for a stairwell. They pass two intersections and several employees, who give them odd stares, but don't try to stop them. When the hallway ends in a T, they finally see the stairs at the edge of the left turn. Lala starts toward them, but Maggie stops her. "Hold on. Let me text Pearl. Someone needs to know where we're going." Her thumbs tap out a lengthy message, and she hits send. "Let me make sure it goes through." After a moment, it does. She tucks the phone in her back pocket. "Okay. I'm ready."

They descend two flights and stop outside the tavern's door. A window gives them a view inside. The lighting is dim, but there are several groups of people sitting at high-top tables. Trails of smoke float throughout the space, and drift toward an opening next to the bar. "I'm going to have to wash my hair after going in there. Yuck," Lala says.

"Tell me about it. It looks miserable in there." Nicole lowers her voice and leans toward the others. "What if Brandi stays out here while we search for Trev? If he's in there, we can tell him something happened to her. We'll see how he reacts."

Brandi gives her shoulder a squeeze. "Yes. Do that. See how the asshole reacts to bad news about me." She looks around for a place to hide, but there's nothing visible. "I'll go up one flight and wait on the landing. You have three minutes. If you don't come out by then, I'm coming in after you."

Lala nods. "Excellent plan. See you soon." She gives Maggie and Nicole a look while they wait for Brandi to climb the stairs. When all is silent, they push inside.

Smoke overwhelms Nicole as soon as she enters. She breathes through her mouth while scanning the tables. There are more men than women seated, more choices for our villain, so splitting up makes sense. It will be more efficient. She points to the left side of the room, making sure Maggie and Lala see the gesture before she peels off.

She stalks the tables along the perimeter. No one wears a uniform, which makes identifying non-crewmembers more difficult. She approaches the first table, but the two men seated there look nothing like Trev. Same with the second, third, and fourth. She's striking out.

Nicole loops around and starts on the next row of high tops. The first three aren't matches, but then she spots a man and woman hunched over an ashtray at the last table. From behind, the guy resembles Trev. He's got long dark hair, a slender build, and he's wearing a leather jacket. Nicole approaches slowly, not wanting to alert the couple to her presence until she's had time to scope them out. A few more steps bring her behind the woman. She holds her breath, partially to block out the smoke, partially to conceal her presence. After thirty seconds, the man raises his head.

And he's not Trev. Dang it. Where can he be?

A noise at the bar interrupts her frustration. Lala is talking to someone on a stool, and their voices are raised. Nicole rushes over, and Maggie meets her there. The man yelling at Lala is facing away from her, but she recognizes his voice. And his reflection in the mirror behind the bar. Lala found him.

"Leave me alone," Trev shouts, his words slurred. He pushes up from his seat, stumbling as he moves. He grabs the bar to steady himself. "I came down here to get away from everyone, but you followed me."

"But Brandi's hurt, Trev. Don't you want to help her?" Lala asks.

"I don't care about that bitch. Whatever happened to her, she deserved it." He staggers toward the exit but stops when Brandi bursts through the door.

"What did you put in my drink, Trev? Tell me." Her eyes bore into her boyfriend. He shifts from foot to foot under her glare.

"Nothing. I didn't do nothing." His whine is piercing. "You're the one who hurt me. I had a right to defend myself."

"I hurt you?" Brandi steps closer to him. "You're delusional."

"You hurt me when you lied to me. About the bastard baby you're carrying." Trev takes a step back, his body bent as far away from Brandi as possible. "Yeah, I knew about you and Dante. He told me everything. How he knocked you up after one shot. How he was going to take the baby from you as soon as it was born." The color leaves Brandi's face, and uncertainty fills her eyes. "Bet you didn't know that part, huh? He was going to tell the court how abusive you were to me, and I would testify in his favor. The judge would have no choice but to grant him full custody." Trev laughs, a nasty, hollow sound. "And Dante was going to pay me big for my sob story. There were going to be fake tears and bruises on the stand. I was going to do whatever it took to bring you down."

Trev's mouth twists into a sneer. "All he had to do was stay away from the band, and everything was going to work out fine for him and his son. And for me. Dante had more than enough money to survive—he didn't need ABOS—but he has no self-control when it comes to the band. The idiot showed up to practice and started ranting and raving because he was dead set against Pearl taking over as singer."

"What does that have to do with anything? Pearl is a far better singer than he ever was," Maggie interrupts. "How about leaving my wife out of this? You don't deserve to say her name."

"Shut. Up," Trev bellows, his hands balling into fists.

"No, you shut up," Brandi says, voice loud but strikingly calm. She stares at Trev, her lips raised in a snarl. She takes another step closer. Then one more. Venom drips from her voice when she speaks. "Dante was pathetic, but you're even worse. You were going to do whatever he said, all for some money. So much for being the alpha male you fantasize about. Listening to an idiot like Dante put you deep into beta territory." She shakes her head. "Definitely pathetic. Worse than any man I know."

"You have no idea what you're talking about." His words are a whine. "Our plan was to put you in your place. You don't deserve to have a son. There's no way you'd raise him right." Trev wobbles backward, grabbing the high-top next to him for balance. "Too bad Dante complicated things instead of lying low. Don't you think that makes him the beta? He had no self-control. Not like me."

A laugh bursts from Nicole's throat before she can stop it. Everyone turns her way. "Self-control? That's the funniest thing I've heard all day." She faces Lala and Maggie. "Where does he get his confidence? He must drink it from Loser Lake."

Lala lets out a giggle. "Yeah. And then he eats a bite of pathetic pizza."

"Followed by some crybaby cake," Maggie adds.

After the words leave her mouth, Brandi shrieks, "Watch out!"

They turn to see Trev rampaging their way. His lips pull back in a terrifying grimace, his crooked teeth gnashing the air as he runs. His bloodshot eyes bulge in their sockets, matching his bright red cheeks. Feverish. Wild. Furious.

Before they can react, Brandi charges, low and quick. She has a protective hand on her belly, and she drops the opposite shoulder inches from Trev. He doesn't see her. His tunnel vision trains on his three targets.

A second before she reaches him, Brandi raises her shoulder and slams into Trev's back. The drummer topples into a table, and crashes to the floor, landing hard with a grunt. Brandi flies to the side, but she stays upright.

A grin fills her face. She looks triumphant and completely unharmed.

From the floor, Trev tries to rise. His hand reaches toward an overturned chair, and he grabs it, pulling his upper half up a few inches. After a moment, shakes wrack his body. He loses his grip on the chair and collapses into a heap, eyes closed and mouth silent.

All at once, Nicole's world expands. She'd been so focused on Brandi and Trev that she's forgotten about everyone else in the bar. The people who were sitting at the tables rush to them, asking if they need help. A long-haired woman is bent down, checking Trev's neck for a pulse. She gives a thumbs-up when she feels a beat.

Outside the bar, footsteps pound on the stairs. Within seconds a group dressed in navy uniforms bursts through the door. The man in front speaks up. "I'm Wilson McGavit, head of security. Does anyone need medical attention?"

The woman bending over Trev raises her hand. "This guy does." A pair breaks off from the security group and runs to assist.

"Nicole. You're okay." She barely has time to look in the direction of the voice before Jake sweeps her into his arms. He squeezes his wife against his chest and rains kisses on her head. "I was so worried."

"I'm sorry. I didn't know it would get this bad." Nicole raises her chin and smashes her lips against his. He snuggles her hard, and the couple stays like that until Nicole feels a tap on the shoulder.

"Excuse me, ma'am. I hate to interrupt." She turns her head toward the voice. It's William. No, Wilson. The head of security. "But the women over there said you were part of the group I needed to talk to." He points to the left, and Nicole sees Brandi, Lala, and Maggie seated at a table.

Jake lowers his wife to the ground, then crosses his arms over his chest. "How long will this take?" he asks Wilson.

"That depends on the situation. How complicated it is. I'm required to take statements and collect everyone's contact information. You know, compile all the relevant details for the police," he says.

"Can I ask you a favor, Wilson?" Nicole points to Trev, who's starting to wake up from his fall. "Will you handcuff that man? He's already killed one person, and I'd hate to see him murder anyone else."

Wilson's startles. "So, it wasn't just domestic violence."

Nicole raises her eyebrows. "Just?" she asks.

"Sorry. That was insensitive. We got a call about a relationship fight, but this sounds like something worse." He glances at Trev, then back to Nicole. "Will your friends back you up?"

"One hundred percent."

"Okay, then. Let me restrain him, and then I can take your statements." He shakes his head. "Going to have to call the FBI in on this one. That's a first for me." He shakes his head again, then jogs to Trev.

Nicole gives Jake another kiss, then joins her girls at the table. They wrap their arms around each other and watch as Trev Branch, former drummer of A Box of Stars, is placed in handcuffs and led out of the room.

Breaking News < Clementine County < City of Clemons

Karina Belmore, woman who confessed to celebrity murder, released from Clementine County Jail

By: Devora Maltrusic • March 21, 2023

Karina Belmore was released from custody this morning after prosecutors dropped pending charges against her. On February 12, 2023, Belmore made national news when she confessed to murdering her boyfriend in a viral online post. Her boyfriend was Dante Wilder, the lead singer for A Box of Stars (ABOS), an indie rock group founded in Gainesville, FL. While Belmore was eventually charged with conspiracy to commit a felony and not murder, she was being held in criminal justice custody after entering a guilty plea.

What changed Belmore's situation was an incident that occurred last week. The remaining members of ABOS were slated to perform during Rage on the Waves, a weeklong music-focused cruise. The ship launched on March 13, 2023, leaving from Miami, FL. Shortly after setting sail, Trev Branch, the ABOS drummer, went on a drunken rampage that began with an attempted poisoning and ended with a confession. During questioning, Branch admitted that he was responsible for Wilder's death. He poisoned the singer with nicotine derived from multiple vape cartridges, which led to Wilder's sudden cardiac arrest.

At the press event after her release, Belmore said the following: "I am grateful today. Not only have I reclaimed my freedom, but the person who killed Dante is finally facing the consequences of their actions. Justice will finally be served."

Chapter 21 – Karina

{November 10, 2023}

When they released Karina from jail, she was grateful for her freedom. When the film offers started rolling in, she was in heaven. As stupid as her Romeo and Juliet idea was, people wanted to hear about it. And they will. She has a movie coming out next February and a book releasing in March.

There have been interviews where she's divulged some of what happened. And, of course, there was Trev's trial, where everyone got an earful about how women were bringing down the world and how Trev was just trying to claim his rightful place as alpha male. Blah, blah, blah. From all that, society has an idea of what went on with ABOS in the beginning of 2023.

But they don't have the whole picture. And while Karina's film and book will give them a better idea about what occurred, they'll never know the entire truth.

Hell, she just learned it herself when Brandi spilled the details a few months ago.

In May, Brandi reached out after returning from a trip to Belize. Karina was surprised to hear from her. They'd ended their friendship on bad terms. There were a lot of "I hate yous" thrown around. Maybe some "I'll kill yous" too. You know, the heated words people exchange when someone gets on their bad side.

But since her brush with the criminal justice system, Karina has been working on improving herself, and mending old hates is part of the process.

With a newly freed Cici as her guide, she communicated with Brandi, and the former besties were able to reconcile over text and phone calls. After two weeks, they decided to meet in person. Brandi flew Karina to her new house, a cute a-frame in the Boulder mountains, and they talked for hours in front of a roaring fire.

About high school, about their fight, and about how Brandi killed Dante.

Brandi was working on herself, too. She was pregnant and glowing, and she didn't want to give birth with untruths clouding her mind. She thought if she told someone her darkest secret, she'd enter motherhood with a clean conscience. Karina agreed to listen but never tell, and she's sticking to that promise. Not a word of Brandi's confession will make it into her book or movie.

It was the third hour of their heart-to-heart when Karina's friend opened up. The fire was crackling, and they relaxed on a cushy green sofa warming themselves. Brandi was hesitant when she started talking. "K, have you ever done something awful? Not like petty theft or cheating on your partner, or anything at that level. But something truly evil."

Karina thought for a moment and shook her head. "I've done stupid stuff. The whole deadly nightshade idea was probably the stupidest. But I've never done anything I'd call evil."

"I have." Brandi lowered her voice to just above a whisper. "But you have to promise not to tell."

"I won't do anything to ruin our friendship again, Bramble." She held up her pinkie. "Promise."

Brandi smiled at the nickname. "I missed you. I missed this." She hooked her finger into Karina's. "I want a clear mind when I have my son, and I think getting this off my chest will help." She withdrew her pinkie and leaned close. "Trev didn't kill Dante. I did."

Karina's breath drew in sharply. "What? How is that possible?"

Her words rushed out in a high-pitched voice. She sounded scared, so unlike the Brandi from high school. "You can't judge me, K. Please. It wasn't my fault." She placed her hand on the swell of her belly. "Have you ever heard of gestational myxedema?"

Karina shook her head and Brandi continued. "Me either. Until last month, when I learned that pregnancy messed up my thyroid. Like really messed it up. I was having psychotic episodes and didn't even know it." She grimaces and pulls her sweater tight. "Luckily, I picked the right community in Belize because I ended up staying next to a retired endocrinologist. Dr. Phillips. Edna, I mean. She's a real sweet lady. And a lifesaver. I wasn't aware of this when it was happening—Edna told me everything later—but two days after I arrived at my rental, she noticed me roaming around the garden in the middle of the night. I was pawing through the dirt and smearing it on my cheeks. I even ate a few bites of a palm tree. Just chomped right through some leaves and swallowed them down, all with a crazy grin on my face."

"Oh my God, that's awful." An image of a dirt-streaked Brandi filled Karina's head. Her friend had lost control of her body. She must have been terrified.

"I know." Brandi shivered. "Edna saw me and brought me to her house, and after an exam in the kitchen, she brought me straight to the hospital." Tears welled in her eyes, and she gripped her stomach harder. "My thyroid levels were low. Dangerously low. I was given some meds to fix it, and they gave the baby a bunch of tests to make sure he was okay. Thank God he was. And pretty soon, I was too."

Karina reached over and wrapped Brandi in her arms, holding tight for a few moments. "Good thing your neighbor saw you. And good thing you're feeling better." Karina raised an eyebrow. "Are you back to yourself?"

"I am. It's amazing what a little pill can do." She let out a deep breath. "After I got out of the hospital, I realized some of my memories were missing. Whole days were a blank. Like completely black, no recollection, nothing. But after taking my medicine for a couple of weeks, I remembered what I had done during my missing days. Those chunks of time were when I plotted against Dante. And killed him."

She paused and smiled, a weird reaction to a murder confession. "You know what's funny? I don't regret what I did. The jerk planned on taking my son from me. And he hurt women like you. Lots of women. If anything, I made the world a better place."

Brandi was right. Even though Karina had gone to jail since Dante's death, her life had improved. She no longer walked on eggshells. Or checked that her bruises were covered before leaving the house. "Tell me what happened," she encouraged her friend. "You're right about the world being better off without him. I'm glad that he's gone too."

And with those words of support, Brandi told Karina what she'd done.

She knew Dante was going to crash practice. She learned it from a text message she spied on Trev's phone. Right away, she went into action mode, her thyroid-induced psychosis leading the way.

Apparently, her cousin lived in Georgia, just a short drive from the band's BnB, and she was looking for work. Brandi sweet-talked Dylan into letting her cousin stock the practice house before the band arrived. The Georgia relative loaded the kitchen and baths with food and toiletries, but she also brought something special—a bottle of Dante's favorite whisky, the kind only he drank. Everyone else in the band thought it tasted like lighter fluid, but the singer downed the harsh liquid like water.

Before sending it to her cousin, Brandi doctored the whisky. She laced it with a lethal dose of nitazines, a powerful drug most medical examiners don't test for. She then mailed the bottle off to Georgia and instructed her cousin to place it in the practice space where it would be seen by anyone entering the house from the basement. She wanted it to seem like a welcoming gift for the singer. A gift everyone else would ignore because they hated the stuff.

What she hoped for happened. Dante drank the tainted drink.

After Trev was captured on the cruise, Brandi fished information from Nicole about what happened when the singer died. She learned that an open bottle of whiskey was found next to Dante's collapsed body. The bottle of whiskey she had planted there. Brandi knew that with even the smallest sip, the man had been dead before he hit the floor. Her poison had worked epically well.

And she was right about the medical examiner. They didn't test Dante's body or the dropped whisky bottle for nitazines. They only searched for more typical substances, plus the deadly nightshade Karina claimed to use for her idiotic film idea. They didn't discover Brandi's murder weapon at all.

During his trial, when Trev confessed to killing Dante with nicotine, Brandi couldn't believe they chose the same method for administering their fatal doses. Apparently, alcohol is a popular way to deliver poison. Agatha Christie even used it in some of her stories.

And while Brandi's cousin placed her tainted whisky inside the practice space for her, Trev did all the dirty work himself. Right before Dante crashed practice, the singer texted Trev, letting him know it was time to unlock the BnB's back door. The drummer excused himself and snuck outside for a double shot of smoky whisky to celebrate what Dante thought would be his grand return to ABOS.

Unknown to him, a comeback would never happen because while Trev's glass was filled with regular booze, Dante's was loaded with a deadly nicotine mixer. A dose close to 200mg from the vape cartridges stashed inside Trev's shoe boxes. The whisky flavoring masked the poison well.

Hidden behind the trees lining the practice space, the boys clinked glasses and swallowed their shots down. Both men felt the liquid's warmth as it rolled down their throats. One of them didn't know an additional ingredient flowed into his body, seeping into his organs.

The timeframe from drinking to death would have been about thirty minutes. Even if Brandi hadn't killed him first, the singer would have died from Trev's poisonous intervention.

So, long story short, Dante Wilder got double murdered.

You can't make this shit up.

Tour Wives, 2025
written September 2023 - January 2024

Thank you, readers!

I was inspired to write this book by my years as a tour wife. I started dating my husband in 2016, and for the first six months we were talking to each other, he was on tour most of the time, across the U.S. and Europe. So, right away, I got a taste of the tour wife life.

I love thrillers and mysteries, and it was a blast to write about A Box of Stars and their downfall, all from Lala, Maggie, Nicole, Karina, and Brandi's perspectives. There may be another book in the works since I want to hear more of what some of these women have to say.

Thank you for reading. It really means a lot :)
-Leigh